THE SUMMER HOUSE MURDER

Also available by Ava Roberts

The Thistler Thrillers

The Perfect You

The Perfect Boyfriend

The Vanishing Neighbor

Juniper Isle

THE SUMMER HOUSE MURDER

A NOVEL

AVA ROBERTS

NEW YORK

Books should be disposed of and recycled according to local requirements. All paper materials used are FSC compliant.

This is a work of fiction. All of the names, characters, organizations, places, and events portrayed in this novel are either products of the author's imagination or are used fictitiously. Any resemblance to real or actual events, locales, or persons, living or dead, is entirely coincidental.

Published in the United States by Crooked Lane Books, an imprint of The Quick Brown Fox & Company LLC.

Crooked Lane Books and its logo are trademarks of The Quick Brown Fox & Company LLC.

Library of Congress Catalog-in-Publication data available upon request.

ISBN (hardcover): 979-8-89242-484-4
ISBN (paperback): 979-8-89242-485-1
ISBN (ebook): 979-8-89242-486-8

Cover design by Lauren Harms

Printed in the United States.

www.crookedlanebooks.com

Crooked Lane Books
34 West 27th St., 10th Floor
New York, NY 10001

First Edition: February 2026

The authorized representative in the EU for product safety and compliance is eucomply OÜPärnu mnt 139b-14, 11317 Tallinn, Estonia, hello@eucompliancepartner.com, +33757690241

10 9 8 7 6 5 4 3 2 1

CHAPTER 1

Esme

IN A THREE-HOUR car ride, I've thought of at least three ways to kill him.

Moments like these, when I have time to stop and think about what he's done, are the worst.

I look over at Greg. My husband's hands are on the steering wheel. He's blasting some progressive rock jam band—awful music and nodding his head in rapture. Our twin girls are in the back of the SUV. Both have their pink headphones on, each watching a different movie on their own iPad. The pine trees outside are getting larger and larger, the mountain road winding endlessly up and up as we climb toward our destination.

I pinch my fingernails into the pads of my hands. What a beautiful family we have. Why is he destroying it? For what?

Now is not the time to fall apart. My sisters will both be at our summer house. The last thing I need is their judgment. I can imagine their shock if they knew the truth.

His phone pings. My heart rate picks up. I know who it is.

I sneak a look over at Greg. He's oblivious. He's rocking out to his music. The music that I've told him, repeatedly, I don't like to listen to.

I wonder if *she* likes his music. Do they make love to it?

Greg reaches down for his black stainless-steel water bottle. I watch his Adam's apple bob as he drinks thirstily before returning it to the console cup holder.

"I'd like to use the restroom," I say.

"We just stopped." He frowns and looks at the GPS. "It's only a half hour more. You can wait."

I want to protest but bite my tongue.

His phone beeps again, and I look at Greg to gauge his reaction. No emotion.

"Going to check your messages?" I ask.

He's silent.

I press on. "Your phone has been going off for the past half hour. Could it be important?"

For the first time during the three-hour car ride, I feel Greg's eyes on me. The road is particularly narrow in this section.

"Watch out," I say, as another car speeds by us from the opposite direction. Greg looks back at the road and overcorrects, swerving to the shoulder of the road. There's not a lot of room between the shoulder and the low gate barrier. Beyond the barrier is a steep mountainside. An image of our car flying down the embankment, flipping over and crashing at the bottom, flashes before me.

I let out a small scream and grab onto the door handle as Greg shifts back into our lane from the shoulder and presses on the brake to regain control of the SUV.

The other car is long gone.

"Watch the road, please," I say, breathless.

I glance back at the girls in the backseat. Gracey lifts her eyebrows up in question, and I nod and smile, reassuring her. She looks out the window briefly, and then back to her movie. Brielle's eye's never leave her screen. Unfettered access to screen time—a privilege for the car ride—has absorbed their attention, and for that I'm grateful.

We travel in silence until I see the sign that we're entering Lake George. It's the same sign, the one with the bear and a pine tree, that welcomed me as a child.

"We need to stop in town at the grocery, before we get to the house," I say to Greg.

"Why?"

"To fill the refrigerator and cabinets with supplies, obviously."

He groans. "Why did you offer to cook tonight?" His words are short, the way he speaks when he's annoyed. "I just want to get to the house and relax."

"You know I like to cook the first meal of the trip," I say. I make a meal schedule so my two sisters and I spread out dinner duty, rotating nights, over the two weeks we're here each August. I've found that if I don't make a schedule, I end up doing all the cooking.

"It's fine," I say. "I'll go back out to the store. Let you and the girls get settled."

That appeases him. We travel the rest of the way in silence.

I push thoughts of his phone beeping from my mind. I have a plan for how to handle those messages, but now is not the time.

A half hour later, our tires crunch against the gravel as Greg turns onto the road that leads to our house. It's an isolated swath of the lake, devoid of other homes. The property was purchased years ago by our great grandparents, before it became conservation land and building was prohibited. We were grandfathered in—ours is the sole house standing in the area. My mother, Audry Howard, tells the story of how her grandfather Charles Goodall chose the property perched on a massive crystal-blue lake, such clarity he'd never seen before or since in a body of water, and old-growth pine trees as far as the eye could see. The perfect spot to expand his logging business, and establish the Goodall family legacy. Shortly after he built on the land, though, the government deemed the area a preserve to keep it from being logged. Since then, the population and tourism have exploded on the other side of Lake George, leading our little alcove to be a respite, miles away from any neighbors, but close enough to drive around the lake and into town for a meal or shopping.

The trees are thick overhead as we drive deeper into the forest along the long, narrow road that is the only access point to our house. The road follows the curve of the lake, and I can see the blue water sparkling in the sun. The house appears before us. It's a white Victorian with a covered porch and turret on the left side, with an expanded three-car garage and six bedrooms.

"Girls," I say. "Girls," I say again, louder. "We're here."

The girls break from their daze. Brielle throws off her headphones and her eyes widen with excitement.

Gracey pops her headphones off, too, folding the cord neatly and tucking it in its case. "I can't wait to see Aunt Piper and Aunt Regina." she says.

"They may already be here, or arriving shortly, if not," I say. I smooth down the skirt of my dress and brush my blond hair behind my ears, and quickly check the mirror that my lipstick is still fresh.

"I can't wait to meet baby Preston," Brielle says, clasping her hands together at the thought of her four-month-old cousin.

She's going through a baby fascination stage and has been asking Greg and I endlessly if we're going to have another child. To which the answer is a firm, but gentle, no.

"I can't wait to play with Cousin Lana," Gracey says. Lana is five years old, just one year younger than my girls.

My mood lifts. This is why we come here every year. Why we've spent money from our own pocket to renovate and expand the house I share with my sisters. Granted, my sisters didn't contribute to the renovations fund—even though we own the house evenly—and they'll benefit from the improvements.

There's an agreement. When my mother was diagnosed with cancer two years ago, she put her type A personality to work and spent a great deal of time planning for her own demise. Dictating the funeral details, allocating her jewels and artwork to each of us as she saw fit, making sure her social contacts and charity binders were in order and ready to pass on to her successor. And, finally, making a plan for our cherished family summer house.

My mother willed the three of us daughters, the Howard sisters, this house with the clear stipulation that we must all occupy it for two weeks in August. Together. Failure to do this results in forfeit of the share in the house. My mother, ever the stern director, even from beyond the grave.

I'd come here regardless of the rule. I'd like to think my sisters would, too. Either way, for me, the joy at bringing the girls together with their cousins is worth it. The cousins, at least, get along.

Last year was our first year here after my mother's death. We three sisters and our families all gathered here in August, as instructed, new owners and without my mother to hold us together.

It was strained at best. I'm not sure any of us were our best self. Piper was still trying to get pregnant after years of struggles. She seemed more anxious than ever, which is saying a lot for Piper. Regina and her husband, Bryce, fought the entire time, and Greg and I were going through a rough patch then, too. Though we'd never show it by screaming and shouting about money troubles like Regina and Bryce did into the late hours of the night. When I'd politely asked them to keep it down, the shouting became directed at me. How I'm terribly uptight and Miss Perfect.

Hopefully, this year with my sisters will be different. Now that Piper, our middle sister, has baby Preston. Maybe this year, she and Regina and I can get along. Move forward from the strife that always follows us.

Finally, Greg pulls to a stop in front of the house. I swing open the door of our SUV and inhale the scent of pine needles and clean air.

I catch sight of Greg, head bent to his phone. My eyes narrow.

This won't do at all.

CHAPTER

2

Regina

GOD, GRANT ME patience. She's doing it already—holding court. My gaze rests on my oldest sister, Esme, seated at the head of the dinner table.

She talks to us like she's on stage answering one of her pageant questions posed to her by a judge. She even looks pageant ready with her long blond highlights, toned frame, and perfectly proportioned features enhanced subtly with the help of injectables.

In the car on the drive up, I'd been telling my husband, Bryce, how her pageant voice drives me nuts. I squeeze his hand and open my eyes wide, giving him the look. *See?* He frowns and gives me a slight shake of his head.

It's our first meal all together at our summer house, and he wants it to go smoothly.

Esme smiles, her white teeth gleaming. "My favorite part of being here is cooking for everyone. Making some of mom's favorite recipes." She nods at the table. She insisted on cooking, and the spread is impressive. Chicken Française. Mashed potatoes. A breadbasket with warm rolls. Freshly baked apple pie.

I look at her with a mixture of envy and disdain. *Doesn't it ever get tiring to be so extra all the time?* But then the voice is there, in the back of my head. That I don't try simply because I can never be as good as her.

I'll always be the baby of the family, looking up to my poised, eldest sister—Mom's favorite—both so alike.

Glancing down at my white T-shirt and cutoff shorts, contrasted with Esme's pretty summer dress, I think how different we are. I'm concerned with comfort and practicality, while she's always *on.* I smooth my hands over my chestnut-colored tangled layers, comparing them to her straight, smooth hair.

"Dinner is amazing, thank you, Esme," our middle sister, Piper, says. Piper is petite in stature, like Esme, but a pared-down version. Her brown hair has never been touched by a colorist, and she hardly wears makeup. "It's nice to have one of Mom's recipes." Piper and her husband, Paul, have named their baby son Preston to keep the P tradition going. It's cute. Not my thing, but cute. It's what she's always wanted, a baby of her own.

My own daughter, Lana, is seated next to me. I wink down at her. "Good?" I ask. She's notoriously picky.

"Mmm," my daughter answers loudly. "The best. Mommy, why don't you make food like this?"

The whole table turns their heads to look at her. Esme chuckles from her end of the table. "I'm sure your mommy prepares you very nice meals, but thank you, sweetie, for the compliment."

"Oh, no, she doesn't," Lana answers happily, taking a giant bite of buttered bread.

"Hey," I say, offended. "You love takeout." I feel the need to defend myself. "She asks for it every night."

Everyone nods politely.

"*My* mommy is teaching us to bake," says one of Esme's twin daughters. I'm ashamed, but I can't tell which twin she is. Esme usually has Brielle in a pink bow and Gracey in a blue bow. I check the bow of the girl speaking. Pink. Brielle . . . I think.

"Baking. That's fun," I say, chewing a bite of my chicken. God, it's tender. So flavorful. It does taste like how Mom used to make it. Maybe even better.

Seated next to her, Greg, Esme's husband, takes his cell phone out from his pocket and begins tapping away. It's beeped a couple of times already.

Esme's pink lips purse. "Honey, not at the dinner table." Her tone is apologetic as she turns to the rest of us. "Greg has a hard time unplugging from surgeon mode. He's used to attending to his patients' every need. But this is supposed to be a time to relax. Not work." She says the last bit with an edge to her voice.

Beside me, my own husband is practically groaning as he eats, such is his enjoyment of the meal. I know he, at least, won't take out his cell phone at the table. He usually can't even find his phone. He's a true outdoorsman. Fishing, hiking, camping. He loves coming here every summer, and so does Lana, our daughter—an only child who loves seeing her twin cousins. If it weren't for them—and a favor I need to ask Esme—no way would I come back to this place. Not after all that's happened here.

A loud wail rings out. Baby Preston begins to cry, suddenly and shockingly loudly. Piper, or middle sister, sets down her fork with a flustered expression. "I don't get a moment to eat." She hesitates and looks at each of us anxiously before scooting back her chair. She picks up Preston from the bouncer

"Are you hungry, Pressi?" she says to him in a high-pitched voice, holding him in the crook of her arm. "I'll make you a bottle." She sets him back down, which causes him to wail even louder.

Another bite of mashed potatoes melts in my mouth. A perfect combination of butter, garlic, and a hint of cream.

Piper has the baby's bottle supplies lined up on the kitchen counter. She measures formula and heats up the water to make the bottle with frazzled, harried movements, darting around the remodeled kitchen.

"Not breastfeeding then, Pipe?" Esme asks her over Preston's cries.

Piper picks up Preston and attempts to get him to take his bottle. "Um, no," she says. "Come on, baby boy. Here's your bottle. Come on," she coos to him with a hint of panic.

"My girls loved breastfeeding," Esme says, turning to the rest of us with *the voice*. "Breastfeeding twins was exhausting. I wanted to do the bottle, but they just loved breastfeeding. And you know what they say . . ."

I wince, worried at what she'll say next.

"Breast is best."

And there it is.

Piper looks at Esme and tears immediately well up in her eyes.

"I tried to breastfeed," Piper chokes on the words. The baby, mercifully, starts sucking at his bottle. Piper turns away and walks briskly to the living room. She sits down on the new sectional sofa, cradling Preston as he continues to eat.

I put down my fork. "Nice, Esme," I say. "That clearly was what she wanted to hear."

Esme's mouth makes a round O. "I didn't mean—" Her cheeks turn slightly pink. "I shouldn't have said anything. I just meant, that's what I've always heard. For me. That's why I did it. The bottle would have been great."

"What's breastfeeding, mommy?" Lana, never one to shy away, asks me.

"It's when milk comes out of your boobs," I say. "To feed a baby."

"Like when a cow gets milked?" Lana asks.

"Yes," I say.

"Eww. We saw that at a farm," Lana says.

"We did." I nod.

"It's not quite like milking a cow," Esme says.

"I mean, it is," I answer defensively. Why am I getting so worked up about breast milk?

My husband, Bryce has already finished his dinner and looks around the table, eyeing seconds. He reaches for the potatoes.

"The house looks terrific with the renovations," says Paul Piper's husband nervously, desperately trying to change the subject, no doubt. "The addition is awesome."

Esme paid for—overpaid for, probably—and oversaw a huge makeover of the house over the past six months. I preferred the house before—the older cabinets, the intricate woodwork, the floral wallpaper.

Now, the wood floors have been refinished. Walls knocked out to reconfigure the kitchen to allow for a massive marble island and a six-burner stove with a commercial range hood. The updates look beautiful. But the house is lacking the authenticity it once held as an Adirondack home from the turn of the last century. On the lower floor, past the living room, she added a rec room, complete with pool table, foosball table, pinball machine, and a bar area with a sleek top-of-the-line beverage cooler. Beyond that is a new powder room and guest bedroom that doubles as an office. On the other side of the house, our old garage was torn out and then extended to hold three vehicles. It's all a little much.

"It looks great," I offer. "It's much bigger now," I add, not sure what else to say.

"Well, it wasn't cheap," Esme brags. "But the old house badly needed the updates. So—"

"Right. I mean, it looked cool before. Timeless. Cozy," I add.

Esme looks at me and frowns. "Sure, Regina. But it's clearly better now."

I shake my head. "Better for you, maybe. But I'm allowed my own opinion. It's a lot of money to suck the charm out of a place."

Oops. I'd promised myself I'd be on my best behavior. *Keep passive-aggressive snark to a minimum.*

I look down at Lana. She's old enough to sense tension and fighting. I have to keep myself in check.

I sigh. "You're right, Esme. The house needed this. Change is just hard for me, I guess." I give her a tight smile.

"You've always been sentimental," she oozes.

CHAPTER

3

Piper

Baby Preston is halfway finished with his formula. He moves his head away from the bottle, unlatching, and squirming frantically as if he wants to get up and walk.

No, baby, finish your bottle.

Panic rises inside me. Feeding him has been an issue from day one. Breastfeeding didn't work. I had low supply, the lactation consultant told me. The bottle worked just fine. Initially.

But now, at four months old, he's just not interested in drinking his formula. It stresses me out to no end. There are a few ounces left. *He needs to eat.*

I'd hoped I could ask my sisters for advice. I'd imagined Esme taking Preston, soothing him, showing me tricks of how to feed him that would make him eat like a champ.

Instead, I'm invisible, as usual. A few critical comments thrown my way, and I'm forgotten.

Preston lets out a wail, and I see my sisters' glance at me from the dinner table, then continue with their conversation.

Tears cloud my eyes.

Why is this so hard? Finally, I have my own adorable baby, after trying so long. Finally, on equal footing with my sisters.

I'm a new mom. My time to feel special, in the limelight. But I'm still an afterthought to them.

When I'd first arrived, Esme gave a cursory kiss and *ooh* over Preston. Then she went right back to cooking. She hardly cares about Preston. Other than to judge my bottle feeding him.

And Regina looks miserable. Can't she for once push down her misery and be happy for someone else?

Was I silly to think my sisters would see how much this means to me? Am I just not fun enough? Not special enough? Too boring and plain?

There was a period in my twenties when I thought I'd get married right out of college and have kids. But then time went on. I started working in accounting at a small firm and didn't meet many single guys my age. My sisters both got engaged. Then they both got married. I caught the bouquet at Regina's wedding, even. Watching my younger sister get married before me was a new low, and catching the bouquet felt like the final humiliation.

I'd about given up when I met Paul. I'd signed up for a cooking workshop, and he's a part owner of the restaurant where the tutorial was held. When he came in to meet the class, I noticed his kind eyes right away.

I tend to be anxious—high-strung, or a worrywart, my mother used to call it—but Paul put me at ease. He told me he was going to take me out to a Michelin star restaurant for dinner the next night and didn't leave until he had my number programmed in his phone.

He's a relaxed, happy, outgoing guy, which balances out my tendency to fear the absolute worst outcome in any situation.

Moreover, Paul didn't seem to mind my being plain. To him, I was natural, beautiful. Not overshadowed by the polished veneer of Esme. Nor the quiet, boring older sister of Regina, who growing up always was witty and funny and edgy.

Paul made me feel that I was more than the forgotten middle sister.

"You don't have to worry when I'm around," he'd assured me after our first date. I'd been anxious that I wasn't impressing him with conversation or my knowledge of fine food. But that didn't matter to Paul. With him, I started to feel safe.

We had our own little peaceful world we'd built together. Becoming a mother was the piece that was missing; I'd watch other moms push their strollers and wonder what I'd done to be excluded from that gift.

My worry had spiraled, and then we tried IVF. Nothing seemed to work, and the more I stressed about it, the worse it seemed to get. Until, three years after first trying, we went on vacation, and I got a positive pregnancy test two weeks later.

But being a mom has been harder than I thought. So much could go wrong with my tiny, vulnerable baby. Is he eating? Sleeping? Breathing? I feel myself getting more and more anxious.

Worse, my worry seems to have gotten turned up a notch since I arrived here. The postpartum hormones are suddenly amplified. I feel my eyes darting around uneasily.

Being back in this place is toxic to my well-being. Even though the kitchen's redone, it's still the same lake house. Creepy. Haunted with memories . . . some of the worst times of my youth were spent here. I shudder and push my brown hair behind my ears.

Tiredness tugs at my brain. Maybe I just need sleep.

"I'm going to try to get Preston to sleep," I say to the others as I head up the stairs. They hardly acknowledge me.

That's the funny thing about being invisible. No one acknowledges you. No one cares what you do.

I look down at Preston, and my dark thoughts dissipate. Love surges through me. He's better than this house.

The hallway is dark. The downstairs may be renovated, but the upstairs must be phase two. Because it looks exactly the same as when we were growing up. Oak floorboards that creak, green walls, and pine paneling. Its Victorian roots from the 1890s are infused in every inch.

I step into my old bedroom. Lana and the twins' toys are scattered around. I can't help myself; I lift up the rug that covers the center of the floor. Sure enough, the charred wood floorboards underneath the rug are still there. I drop the rug quickly, arranging it back in its place.

Shaking away a feeling of unease, I close the girls' bedroom door and take Preston down the hallway to our room. As I open the door, the sound of glass shattering pierces the air. Shards of glass shoot out of the window, landing inside and covering the floor. Preston's crib that Esme had ordered and white-glove installed for him is full of glass. I pull Preston close to me and slam the door shut.

Then I glance down at the jagged, thin white scar on my hand, remembering.

I hear footsteps nearing us in the hallway.

"What happened?" My husband, Paul, is behind me.

"The glass, it's everywhere." Preston is half-asleep in my arms, but he starts to fuss.

Paul opens the door and observes the scene. "How'd the window break?" He steps into our bedroom, unbothered by the glass, his large frame filling the space, his middle thicker from tasting his dishes at the restaurant.

"I don't know how it happened, Paul," I say miserably. "It just shattered right as we walked in." I feel my eyes welling up again as though I am responsible for the broken window. Having Preston's crib filled with shards of glass is almost more than I can bear.

"I'll get a trash bag and start cleaning this up. I'll need tape and a tarp to seal the window. Let's ask Esme where to get them." His voice is calm and steady.

We walk down the creaky hallway. I grasp onto the banister as I go down the steep stairway, Preston in the crook of my right arm.

All eyes are on us as we approach the dinner table. Esme's getting out coffee cups and saucers and dessert dishes.

"What on earth was that sound? Sounded like glass breaking." Esme frowns at me, her brow frozen from injectables, but I can see the strain of her displeasure on her face.

"I walked into our room and the window broke. Glass is everywhere," I say helplessly.

"Do you have tape and a tarp?" Paul asks them.

Greg, Esme's husband, puts his phone down and nods. "Let's go in the garage. See what we can find."

Paul gives me a reassuring nod. "We'll get it cleaned up."

Our husbands leave through the side door that exits to the new three-car garage.

"How did the window break?" Esme asks, accusation thick in her voice.

"When I opened the bedroom door, it just broke."

"Broke, how?" Regina is incredulous.

"I don't know. I didn't see anything hit the glass."

"Well, that doesn't make sense," Esme says.

"Why don't you check the security cameras?" Regina says to Esme. Knowing full well we've never had any alarm system let alone video surveillance here.

Esme looks offended. "We don't need cameras. It's the safest place in the world way out here," but she doesn't look so sure, and bites her lip.

"It's the one thing in a huge, fancy reno that might have been useful," Regina says under her breath.

Bryce, Regina's husband, shifts his eyes between the three of us sisters, and then looks longingly after where the husbands have gone. He stands up. "I'll head outside and see if there's anything out there that could have broken it. Maybe a branch hit the window."

Their three little girls finish up their desserts, apple pie smudging the sides of their mouths. Lana's fork clinks on her empty plate. "Mommy, can we go play?" she asks Regina.

"Sure," Regina answers. "Why don't you show your cousins the toys you brought?" The girls get up excitedly from the table and run to the living room, which is now open and visible from the kitchen, thanks to the renovated open floor plan.

"I need to put Preston down to sleep," I say, hearing the tremor in my voice. "But there's glass all over the room."

"This reminds me of that summer." Esme's tone is sharp. Her insinuation hurts. I pull Preston closer.

I was eight years old the summer when the incident happened, just a little older than Lana is now. I'd been mad. The mirror in my room had been broken. I remember being angry, the shattered glass, and the cuts on my knuckles. My mother's disapproving gaze as she wrapped a white gauze bandage around my hand.

"I don't know what happened up there! It wasn't me," I say back. The way everyone keeps looking at me makes me pause.

What really did happen up there? Am I missing something?

"You look exhausted," Esme says. "You can lie down in our room. Both you and Preston can use it. I'll grab one of the baby loungers I used when the twins were nursing. I still have them."

Esme sweeps past me, her perfume wafting by as she leaves to search the downstairs storage closet.

Regina regards me. "You okay?"

Ignoring her, I look down at Preston, suddenly worried he's bleeding. Did the glass cut him?

His face is calm, and he is sleeping. His white and gray striped onesie is clean and unscathed. His eyes are closed peacefully, his small mouth pursed in a sucking motion. He looks like he's dreaming happy dreams about drinking his bottle.

"Piper?" Regina says again.

"I'm fine," I say absently, still staring down at Preston.

"You look as if you've seen a ghost," Regina says.

Maybe if my sisters would help me, rather than attack me and keep asking me if I'm okay, then I would be better.

I open my mouth to tell her this, but instead, my voice rises as I reply, "Well—There are ghosts here, aren't there?"

Esme returns with the bedding and baby lounger. I follow her gratefully up the stairs again, past the closed door of my room with the shattered glass, and into the primary suite—Mom and Dad's old room.

She plops the extra blankets and lounger down, and wordlessly leaves the bedroom.

I close the door behind her, and flip on the single bulb that hangs from the closet door, searching for an extra pillow. And that's when I see it.

Etched crudely into the inside of the closet is one word. "Help."

CHAPTER

4

Esme

STRONG ARMS WRAP around my waist and pull me closer.

"Ugh, stop," I say, wriggling away and rubbing at my eyes. The room is still dark, the blackout shades pulled down, but I see the faint outline of the early morning sun beyond them.

My husband pulls at me again, moving his hand up and down my thigh.

I flip the covers of the bed, letting the warmth escape. I swing my legs out of bed and sit up. "I'm going to run back to the store before everyone wakes up."

Greg's voice is petulant. "We're on vacation. Come back to bed."

I wish I could. How easy it would be to roll back into bed. Take him in my arms and be close to him again.

It's a thin line between love and hate, they say. Two ends of the same spectrum. I never understood this, but ten years of marriage will change a person's view. I see now how someone you love can engender such raw emotion. When they hurt you, the love you have for them boils over into unbridled rage.

Mother always taught me that showing such emotion, however, is a stain on one's personality. Unbecoming.

"Not now," I say.

He flips over dramatically with a sigh and pulls the covers back up.

It's our first morning here of our two-week stay. I need to fully stock the cupboards, and I want to have fresh pastries and breakfast ready before everyone wakes up.

Hopping out of bed, I move to the small closet and sift through the clothes I unpacked and hung up last night. I quickly pull on a pair of white shorts, a navy V-neck tank, slip on my Cartier watch and a pair of leather sandals. In the bathroom, I brush my teeth, run a brush through my straight blond hair, and apply a coat of lipstick and mascara.

Shutting our bedroom door gently behind me, I tiptoe down the hallway past Piper's room. Paul taped up the broken window with a plastic tarp last night. Piper spent hours vacuuming and going over every inch of the room for glass.

"What if the baby gets cut by a sliver of glass? What if he swallows a chip?" she'd said, her eyes wide, haunted. After hours of cleaning and searching, stripping the bedding and cleaning some more, she finally agreed to sleep in the room and allow Preston in his crib.

The floorboards creak as I pass Regina and Bryce's room next. Their door is closed. I assume they'll sleep in. Regina always was the last one up in our family. Mom would remind her a million times, gently at first, and then more sternly, that it was slothful to sleep too late.

I glance at the kids' room at the other end of the hallway. Our twins shared the bottom full-size bunk bed and Lana had the top single bunk, though I suspect all three ended up in the lower full bed.

We three sisters used to share a bed on trips. All of us huddled together under the covers, a flashlight glowing. I'd read out loud to them or tell them stories.

Those days seem so far away. Almost like another lifetime. What would it be like to be close to my sisters now? I long for that. But so much has happened.

I walk down the stairs and am greeted by the quiet, empty great room and kitchen.

I spot Greg's cell phone on the charger. Quickly checking to make sure he's not coming down the stairs, I unplug his phone and swipe in the code I observed him typing last night. Don't mind if I do.

His message app says he has three messages waiting from B.

I click on the first one: "Baby, I miss you already. I hate waiting. But soon we'll have a whole week to ourselves."

A whole week? Is he planning on leaving here early? He wouldn't dare. Would he?

The next message reads, "Thinking of you."

I do a double take as I scroll through the next one. It's a photo, and my eyes widen in horror as I recognize what on earth it is.

Two round, full breasts.

My nausea hits like a punch to the stomach.

I take a deep breath and start typing "Greg's" reply. I reread it quickly, glancing up at the staircase to make sure no one sees me. I hit send.

The arrow shows the message has been delivered. Then I push delete on the message thread.

I plug the phone back in, dropping it like it's a snake.

Fishing my keys out from my purse, I head out.

My hands shake as I drive to the store. I barely register what I'm doing and have to force myself to focus on the road.

Did I do the right thing? My mind can't fully process the repercussions of what I've just typed.

I pull into a space up front in the parking lot of Gents, the local grocery store. It's the same store we went to when I was little. It's been remodeled, the aisleways large and stocked with fresh local produce and organic, specialty pastas and cheeses.

Pushing thoughts of Greg and *her* out of my mind, I inspect a block of goat cheese. I'm considering what to make for lunch, perhaps deli sandwiches and a cheese board for everyone to nibble on—this is a hungry group—when I spot the profile of a woman.

My heart skips a beat. I drop the cheese into my cart and navigate closer to where she stands. Could it be her?

It's early morning and hardly anyone is in the store other than the clerks and a few shelf stockers.

She rounds the corner. I follow behind her, with wheels squeaking against the linoleum floor. Her sandy-blond hair bobs as she pushes her own cart.

"Excuse me." A small, older gentleman pulls out a large cart in front of me, blocking me from following the woman down the aisle. He's planted his trolly of cans in the middle of the aisle, and I can't squeeze past without knocking into him. He begins to stock soup onto a shelf.

I watch as the woman rounds the corner. The man seems in no hurry to make room for me to pass him.

"I'll just go around." I turn my cart 180 degrees and take a left into the next aisle. But the woman is gone. I quickly push the cart forward, my breath coming in puffs. I must be imagining she's here. She can't be . . . It's impossible. But it looked just like her.

I have to find the woman. To know, for sure.

Pushing my cart into the large area that leads to the checkout counter, I scan the area. It's empty, save one lone checker who smiles at me.

I go up and down the main aisle again, checking each row. The place is empty of other customers.

She's gone. Or had I imagined her?

I quickly fill my cart with the essentials, absently throwing food into the cart and ignoring the list I'd carefully written out.

At the checkout counter, I place my items on the rotating belt. "Morning," I say and smile at the clerk. "Did you happen to see a woman here? Sandy-blond hair, who just checked out before me?"

She pauses with a box of organic grain-free crackers in her hand. "No, ma'am. No one's been through here this morning yet. You're my first customer."

My hand is unsteady as I provide my credit card. "Mmm. My mistake."

The woman leans into me and lowers her voice. "Be careful out there."

"Excuse me?" I say. "Why?" My knees feel weak. My eyes shoot around, looking for danger.

"It's going to be a hot one." She laughs, causing her short curls to spring up and down.

"Oh, yes," I say, and wave absently to her, pushing my cart through the doors of the store and out into the heat.

I roll the cart to my car and scan the parking lot. I see a few cars parked at the back of the lot, but they're empty.

The main street of the town is quiet. Most shops won't open until nine or ten AM. The only activity I see is at the corner coffee shop, where a few people are eating and sipping their iced coffee on the patio. There's no sign of the woman. That hair. That profile . . . the nose with an upward slant and a sprinkle of freckles. There's no mistaking it was her. The more I think about it, the more certain I am.

After loading the grocery bags into the hatch of my SUV, I climb into the driver's seat and turn on the ignition, letting the cool air blast me.

I put the car into reverse and make my way over to the coffee shop.

CHAPTER

5

Before

Esme

My mother's heels echo down the white hallway. I wrinkle my nose; it smells like bleach and cafeteria food. We enter a small room. My mother sets flowers on the table next to a woman lying in a hospital bed.

"Esme, sit here," my mother says. I sit on a plastic chair, my legs dangling. The smell is worse in here, and I wonder how long we have to stay.

I look up at the two women. My mom stands over her sister. She's hooked up to tubes and is lying propped up on pillows. I don't recognize my aunt. She's not one of the family members we usually see at gatherings and holidays.

Her eyes are half-open. She looks up at my mother. "You came."

"I didn't have a choice. I understand there isn't much time left," she says.

"We have to talk about Alexis."

My mother stiffens. "Where is the girl?"

"She's at our neighbor's. But she can't—You have to take her in. Promise. She belongs there. With you . . . and Frank."

My mother's voice is cold. "I don't imagine there are many other options. Is there no one else who can look after her?"

My aunt shakes her head, and grabs my mother's hand. "Please."

My stomach feels funny watching them talk. My mom seems so mad, not like herself at all. So I try to focus on the tiles of the floor. They're light green and yellow and white, and if I squint they blur into one color.

"Audry. Alexis is innocent in all this. Tell me you'll do it."

"Fine. She can stay with us." At this, my ears perk up. What is my mother talking about? Who is Alexis? I don't want anyone to stay with us.

The conversation doesn't last long. Mom says goodbye over her shoulder, and grabs my hand. I don't look back at my aunt as my mom leads me out the door.

In the hallway, I glance up and see her eyes are watery, and her face is a little red. I can't tell if she's angry or sad, or both. "Mom?" I croak. "What's going on?"

We get to the end of the corridor and my mother leans down to me. "Esme," she says, and pulls me into a hug. "My dear, sweet girl."

She cups my face in her hands, and gives me a gentle kiss on the forehead. "I love you so much. You're the oldest of your sisters. Such a smart, responsible girl. I see so much of myself in you. There are some things that I think you're old enough to know now."

My mom leans in, and she tells me a secret.

* * *

I finish outlining the hopscotch grid on the driveway outside our summer house. "I'll go first," I say to my sisters and cousin. "Then Regina next, then you, Piper . . . and then Alexis," I add, remembering mom told me to include Alexis now that she's "joined our family."

I hop on the number one with my left foot, and then jump with both feet on the two and three squares. My sisters watch on in rapture, waiting their turn. And then I hear *her* voice. "This is boring. Hey, want me to teach you how to cartwheel?"

It's Alexis. I jump on one foot to the four, but I've lost my sisters' attention.

Alexis runs to the lawn and throws her hands into the air before leaping up, and then turning upside down on her hands, legs outstretched, and landing on the other side.

"Teach me," Regina says eagerly.

"Guys, we're playing hopscotch," I remind them. "Come on."

Piper looks back at me, but I can tell she wants to cartwheel, too.

Alexis lets out a huge laugh, doing another cartwheel, her long wavy hair flowing behind her. When she lands again, she smiles, a dimple appearing on her cheek, making her look even prettier.

"No one wants to play your boring hopscotch, Esme," she says.

Regina pitches herself forward, but crumples halfway over, her legs bent, not able to reach a full circle. She lands in the grass but lets out a squeal of laughter. Alexis bends over her, grabbing her hand to help her up.

"Good try. Next time, be sure to keep your legs straight, like this."

I cross my arms and watch them. Finally, Alexis looks back at me. "What's wrong, Esme, are you afraid to try?"

"I'm not afraid," I say. "I just don't want to."

She smirks. "Esme, it's easy, watch!" She peals out in laughter as she does another flip, and I notice my sisters smiling at her in awe. "Esme doesn't want to get her pretty dress dirty. She knows she'll fall if she tries."

I want to tug on those long curls of hers. Tell her to go back home. I understand that she can't—that her mom just died a few weeks ago, and her dad has been dead for years—we're her family now. But I don't want her here. I frown, stomping my feet.

These are *my* sisters. *My* family. We play the games *I* like, and it's fun.

This isn't fun. Bossy pants Alexis is ruining everything. She's only been here three days, and I can't stand her. I'm the oldest, ten, to my little sisters' eight and seven years, which means I make the rules. But Alexis thinks that because she's ten, too, that she's in charge.

"Piper, Regina," I call to them. "I have a secret. Come here."

Both of my sisters' eyes light up. There's nothing like a good secret to excite them.

They huddle close, and I whisper in their ears. Alexis stands off to the side, pretending not to care, but I can see her watching us.

"We're going to play a special game," I whisper to them. "A hidden treasures game."

Alexis walks over, listening in. She can't help herself. "I want to play."

An idea pops into my mind. I'm going to make Alexis wish she never came here, and I think I have just the way to do it.

CHAPTER

6

Regina

I HEAD DOWN THE stairs, rubbing the sleep from my eyes. I'm wearing an old AC/DC T-shirt, cutoff jean shorts, and my dark layers are tossed up in a high bun. The kitchen is empty and so is the coffee pot. That's just a travesty.

Groaning, I fill up the coffee machine with filtered water. Then I locate ground coffee in a crock nearby on the counter. I fish out the scoop and add the fragrant grounds into the basket. I press the "on" button and wait for the hot liquid to be ready.

Looking around, I see Esme's touches everywhere in the new kitchen. It's gleaming and polished, just like her.

"Hey."

I nearly jump out of my skin.

"Morning, Piper. You're up early," I say, responding to my sister's arrival. I tap my fingers, watching as the carafe slowly fills, drip by drip. I consider taking it off the heat plate early and pouring some in my mug. But then the coffee flavor gets messed up. I know from my years working at the bar that good coffee is an art form, essential to remedy a hangover. I can tell by my throbbing temples that I overdid it with the tequila last night.

"I never sleep more than a few hours at a time with Preston," Piper laments. "He's stirring, probably ready for his morning bottle." Her eyes are large with dark circles underneath them. She heads to the sink and fills a pot with water to heat on the stove.

Piper looks worse for wear. I was tired with Lana, sure, but I don't remember being completely beside myself with exhaustion.

"Do you remember Alexis?" she asks softly. Suddenly.

I blink hard. "Come again?" I'm not sure I'm hearing her correctly.

"Alexis," she says, turning her large eyes to me. Her skin looks super pale in the morning light, with the white and gray marble countertop reflecting against her skin.

A chill goes up my spine. Why is she bringing up Alexis?

"Yes, I remember her," I say. The coffee is more than halfway processed. I reach into the cabinet and take down a large travel mug and ceramic cup.

"I saw something of hers yesterday."

I tilt my head to look at her, feeling creeped out. I'm really starting to worry. First the broken window. Piper went on and on about how it was broken before she got in the room, but I'm starting to wonder. On one hand, Paul noticed several large rocks below the bedroom window. Could someone have thrown one and broken the glass? A local vandal? But no rock came through the window and landed in the room. Besides, we don't have any neighbors for miles on either side, so who would have done that? No one who isn't from here would even know about the road to the house. Even Bryce missed the turn for it yesterday. There are no distinguishing markings identifying the road.

Or did Piper break it herself? Like before . . . ? She's not known as being the most emotionally stable Howard sister.

Now, this. Bringing up Alexis. I really need that coffee.

"Look. It's been years . . . What could be hers, in the house? I mean even if she wanted to get something here, she wouldn't break a second-floor window. Especially since we were all in the house," I say, trying to reassure her. "I'll bet it has something to do with the renovation. The workers may have moved a beam, or all the hammering could have caused the old window to weaken and suddenly break."

She looks down at the baby bottle warming in the pot of water on the stove. "You're probably right."

"I mean. What was it . . . ? What did you find?" I ask, my curiosity piqued. It feels like Piper is talking in riddles.

"It was a toy. A doll."

"Probably one of the girls'," I say, patting her on the shoulder.

"It was hers," she insists.

Finally, the sweet, aromatic coffee is ready. I pour the steaming liquid into the to go mug. I'm not sure why Piper is going on and on about a doll, but I hope she's okay.

"Here, have a sip." I offer her the mug of coffee. "You doing all right?"

She stares at the cup blankly. "Yeah. I just wonder—"

Bryce trots down the stairs just then and joins us in the kitchen, grabbing a banana.

"Let's catch up when we get back," I say to Piper. "Bryce and I are heading out to fish—he says early morning is the best time for it. Esme should be home soon." I hold up a note Esme left saying she's at the grocery store and will be back, along with a detailed itinerary for the day. "The twins and Lana are still sleeping. When the girls wake up, can you look after them until Esme's back?"

Piper looks around helplessly. "Sure. Why not?" she says. "Preston will be up soon. I can look after all of them." She checks the baby monitor and nods.

"Thanks. We'll take the girls swimming when we're back." I glance at my husband. I can tell my sister doesn't want to look after the girls, but Bryce and I really need time to talk.

Bryce slips on his hiking boots and grabs his fishing rod. "Ready?" he asks.

I pull on my own boots and grab a small backpack that I've packed with two water bottles and some snacks, along with my precious coffee to go. "Let's do it."

I feel a little pang of guilt as I wave to Piper. She gives me a half smile and waves the milk bottle back at me. I close the door behind me.

We head out into the heat. I take in the view of the lake and the tall trees, which provide much-needed shade. The vista is beautiful. Serene. Every step I take away from the house, I feel stress draining from my body. Getting out into the open air, and away from the claustrophobic house, is just what I need.

We're about to turn onto the footpath to the lake when a police cruiser appears on our lane. The SUV drives up to us, pulling to a stop. The door swings open, and a man with dark hair and a few strands of gray at his temples gets out.

He looks familiar, though I'm not sure why.

"Morning, folks," he says to us. "I heard there were cars up here." He focuses his gaze on me. "Are you the threesisters who always visited, way back when?" A smirk rests on his lips, and I don't like the way he's looking at me. How would he know we used to come here on our yearly family trip? Up until I turned eighteen, when I stopped coming. I haven't been back here since then, not until last year, now that I've been forced to be here.

"Uh, yes. This is our family home we've been coming to."

"Rock on," the officer says, smiling and nodding. For a moment I have no idea what he's talking about, and then I realize he's looking at my AC/DC shirt.

"Ha, yeah," I say awkwardly, looking to Bryce. He steps in.

"What can we help you with this morning, Officer?"

The uniformed lawman nods to the fishing pole Bryce is holding. "Going out to try your luck?" he asks. His mannerisms are odd. He stands very still, his muscular arms crossed, feet wide apart.

Bryce nods, "Yes, sir."

"Well, just wanted you all to know there is a red flag fire warning in effect right now. Extremely hazardous conditions for forest fire. All campfires, bonfires, anything with a flame is prohibited."

He looks at me again, and that's when I know exactly who it is. His dark hair has specks of gray in it now, but it's him. My stomach drops.

The fire. From before. I know who he is. Is he taunting me?

"Are you Ben?" I ask him. "I think I knew you back in the day."

Now his smile widens. "That's right. Regina."

"How have you been?" I ask absently. It's coming back to me. He was a local. He invited my sisters and I to the lake. The night everything happened.

"I've been great. Work is good. I made sergeant." His jaw clenches. "Going through a tough divorce, though. She's trying to drag my name—" He stops venting abruptly. "But it's all good," he says now with a smile. "Living the dream."

"How nice," I toss out, looking at the lake, itching to go.

"Not too bad—for a local," he says, a shadow crossing his brow as he meets my gaze.

"Hey, thanks for the fire ban warning," Bryce replies amiably. "We better be on our way."

At that, Ben gets in his cruiser, but not before giving me one last, lingering look.

"That was weird," I say to Bryce as we make our way to the head of the path.

"I suppose," he says. "Just doing his job to warn people about the fire hazard. Out of towners like us might not know the dangers."

I roll my eyes. Bryce can be so dense.

"Besides, the local law here likely doesn't have a heavy work load in such a sparsely populated area," he says.

"Babe, that was strange. It was like he purposely wanted to run into us," I explain, but then stop talking since Bryce is clearly not picking up on my concern. So we continue walking in silence. Except I can't stop thinking about Ben the cop.

"I'm not going to last two weeks," I say to Bryce's back. "Poor Piper is losing it, and Esme is already driving me nuts. Now this weird dude we used to know shows up." I pause. "Maybe we should leave tomorrow."

"Leave?" He turns to look at me and adjusts his fishing rod carrier. He's frowning. "What about the will? Your mom's stipulation?"

I wave my hand. "That's not real. Remember that attorney, she said it's not actually enforceable. It was just a weird thing Mom put in—a last wish. The house is still one-third ours, whether we come here or not."

He shrugs. "I'm not so sure. And what about the other thing? The real reason we're here?" He glances sideways at me.

I kick a rock off the path with my boot. A plume of hot dust covers my leg with dirt. "I know. I'll get around to asking her." My eyes narrow. The air feels stifling at the mention of Esme.

Asking her for money is the last thing I want to do. She already looks down on me. To have to bow down to her and beg for money? I clench my hands into fists.

"I just really want to go. I can ask her tonight, and we'll leave tomorrow."

"How would that look, Reg?" Bryce strokes his fishing pole as if it's made of gold. "Plus, I like it here."

Why did I expect support from him? With unlimited fishing and home cooked meals, plus the possibility we'll get some cash from my sister, he's not going anywhere.

"Have you thought about what you'll say?" he asks, snapping me back to the conversation. "To your sister?"

We made a plan. Ask Esme to buy us out of our portion of the house. I even printed out some real estate figures to show her what it'd be worth. Sure, it's a lot of money for someone like me. But to Esme, it's pocket change—and we need it. Badly.

"I'll ask her to buy our share, like we planned. I just hate groveling to her." I snap a thin branch off one of the trees and toss it aside. Nothing is ever straightforward with Esme. Sure, buying us out would be easy for her. But I know she'll stretch it out and find a way to make me feel terrible about myself.

"She's not so bad," Bryce says.

Traitor. His defense of her feels like rubbing salt into an open wound. "Maybe it's a sister thing," I say. "You wouldn't understand."

A noise from the bushes startles me. I glance to my right where I heard the sound. I slow down. "Shh. Did you hear that?"

Bryce clods on, unconcerned. "Just a bird or a squirrel. Chill out and try to enjoy nature."

I snap another twig off a branch and consider whacking him with it.

The crunching in the forest causes me to pause again. It's closer this time. Whatever is causing the sound, it's not a squirrel or bird.

Even Bryce can't help but notice. He slows down and looks to our right, where the sound is coming from. By the disturbance it's making, I'm picturing a bear or mountain lion. The trees are dense, and aside from the path ahead of us and behind me, we're trapped. It would be impossible to run into the woods on either side of us. I can't even see farther than a few feet into the forest on either side.

"There's a clearing up ahead," Bryce says, picking up his pace.

I let him walk a few paces ahead. I hope the bear, or mountain lion, eats him first.

We continue on silently for another few minutes, passing our old boathouse on the left, and the rustling eventually stops, so I assume we've avoided being eaten by whatever was stalking us.

The pebble beach that leads to the lake is really pretty, I'll admit that. The hills of the old- growth forest surround the area in a fortress of spruce and pine trees, sloping down to the focal point of the water. Bryce puts his bag and fishing pole on an old log strewn on the beach.

I sit on the log and take out my water bottle. I put on my sunglasses to combat the glare from the lake.

Peaceful. I try to take deep breaths in. Let my stress melt away. But there's a tightness in my chest. I stretch out my legs.

Bryce casts into the air, and I hear the gentle *thwack* of his bobber hitting the lake. He does fly fishing—the only respectable type of fishing, he tells me often with a grin. He angles the rod and reels the line back in slowly, hoping to entice a fish to bite.

"Should be the perfect spot for some trout or bass, maybe even pike." His voice vibrates with excitement.

I ignore him. My mind is stuck on my sister. I can't believe he thinks Esme's "not that bad." It's like he never met her. Maybe he's just not paying attention. Because being around her for more than five minutes, even the least observant person would see what she is.

Phony. Entitled. Mean-spirited.

My whole life, people have acted like Esme walks on water. But most people aren't very bright. Is my husband fooled by her, too?

Lana springs to mind. She so loves her cousins. I don't mind her playing with them, getting close. But does the apple not fall far from the tree? I hope those twins won't be mean to Lana. Make her feel less than. Like their mom always does to me.

"Woah!" Bryce's whole body goes stiff as he hooks a fish on the line. His energy is focused solely and fully on the potential catch.

I can't help but wonder what it would feel like to have him care half so much about me, our predicament.

He reels in a small trout and holds it proudly up in the air. I grab my phone to take a photo.

"Good catch, babe," I say, snapping a picture.

He unlatches the hook from the fish's mouth and gently places it back in the water, allowing it to swim back out. He grins widely. "First catch of the day. It's going to be a good one."

In this moment, I don't imagine this to be our last peaceful day by the lake. But it is.

CHAPTER

7

Before

Alexis

THE SOUND OF water rushes over my head as I swim. I come up for air. I gasp for a breath, and then dive back in. The cool lake feels amazing after the heat of the sun.

Something tickles my shoulder, and I look underwater to see my cousin's long blond hair. Breaking the surface, we both tread water. She motions for me to follow her.

We glide through the lake like mermaids. Kicking our feet in unison, cupped hands pulling us forward as we swim.

We reach the shore, and I climb out of the water, the rocks rough against my soles. By the end of summer, my calloused feet will have become thicker, and I'll barely feel the shells and pebbles as I step.

"You have to see what I've found," she says, a wide smile on her ruby lips.

I follow her onto the shore. We're hunting treasure now, our footsteps quickening with every step.

Leaving the lake behind us, we make our way through a meadow with tall grass and wildflowers. My hair is quickly drying, the drops of water on my shoulders already having evaporated in the heat. My legs begin to burn, but still I follow her, the long, wispy weeds stinging against my legs. We come, finally, to a clearing.

"What is it?" I ask for the tenth time.

"You'll see."

Usually our treasure is something we've found in nature. A smooth rock. A white-tipped feather. An old key, or a plucked wildflower.

She moves toward the edge of the forest, away from the meadow, into the shady canopy of the trees. I follow her to a group of large rocks under the trees. She puts her hand in a crevice, feeling around behind the boulders, searching for something. She smiles as she slowly lifts out her prize and holds it out to me.

CHAPTER

8

Piper

MY EYES GENTLY shut and then snap open. I mustn't drift off. The twins and Lana are playing a board game, and Preston is sleeping, but I'm on babysitting duty. I can't drift off. That would be irresponsible, and I need to show my sisters I'm competent. It's only nine in the morning, but I feel like I've lived a lifetime since Regina and Bryce left to go fishing.

Paul had come downstairs right as they left. He whipped up an omelet in the kitchen. As we ate, I told him I was on duty to watch all the kids once they woke up, and that I was worried about what to make for our turn at dinner tonight. Thankfully he offered to cook for us, said he'd go hike the trail to forage for herbs and dandelion leaves for the meal. The minute he kissed Preston and I goodbye, the three girls had stumbled down the stairs, hungry for breakfast and bouncing wildly around with excitement. Greg followed wearing only shorts and let us know he was heading out for a run.

I made the girls breakfast of toaster waffles and microwave bacon to hold them over until Esme returned, wishing I'd thought to ask Paul to make something before he left. Instead, I juggled holding Preston while I tried to get their food ready, putting Preston down every few minutes in the bouncer. At which point he'd begin to wail, and I'd pick him up again. Repeat.

The girls gobbled up their breakfast, sitting on the stools at the kitchen island, leaving crumbs and plates that I didn't have time to wash. After breakfast they ran around playing and scattering toys around the living room. They finally settled down and agreed to play a board game. Brielle is now directing the others to follow the rules, while Gracey and Lana are much less concerned with the exact instructions.

The thought tantalizes my brain . . . I could be napping right now. Why did Regina leave me to mind the three girls and a baby while she goes fishing with Bryce? Is that not a little selfish?

But no. She must think I'm capable. That's good. I want her to depend on me. We're equals. I'm a mom now. She knows her daughter and the twins are in good hands with me.

And they are . . . I push down the appealing thought of sleep. If I closed my eyes for a few minutes, no one would notice, would they? The girls don't need me. Preston is sleeping . . .

I jolt awake.

A figure looms over me.

I yawn and sit up, disoriented.

"Where are the girls?" Paul asks.

"What?" I scan the living room. Remnants of a board game are strewn across the table. I glance over to the empty kitchen. There's no sign of the girls.

I pick up the monitor. Preston's sleeping body, curved onto his side in his crib, is thankfully there. My eyes lock with Paul's.

"You haven't seen them?" I ask.

"No, I just got back from my hike and found you sleeping. Were you supposed to be watching them still? I don't see them."

My eyes widen in horror. "You search the house and the pool . . . I'll check the lake." My brain is still groggy from my nap, but I'm propelled by fear and adrenaline. I remember Lana saying she wanted to go on the boat, could they have gone out there?

"I'm sure they're fine," he calls, but I don't wait for him to finish before I zip out the door.

The lake glistens blue. From the front porch I don't see any movement at the small beach that leads to the water, or at the boathouse to the right of the beach.

I run out in my bare feet, grasping the baby monitor. I'm not sure how far it will get a signal, but I don't have time to go back and bring Preston with me. Paul won't always pick him up right away if he cries, the way I like to.

I move quickly down to the shoreline, and the hot pebbles and dirt cake my feet instantly. I reach the lake, scan the water. No sign of the girls. I glance down the shoreline and see two figures. It looks like Bryce in a ballcap casting his fishing rod and Regina sitting on a log near him.

"Holy smokes," I mutter. What would Regina do if I lost Lana? What would Esme do to me if I lost her girls?

I hurry to the boathouse and enter the open area under the peaked roof. The deck boat is there secured by ropes. The water is still. No sign of the girls. I turn back, panicked, and try taking deep breaths to calm myself. To no avail.

Terrified, I take off running back to the house. My left foot catches on a rock. I stumble and howl in pain, both hands flying forward into the dirt as the monitor drops from my hands. My hair splatters into the dusty earth. I grab the monitor, wiping at my face, which only serves to get more dirt into my eyes. Picking myself up, I start off again for the house, watching more carefully where I'm going but still trying to search the area for the girls.

The door to the house is open, and I rush in. There's a trail of water leading from the back patio to the kitchen. Gathered around the kitchen island, wrapped in towels, are the girls. Paul is getting them juice boxes from the refrigerator.

"Were they in the pool alone?" I ask Paul, guilt gnawing at my stomach.

"Afraid so. They weren't in the house, so I figured I'd try there. I told them to wait until we have a snack, and Preston wakes up, and then we'll all go out to swim."

I nod, grateful he took charge of the situation.

"You okay?" Paul asks.

I look down and realize I'm caked in dirt.

Just then, the door to the garage opens and Esme walks in. Her eyes widen as she takes in everything—the wet girls, me covered in grime.

"What on earth?" she asks me.

"I fell asleep, and we couldn't find the girls—just for a moment—but Paul found them," I say breathlessly. "And then I fell—"

Esme's face registers horror. "Were the girls in the pool alone?" Her eyes dart to me. "How could you?"

She pushes past me to the twins and wraps them each protectively in her arms.

"I'm sorry . . ." Any excuse will fall short. I shake my head and shrug. There's no good explanation I can give.

"Why don't you go get cleaned up," Paul says gently to me. "We've got it from here."

I turn around and make my way to the stairs, head hanging in shame. Halfway up the staircase, I pause, and overhear Paul and Esme speaking in low tones. They're talking about me. I catch a few words here and there. *Newborn . . . no sleep. Irresponsible . . . Happening again?*

My face burns. It's embarrassing to be spoken about like an invalid. I make my way to our room.

In the bathroom, I'm startled by my own reflection. My face is brown with smudged dirt, and my hair is disheveled. I sit on the edge of the bathtub and observe my feet. I wince as I touch my heel. There's no blister yet, but the skin is shiny and a deep shade of red.

Both of my legs are covered in mud. Turning the shower faucet to hot, I let the water run until the bathroom is steamy. Stripping off my clothes, I step into the spray.

Less than a minute into the shower, I hear a piercing cry on the baby monitor. I stifle a sob from deep within. Why didn't I leave the monitor with Paul? Why is everything I do such an enormous screw up? I can't even take a shower.

I squirt a large dollop of body wash onto my loofa and vigorously rub it over my body, trying to scrub the worst of the dirt off. Another wail rings out, and knowing Preston, he's about to lose it. When he wakes up, he expects to be soothed and picked up immediately.

After scrubbing at my face and rinsing off the soap, I turn off the water and grab a towel. Each wail from Preston is like a stab to my heart. He's waiting for me.

Through the monitor, I hear a voice. "There, there."

My heart drops. I towel off quickly, not bothering to get fully dry.

"It's okay, baby, Auntie's here," I hear through the monitor.

Preston's crying subsides.

That voice. A thought grabs hold of my brain and won't let go. *My baby's in danger. He's not safe.*

I grab the monitor and rush out into the hallway, clutching my towel over my body. I stumble as I turn the corner.

Flinging open the door to our bedroom, I find Esme cradling Preston. He looks content, his little cheeks pink and his blue eyes looking up at her with interest.

"You," I say. "I could've sworn I heard Alexis's voice on the monitor." My eyes dart around the room, searching for our cousin.

Esme frowns. "Why would you think that? It's just me in here."

"Are you sure?" I ask.

"I'm sure." Esme frowns. "Do you think maybe you're having one of your episodes? Like you used to when we were younger? Hearing things that no one else hears . . . Your mind playing tricks on you?"

"No, Esme," I say, though I'm less sure now. "I know what I heard."

"Well, it's impossible. It's just me in here." Her tone softens. "There's a fruit and bagel tray downstairs, fresh coffee. Help yourself. I've got Preston." She moves past me, bringing him out of the nursery and into the hallway.

"I'll take him," I say, my heart still pounding, as I reach for him.

She balks. "Piper, I'm trying to help. You need to accept my help. You seem . . . unwell. Go eat. Really."

I move past her to go to my room, where I absently pull on a tee shirt and khaki shorts. That was Alexis's voice, I'm certain of it—But with each passing moment, my certainty fades, and by the time I head down the stairs, I decide maybe Esme's right, after all.

CHAPTER

9

Lana

"SHOULD WE BE out here?" I say, trailing behind my cousins. Aunt Piper fell asleep, so we crept upstairs and changed into our swimsuits. Now we're outside in the backyard.

Brielle tosses her head back. "Lana, if you're scared, go back with Aunt Piper. You can take a nap with her." She giggles, holding hands with Gracey. I glance back at the deck and the pool.

"I thought we were swimming," I say.

"We will," she says. "We're going to play hide-and-seek first. I'll count, you two go hide," Brielle says.

Gracey shrugs and disappears into the forest to hide. Brielle is covering her eyes and counting. If I don't move fast, she'll find me.

I go the other direction, away from Gracey, on a small footpath. I let out a small cry when a figure steps in front of me.

"Hello." A woman smiles down at me. She's pretty. She bends down. "Have you seen a little dog go by here?"

I shake my head no.

"That's too bad. We were playing in the lake, and I saw him run back down this trail." She pauses. "Do you like puppies?"

I nod my head up and down. "I love them."

"Mine is white and fluffy. Maybe you can help me look for her?"

"Okay," I say. My friend at home has a new dog. She's cute. She licks me and twirls around in circles. I want to see a puppy.

We walk farther down the footpath. "Callie, come here, girl," she calls out. We don't see her dog anywhere, though.

"How old is she?" I ask.

"She's only four months old."

"My neighbor has a puppy, too," I offer, thinking how much I'd like to pet a cute doggie right now.

"Do you live in that house I saw back there?" the woman asks me.

"Yeah," I say, "for two weeks in summer."

She leans in. "Do you know that when I was a little girl, I knew three little girls that used to live near here? We all used to play and be good friends."

"Really?" I ask. "Maybe you played with my mommy."

"Could be. It was a long time ago."

I stop, remembering. "We're playing hide-and-seek. I'm supposed to be hiding. From Brielle. I better go."

I look around the woods. We walked pretty far. I turn back.

"Sure," she says. "Thank you for looking for my doggie. I'm sure I'll find her. And maybe next time you can come play with her. Would you like that?"

"Yeah," I say eagerly. "I hope you find her soon."

I give her a wave and run the other direction. I hope this is the right way home. Did we come from this direction? I keep going, not sure what else to do. It only takes a few minutes before I'm in the backyard. Brielle and Gracey are taking turns climbing on a boulder, then jumping off.

"There she is," Gracey says to Brielle.

"I thought she'd hide in there forever." Brielle laughs like they're sharing a secret. Did they not want to come find me? Well, they are the ones who missed out. I made a friend who they didn't get to see. A friend with a puppy.

"Last one in the pool's a rotten egg!" Brielle yells. She takes off toward the pool, and Gracey is right behind her. They're a year older than me, so they're faster. I can't keep up with them. I want to play with them, though, so I follow behind.

They splash onto the pool steps. I hop down onto the second step, the water up to my knees. I'm not supposed to go in without my parents. With nothing to help me float. I walk down to the third step, water up to my waist. I can go in, just this one time. I splash my hands into the water, getting ready to take the final step.

Brielle is bobbing up and down. Gracey doggie paddles to the edge, her head going under the water and then coming up, gasping for air. She gets to the ledge and pulls herself up.

I'm about to follow Brielle when I hear a voice calling to us. It's Uncle Paul, telling us to come in right away.

I take one last look around the yard, hoping to see the little dog, but she's not there.

CHAPTER

10

Esme

OUTSIDE ON THE back patio, the sun beams over the pine trees in a cloudless sky. I can feel the sweat forming on my face already; mugginess wraps itself around me as if stepping into a steam room. The large rectangular pool glistens blue. It looks much different from the overgrown, greenish-tinted pool we grew up swimming in. I oversaw the entire pool being resurfaced and had the contractors add a raised hot tub to the other side, overlooking the forest. On a clear night, with no city or neighborhood lights, you can see every star in the vast sky.

Lounge chairs with white cushions line the pool, and there's a seating area with a newly built stone fireplace surrounded by a mahogany sectional with white cushions. I set my sunblock and a stack of towels on one of the tables.

"Girls, we all need sunblock on before we get in the pool," I call out. I'm 100 percent sure that Piper did not put sunblock on them, and the girls' delicate skin needs protection.

The girls wiggle impatiently as I apply the lotion on their legs and arms and faces, and then I slip Lana into her swim vest and secure the clip on the back. Brielle jumps into the pool first, making a splash, and Lana uses the steps to carefully get in. Gracey follows Brielle, jumping and landing practically on top of her. My heart drops, but they both bob up in the water, laughing as if it's the most natural and fun thing in the world.

Paul has changed Preston into his two-piece swim shirt and trunks, and has inserted him into a blow-up device that surrounds the baby like a round wheel. Paul gets in the water, avoiding the girl's splashes, where he dips his small child gingerly in the water, testing the baby's toes in the pool.

I slip off my sarong to reveal a smart one-piece that flatters my lean shape. I pull my long blond hair into a low ponytail. I enter the pool gratefully; my relief from the heat is immediate. I take a deep breath and do a quick lap to the deeper end of the pool.

When I resurface, I come up next to Paul. Preston doesn't seem to mind the water temperature, and Paul is gently swishing his feet in the water, while holding the baby safely in his arms.

"He likes the water," I say.

Paul smiles proudly. "He does."

"So tell me, how has Piper been adjusting to motherhood?" I ask.

He pauses, considering. "I've been back at work—late hours at the restaurant—so his care mostly falls on her. As I mentioned earlier, lack of sleep and his feeding issues have been hard on her. She wants to get everything right. But I think coming here . . ." He looks around to make sure the girls aren't listening. "Piper's gotten worse. Paranoid."

"Paranoid? About what?" I ask.

Paul looks as if he's weighing whether or not he should confide in me.

Just then, I hear the sliding patio doors open, and when I turn my head, I see Regina and Bryce heading toward the pool. Regina's chestnut hair is wrapped up in a high bun, and I see that she's removed the dreadful AD/DC T-shirt that makes her look like a teenager. She's now wearing a nice white bikini.

"Catch anything?" Paul calls out to Bryce as a greeting.

"Tons. They were biting like crazy." Bryce cracks open a beer with gusto. "You gotta come out there with me, Paul. Let's go fish tomorrow morning. We can take the boat out."

Paul looks down at baby Preston. "Right, let's do it," he says, but I can hear the hesitation in his voice. He must be worried about leaving Preston in Piper's care after what happened this morning.

Regina gets in the pool to her shoulders, and then wades over next to me in the deeper end. "The girls seem like they're having fun," she says, nodding to Lana and my twins. Their shouts and peals of laughter ring out between splashes. "It's sweet," she continues. "Reminds me of the three of us when we were little."

I nod. Something about Regina feels off. She's being too nice. I look over at her with a discerning eye. She catches my eye and smiles.

"Lana's gotten so tall," I say to her. "Beautiful girl. We've missed you guys. I haven't talked to you since, when is it now, last August when we were all here? I don't think we even received a Christmas card from you." My sister hardly returns my calls or messages, and she doesn't do social media. I saw her last August for our first summer here without Mom. Prior to that, I hadn't seen her in years, not since maybe Lana's first birthday. Piper does a better job of sending messages now that Preston was born, but still, this is our first chance to really catch up in years.

Regina pushes the water around with her hands, and then finds the edge of the pool, pulling herself up to a sitting position so that only her feet remain in the water. "Yeah," she says. "There's been a lot going on. In fact, I'd hoped we could find a time to talk . . . in private."

I knew it. Regina's got a plan. It's always something with her. I wish I could trust her to say a nice word without there being an alternative motive, but it's never happened yet.

"Sure," I say, trying to keep the sigh out of my voice. "Maybe after we swim. We can prepare lunch and chat."

The sliding door opens again, and Greg appears wearing red board shorts, back from his run. His abs are toned, and my gut clenches as I think how handsome he looks. He dives in the pool, gives me a quick wet kiss on the cheek, and then joins the other men as they lounge by the pool steps.

The silence between Regina and I stretches out, allowing me to overhear our husbands chatting up a storm. They discuss topics I have no real interest in. Fishing. Investing in the stock market and crypto. Baseball. All the while, Paul holds Preston and the baby doesn't make a peep. He makes it look easy.

How nice it must be to be a man. They're having the time of their lives, not a care in the world. Meanwhile, Piper is either sleeping or having a nervous breakdown, Regina always looks put upon by the world, and I feel sick to my stomach about my cheating husband, the texts I sent his mistress, and the woman I saw today at the market.

Do men just not have issues? Or do they just hide it better? Maybe they simply don't care as much. That must be it.

Well, I care. *A lot.*

I wade over to where Greg and the other husbands are standing in a circle in the pool. The men all ignore me, but I feel a shift in their mood. I've invaded their masculine energy field.

I wrap my arms around Greg's waist. Maybe he's right. We need to connect. Physically. Get back on track. He pats absently at my arms and gives me a funny look.

"Yeah," he says to Bryce, debating luxury cars. "But have you seen the new model? If I could buy any car, I'd buy that with the V8 turbo engine. What a beauty." He whistles with reverie. Meanwhile, this beauty—his wife—he appears indifferent to.

Running my right hand up and down his back, he flinches, annoyed at my display of affection. He seems to wish I were anywhere but next to him. In fact, now may be a good time to check back on Greg's phone. If B responds to my text the way I think she will, I need to be the one to reply to her—not Greg.

"I'm going to get changed," I say to Greg, and then wade over to tell Regina, who is now laying on a flotation device. She barely moves her head to nod to me in response.

I rinse off in the outdoor shower and then wrap my towel around myself. If I laid out in the sun for even a few minutes, I'd be scorched from this heat and sun. Instead, I quickly towel off then arrange the towel on the outdoor rack to dry.

Once I'm inside the house, I slide the door closed behind me. The cool air sends goose pimples rising on my flesh. I don't see Piper anywhere, nor do I plan to go looking for her; she needs to rest. Heading over to the charging station, I see Greg's phone is no longer there. I tiptoe up the stairs, careful not to wake Piper if she's sleeping.

In our bedroom, I peel off my swimsuit and hang it on a hook in the bathroom. I pick out an outfit from my closet, and slip on the white pleated shorts and navy tank. All the while,

I'm scanning the room, closet, and bathroom for Greg's phone, but I don't see it. I do a sweep of the bed while I pull up the sheet and blanket to make it; not there. I open the bedside drawer on his side; not there. I move back to the closet and check his shorts; bingo. The heavy black phone is there.

Slipping it out and into my hand, I punch his passcode. Darn. There's a new message chain between them.

The first message on the thread, from B, reads, "Be there soon. Excited to see you. XO." Greg, clearly confused since my texts to her were deleted, responded: "You're coming here? No. I told you next week I'm taking you to the Cape."

My nostrils flare and I feel the heat rising in my face. How dare he? I blink, not believing the words. He's planning on leaving here early, which is unforgivable during the one trip our family all looks forward to, but then he plans to take *her* to the Cape, of all places? The place he proposed to me.

B has replied: "Too late. You told me it was urgent. I'm already halfway there. I'm staying at the Bergamont Resort. Meet me tonight for a drink. It's the least you can do."

Oh, someone will meet you, B. But it won't be my husband.

I type out a reply: "Great. Meet me by the front boardwalk near the dock at 9:30pm. X." For authenticity, I've forced myself to sign it with the sickening X I've noticed he uses with her.

Making sure the message is sent and received, I delete the conversation.

CHAPTER

11

Before

Alexis

MY COUSIN STANDS before me, palm open, displaying the treasure. In her small hand is a ring. A thin silver band and a large clear stone in the middle that gleams and glints in the sunlight.

"Is that a diamond?" I ask, my voice hushed in awe.

"Hold it," she says, dropping it in my hand.

I clasp onto the ring.

"Put it on, Alexis," she says, laughing. "Don't be afraid."

I put it on my ring finger, but it's much too large. I move it to my middle finger, but again find it falling off. I move it to my thumb and find it still loose, but it holds on better there.

"Where did you find this?" I ask. Probably not in the rocks. What a lucky find.

Her ruby lips purse. "I just found it," she says with a shrug. "It looks pretty on you. You can keep it."

My belly feels warm and full. It's the first time I've felt at home here. Maybe things won't be so bad.

"Thanks," I say, using my index finger to feel the ring on my thumb, the hard stone set in the smooth band.

"Last one's a rotten egg," she calls out, and spins on her heel. I follow her hair flying through the wind, racing to be first back to the water. But her strong legs beat me by a long shot.

Huffing, I splash into the water. She already dove in, and I watch the kick of her feet cutting through the water. I clench my finger over my precious ring, but it makes swimming harder. I can't lose the ring. I keep going, kicking and using my arms. But I feel like I'm sinking.

I struggle for air. I cry out. "Help," I call. But she's ahead of me, gliding through the water. I look back at the shore I just came from, closer than the lake house shore where we're headed. Should I go back? But what if I get lost trying to walk through the forest and underbrush?

Suddenly, I wish my mom were here. I see her face, her crinkly eyes when she smiles.

Gulping for air, I know I have to keep going. I feel the ring on my thumb. Still there. I keep pushing forward. It didn't feel this far when we swam out. I look around and make out my cousin's silhouette on the beach. Just have to get there . . . Almost there.

But I'm finding every stroke harder to keep going. My limbs scream out to stop moving. My head dunks under. Once, then again. Then I feel myself going under, I can't seem to break the water for air. I dip again.

This time, I'm not sure I can get back up.

CHAPTER

12

Regina

"MOMMY, I'M HUNGRY." Lana's voice wakes me from a semi-slumber and startled, I almost fall off the floating raft in the pool. Lunch. Right. I was supposed to help with that.

"Sure thing, love. I'll go pull something together and call you girls when it's ready." As much as I'd like to continue laying here, and let Esme prepare the food—as I know she will if I don't move—I have to. She roped me into helping, of course, on the condition that we could chat as we make lunch.

The heat of the midday sun has zapped my energy, but I hop off the float and drag myself through the pool. A second cup of coffee will do the trick. Maybe Esme's already prepared everything and I can skip having to help while she's breathing down my neck.

I leave the husbands and the girls in the pool with a final longing look back at my raft, which the girls have quickly grabbed and are now giving one another rides on. I dry off with a towel and slip back on my AC/DC shirt, pausing as I'm reminded of my conversation with the creepy police officer, Ben.

Inside, there's no sign of Esme, or Piper for that matter. The kitchen counter is bare. So lunch preparations haven't even started yet. I glance at the time—12:45. We're behind Esme's itinerary for the day. Unusual.

"Esme?" I call out. But there's no answer. "Esme?" Now I'm starting to wonder if something could be wrong.

I'm about to head upstairs when she appears at the head of the stairs. Her blond hair is combed back and she's dressed in cute white shorts and navy top. Her face briefly flashes a look of guilt, and then her composure is regained, a smile fixed in its place.

"Shall we get to lunch prep?" she says, whisking by me and into the kitchen. "We're behind schedule." She turns on the faucet and washes her hands, then dries them on a dish towel.

"Great," I say, waiting by the sink to wash mine, too. But first I grab a mug and pour the remnants from the coffee pot into it. I plop the mug in the microwave and reheat it for thirty seconds, and then drink it down in four large gulps.

Esme has placed cold cuts, cheeses, fresh rolls, dips, and spreads, as well as lettuce and veggies on the kitchen island.

"Why don't you cut these veggies, and I'll put the meat out?"

She takes out the ham first, and begins rolling the thin slices on the platter. We'll eat buffet style, with everyone making their own sandwich, and choosing their own individual ingredients and condiments.

"Super," I say, selecting a long sharp knife out of the wooden block and setting it on the cutting board. I rinse off a cucumber before I begin to slice. My movements are hesitant, uncertain.

I'll start with small talk. "I heard the twins say they're getting a new nanny. They said they really liked the old one and were upset about it. What happened?"

Esme glances at me sideways, her long lashes flicking with irritation. "They said that?" Shakes her head. "Well, kids don't understand these things."

"What happened? Did she steal from you?" I recall the long list of employees she's had problems with. Stolen food. Habitual lateness. Overuse of cell phone while working. Esme runs a tight ship with high expectations.

At the mention of her nanny leaving, Esme's body tenses and she doesn't answer immediately. "That bad?" I ask. I'd expected her to launch into a gossipy story of an irresponsible employee raiding her closet, but clearly this has struck a real nerve.

She turns to me, eyeing me up and down, as though deciding whether she should confide in me. "Let's just say she crossed a boundary." She continues working on the food prep, but the color rises in her cheeks. "With Greg . . ."

My jaw drops open. I know there'd been an indiscretion on Greg's part before they were married. She'd almost broken up with him, but he'd promised her it was cold feet. Now this.

"No way," I say, disgusted. "I can't believe him. With your nanny?"

She waves her hand. "Trust me. I'm taking care of him. But the nanny is out. I don't care if the girls love her. She's gone." Her voice remains calm. Cold.

"Of course." I lay my hand on her shoulder. "I'm so sorry, Es."

"Don't be." Her voice is hard. "I shouldn't have said anything."

We work in silence for a while. When it seems like she's recovered from talking about her rotten husband, I decide it's now or never.

Deep breath. "So, there's something I wanted to ask you about . . ." I start.

She lets out a small sigh as she continues to prep the food. "Of course. What's on your mind?"

"We've had a really hard time lately, Bryce and I . . . financially. We were hoping you'd want to buy us out of our portion of the house," I blurt it out all at once. I drop the knife and pull out the sheet folded in my purse. "Here. I've printed out some recent home sales on the lake, for price comparisons." I hold the sheet out to her.

"I see." She takes the piece of paper and regards it. "That was so thoughtful of you to print prices of how much you'd like me to pay you." She looks at me. "I suppose you'll continue to come here every summer, and use the house as desired, without the pesky nuisance of contributing financially or being a part owner?"

I can't read her, but I think she's pissed. Everything's a riddle with Esme. I feel like she's walked me into a trap and I don't know how to answer.

"We'd love to still come, sure—if we're invited. And it's convenient for you. But it's up to you." I make one final attempt at what feels like a botched job of this. "We really need the money, and I know you can afford it. And it's not like I can sell my portion to anyone else . . ."

Her eyes narrow, and I know I've really said the wrong thing now. Because we did look into selling just our portion, and found that it would be pretty difficult to do and would need both of my sisters' agreement. The other option would be to bring her to court to try to force a sale. That's not something I want to even consider, especially with how much time it could take. Time we don't have. Not to mention legal fees, which we can't afford, either. Plus, our lawyer said my mom's weird stipulation about coming here for two weeks each August isn't technically enforceable, but could still make it a more difficult process to sell to an outside party.

Esme goes about laying out the cheese, slice after slice. The veins in her neck look strained, but otherwise I'm not sure she's heard me. Is the conversation over?

"Esme?" I venture eventually.

She turns and cocks her head at me. "Yes?" She looks expectantly at me.

"I mean. What do you think about the . . . about buying our portion of the house?"

Her neck veins stretch taut again. She slams down the package of provolone. "I will consider it. I have to talk to Greg."

"Esme, are you okay?" I reach out my hand, placing it on hers.

She flinches and flicks my hand away.

"Are you going to finish cutting those?" She turns to the cutting board and the whole bell peppers and tomatoes. Without waiting for a reply, she grabs the knife and starts slicing. Anger seems to radiate from her petite body and she's cutting with a vengeance.

What will I tell Bryce? I glance out the window. He's on his second beer, lounging in the pool with the guys, fully enjoying his vacation. Little does he know how screwed we are. Will he still think Esme's so great when I tell him she's "considering" our proposition? I'm 99 percent sure that's her way of telling me to fuck off, but Esme is too proper to ever say what she really feels.

I take the rolls and set them in a breadbasket. "I'll let everyone know lunch is ready," I tell her.

"Wonderful," she replies. And that's the end of it.

I consider telling her the truth. How desperately we need the money, and why. But my pride has always been my Achilles' heel. I'd rather die than plead, or beg, or tell her my sob story. I doubt she'd care, anyway. My problems don't fit into her picture-perfect life. I'm a nuisance and beneath her, and why would she want to help someone she doesn't even like?

CHAPTER

13

Before

Alexis

I FIGHT TO KEEP my head above water. Kick. Stroke. Breath. I can't give up. Finally, I feel the muddy soil as my foot reaches the ground underneath. I crawl onto the shore and sit, panting with exertion and relief. My lungs hurt, like they're going to burst, and I struggle to get air in.

I see her blond head above me, the sun shining behind her, making her face a shadow.

"I won," she says.

Squinting up at her, I nod. I hold up my thumb. "I still have the ring," I say breathlessly.

"Good," she says. "Let's go."

We make our way back to the house. The lake house is large compared to the one-bedroom apartment I lived in with my mom for all of my ten years. Coming back here without her this summer, though, feels all wrong.

Inside, we grab sodas and a bag of potato chips. We sit out on the back patio, our feet in the pool, eating the salty snacks.

Eventually, Aunt Audry and Uncle Frank return from their outing with Regina and Piper in town. They tumble out on the back porch. Audry looks at the almost empty bag of chips with disapproval. "Dinner's at five," she says. "Why don't you get washed up and help set the table?" She looks at me.

"Yes, ma'am." I get up quickly. As I brush past her, I feel her grab my shoulder.

"Where did you get that," she says, pulling my hand up to her.

"We found it . . ." I say quietly.

Her eyes are dark. She pulls the ring from my thumb. "Tell me the truth," she says.

Out of the corner of my eye, I see Esme. She shakes her head no. *Don't tell,* she mouths.

"In the rocks—"

"Go to your room, Alexis," she says coldly. "You can stay there without dinner until you see fit to tell the truth."

Up in my room, my stomach rumbles. I wait for someone to come and get me for dinner, but minutes pass and no one comes.

I crack open the door and creep out in the hallway, pausing on the stairs. I hear the forks clinking on their plates as they eat. I strain to hear bits of their conversation.

"Diamond ring . . . little thief . . . that side of the family . . . bad genes." Then, "Look what happened to her mother."

Hot tears run down my face. So that's what they think of me. I thought nothing could be worse than when my mom died, leaving me all alone. But at this moment, I'm more alone than ever.

CHAPTER

14

Piper

When I awake, my first thought is that someone's standing over me. Watching. But peeling my eyes open, the dimly lit room is empty.

My second thought is that the room is too quiet. There's no crying or babbling from Preston. I wipe the drool from my mouth and stumble out of bed, craning my neck to look into the crib. Someone's taken Preston. He's not there. Panic claws at my throat.

It hits me. It's midday, and Paul has the baby. How I fell in the dirt. The girls at the pool unsupervised. Hearing Alexis's voice over the monitor. How Esme and Paul took Preston and relegated me to the bedroom to "rest" as if it were a padded room. I have, in fact, been to one of those types of places long ago. I'm determined to leave that in the past. I've never told Paul the full extent of my history, and there's no need to do so now.

I head to the bathroom. In the mirror I see that my hair is limp and disheveled, and I'm pale. This afternoon, I vow, I'm going to get it together.

I hardly ever wear makeup, but I take out the products I own. I apply a little tinted moisturizer, a few strokes of blush, and a coat of mascara. There. I look more awake. I run the brush through my hair and place it in a low ponytail, so it'll be out of the way of Preston's grabbing hands. He loves to clutch onto my shoulder-length strands and yank with a force that's stronger than his four months.

Downstairs, the long table is filled with the entire family finishing their lunch. I feel embarrassed as all their eyes turn on me. Paul gets up and hands me the baby. "You must've needed the rest. I've had him for hours," he says, as if he's been fighting a great war for months.

Preston's eyes fly open and he starts to squirm. He's hungry, and so am I. I longingly look at the buffet-style cold cuts and sides. "Can you hold him while I fix his bottle?" I ask Paul. But he seems not to hear me—or is purposefully ignoring my plea—as he heads onto the back deck with Bryce, a cold beer in hand.

I feel my anxiety start to rise as I cradle Preston in one arm while making his bottle. Once it's ready, I sit at the table as Lana, Brielle, and Gracey get up. The girls bring their plates to the garbage can to empty them, then place them in the sink. Esme and Regina remain at the table with me.

Preston drinks about two ounces of milk before he starts to fuss. He pushes the bottle away, looking angry.

"Maybe it's an allergy?" Esme suggests, watching Preston.

"We've done several tests—no allergies. But we still switched formulas. I have a special no-gas bottle. Nothing seems to make a difference."

"Look at the way he's eyeing the food," Esme says to Regina, who nods absently. Regina's scrolling on her phone and tapping away. Esme continues, "I think Preston's ready for solid foods. Give him some baby oatmeal. That will fill him up. He's hungry, poor guy."

"The doctor said no solids until six months," I say, shifting Preston so he's more upright, wishing he would just drink his milk. My whole body feels tense. I read babies can sense this. I try to relax, ignoring the perspiration starting to form under my arms.

"Doctors don't know everything. We gave the twins solids before six months. Every baby is different."

Esme gets up and begins to clear the discarded plates. The twins and Lana have actually cleared their plates, but the husbands have left theirs on the table, along with various half-eaten side dishes, condiments, cups, and crumpled napkins.

"I can help you clean up," I say. Preston finally begins sucking at his bottle.

Esme shoots me a look. "Don't bother, really. Your hands are full," she says. Making me feel helpless.

"Well, it's our turn to make dinner tonight. Paul's going to grill filet mignon and make his signature house salad for us." It's as if I've spoken into the ether. Esme is busy filling a black garbage bag and absently nods at me. Regina's face is a slight scowl as she taps on her phone.

I watch as the leftovers are placed in the fridge. I want to ask Esme to keep the food out for me, but I don't want to impose. My stomach growls as I wait for Preston to finish, but I'm grateful he's eating.

Looking down at his face, I feel a surge of love. Such a beautiful boy. And he loves me. I'm his mom. At least I have that.

Setting down the empty bottle, I turn him over gently to burp him. The heavenly smell of baby lotion wafts off him, and his tiny body relaxes into mine.

Everything will be fine. I try to push away the anxious thoughts that have been building. The ones telling me something is very, very wrong. That I'm in danger. That Preston isn't safe. That Alexis is back and wants revenge. She was here. I heard her voice over the monitor. Maybe the broken window was an omen—or something worse? A threat?

Maybe it's best to pack up and leave for home tomorrow. But then I'll be missing the chance to connect with my extended family. Cousins for Preston. I'll look weak. Crazy.

No, it's best to stick it out.

It's just an adjustment. Being here with the baby. The past colliding with the present. *Everything will be fine,* I tell myself. *It's all going to be okay.*

CHAPTER

15

Before

Esme

It's been a few days since my mom caught Alexis with her ring, and I can tell Mom is not happy with Alexis. There's lots to be mad at her about.

Mom calls us to the table for dinner, flipping off the television show we're watching. She's made a pot roast.

"What smells so bad?" Alexis asks.

"Mind your manners," my mom says, shooting Alexis a disapproving look. My dad sits at the head of the table, and my mom takes her place at the other head. Alexis sits across from me. Both of my sisters fight to take the seat next to hers.

"You got to sit next to her last night," Piper says to Regina, pouting. "It's my turn."

"That's not true! You got to be next to Alexis every night this week." Regina sticks her tongue out at Piper.

"Girls," my mom says. "What kind of behavior is this? Regina, go sit next to Esme. Now." Regina sulks, kicking at Piper's chair on the way over to sit by me. My sisters used to fight to sit next to me. I bite my lip, looking at Alexis across the table, who is holding her nose.

"What's for dinner? It stinks." She giggles, and Piper snickers next to her.

"Really, girls, I've had enough of this." My mom's voice is stern. "You will respect the food we make and put on the table, Alexis. Or you can go without."

My father attempts to interject. "Let's say grace. Piper, why don't you begin."

"Dear heavenly father, thank you for this meal we are about to receive. Thank you for bringing Cousin Alexis to live with us. Amen."

Alexis catches my eye and smirks at me and crosses her eyes.

"Mom," I cry, "Alexis is making faces at me during grace."

"Not true!" Alexis calls out. "You're a big, fat liar."

"Girls, enough." My mom is using her sternest voice, and even I know that means to be quiet.

I kick at Alexis under the table, gently, but just enough to bug her. I kick her again, and then again.

"Mom," I say, "today Alexis said a bad word when we were at the pool."

My mom places down her fork, not having had more than a bite, and sighs. "What did she say?"

"She said the 's-h' bad word. For poop," I say. And it's true.

"Did not," Alexis says, though she looks guilty.

"You mean 'shit,'" Piper says.

That sets my mother off. "Piper! How dare you use that language? Go to your room. Right now." Her eyes narrow as she looks at Alexis. "And Alexis. I will not allow you to teach my girls bad manners, and bad language, and stealing. This can't continue. I won't let you influence my daughters. They're younger than you, Alexis, they look up to you. And to Esme."

My mom's face is red, and she looks to my dad. He shrugs and clears his throat. "Yes, Alexis. That's not how our family speaks." He sighs. "Now go to your room."

Piper pushes back her chair and goes upstairs, and Alexis gets up to go, as well, but not before getting in the last word. "It was Esme." She points her finger at me. "She's the one who started it."

It doesn't bother me. She's in trouble. I've won.

I take my first bite of my pot roast. It tastes yummy. Regina is quiet and looking down at her food. I hope she's not feeling sorry for Alexis.

Suddenly I hear a scream and a loud crash. My mother moves quickly, running up the stairs after Alexis and Piper to see what's the matter.

"Stay here, girls," my dad says, as he throws his napkin down on the table and follows. Regina stays at the table, but I climb the stairs to get a peek.

They're in the bedroom, and I hear my mom say, "Oh, my goodness," and my dad curses. "She's bleeding," she says to my dad, and he rushes past me. He goes to the bathroom and comes back with the first aid kit.

I sneak a peek into the bedroom, where Piper is crying so hard she's gasping, as my mother bandages her hands. The vanity mirror is destroyed. Shards of glass lie on the ground.

"What happened?" my mother says. "How did this break?"

I step back around the corner to hide, but continue to listen. Piper is gulping in air and so upset she can't answer Mom. Finally, after a few minutes, Piper calms down enough to speak.

"Alexis told me I was naughty and going to the orphanage. She said that's where they send bad kids. And then she pushed me." Her voice is thick with emotion, and she sniffles as she goes on. "I was mad, so I tried to hit her with the doll, but she moved, and I hit the mirror instead. I didn't mean to." She lets out a wail. "Ow, that hurts."

She begins to moan frantically, and I cover my ears, scared.

"Audry, we need to take her to get medical attention. The blood is soaking through the bandages," my dad says in alarm.

At that moment, I hear footsteps and look over to see Alexis. Her eyes are wide as she waits to hear what's next. She catches my eye then, and sticks out her chin at me, defiant.

My little sister is bleeding and in pain, and I can see it in Alexis's eyes—she's happy.

"I'll take her," my mom says, and she and Piper brush past us in the hallway, my mom holding her wrapped hand. "But Frank, get her under control," she snaps, nodding to Alexis.

My dad appears in the hallway. He sees Alexis and I standing there. In a thundering voice, louder and angrier than I've ever heard him, he points to his bedroom. "Alexis, get in the closet. And do not come out until I say so."

C H A P T E R

16

Piper

I PLACE PRESTON IN his baby bouncer. "You sit right here, you can watch Mommy and Daddy eat," I say to him. I finish setting the table, using Esme's new place settings and cutlery, with our mom's fine china.

Paul comes in from the deck where he was grilling the steaks, and places the steaming tray of meat on the counter.

"We'll let those rest, and be ready to eat in ten," he says. When he's in cooking mode, I usually act as his sous chef. He's used to be in charge in the kitchen and leading his staff. At home, we make a good team.

"What else do we need?" I ask him.

"Just put out some drinks for the kids, ice water for you and wine for us, and we'll be set. First course salad is ready."

"They said they'd be home by now. Hopefully they don't decide to eat out," I say, glancing at the clock, noting it's six forty-five PM. Regina, Bryce, and Lana went with Esme, Greg, and the twins to the local fair in town. They said they'd be back by six thirty for dinner. It wouldn't be the first time they'd changed plans without letting me know. "Maybe I should call them," I say.

Just then, the girls come crashing into the house in a jumble of excitement. Brielle runs up to me and holds out a huge pink pony. "Look what my daddy won at the fair!"

"Wow, it's almost as big as you are," I say.

Gracey is beside her and squeezes her animal close. "Mine's a unicorn."

Lana comes in behind them with less excitement, and I notice a small dolphin in her hand. "What a pretty dolphin that is, Lana," I say. "Such a nice color blue and so soft." I hold out my hand to touch it. "Did you name him?"

She brightens a bit. "I think I'll call him Bluebell." The girls run off with their prizes to the playroom.

Regina enters the large oak door of the house, her brow furrowed. "Do they have to outdo everyone all the time? Esme wouldn't let Greg stop playing until he won both girls huge prizes." She rolls her eyes. "He blew through three hundred bucks trying and then finally slipped the guy a hundred."

"Lana seems happy with her dolphin. Don't worry too much," I say.

Regina throws her bag down. "This heat is brutal." She heads toward the kitchen and pulls out the blender, a large handle of tequila, and some mixer. "I'll make a pitcher to cool down."

Esme, Greg, and Bryce are the last of the group to arrive.

"Great timing," I say. "Dinner will be ready any moment. We'll start with a fresh salad, Paul used hand-picked—"

Esme walks to the dinner table and cuts me off. "Oh Piper, you can't use these dishes. These are mom's special occasion plates. Why didn't you use the everyday dinnerware?" She begins stacking the plates that I set out back up.

"Sorry, I thought since Paul made a nice meal and is pairing it with special wine he bought when he went to Napa for the restaurant . . . I thought we could use them."

She shakes her head. "I don't think so." She places the dishes back in the breakpoint and returns with plain ceramic plates. They don't complement the wildflowers on the table that Paul picked up at the market, but they're fine.

"I guess we're ready now," I say.

Esme calls the girls and they tumble into the kitchen, and Esme instructs them to go wash their hands before they eat.

"Those steaks look amazing. Man, I can't wait to dig in," I hear Bryce say to Paul, slapping him on the back. "Need a hand with anything?"

"Sit, sit," Paul says, bringing out the first course restaurant-style salad for the adults and a plain pasta salad and a crudité plate for the kids.

Paul uncorks the wine as everyone takes their places. The three girls sit together at the end of the table, and Esme is at the head. Greg is to her left, Paul to her right. Regina sits next to Paul, and Bryce sits next to Greg.

Once I'm finished checking on Preston and moving his bouncer to a position where I can see him, and he can see me, I squeeze in next to Regina, with the girls to my left. I feel a bit like I'm at the kiddie table way down at the end.

Paul finishes pouring the wine, just water for me, and takes his seat. He raises his glass. "We're glad we can be here with the family, and that Preston is here to join our family tradition with you all at the summer house. To good times and good health."

Everyone raises a glass and puts their wine to their lips. "Beautiful, Paul, simply beautiful," Esme murmurs in approval.

I extend my hand trying to clink glasses, but I'm too far away from everyone, so I simply take a sip of my water and add, "Agree, I'm so glad we're doing this." But I've missed the moment, and no one replies as they all focus on their food. They dig in with groans of satisfaction.

"Regina, is that blue margarita a good pairing for the steak?" Esme asks. "You know that Paul brought us Cabernet from a vineyard in Napa, especially paired with the filet mignon."

Regina stiffens next to me, places her food in her mouth mechanically, not making eye contact with anyone. She grabs her margarita. "I like tequila," she says, taking a large gulp. She's blocking me from feeling like I'm part of the group.

"Well, I'd like to add to Greg's lovely sentiment," Esme says, clearing her throat. In *the voice*, as Regina calls it, referring to her pageant voice, she begins, "Guys, this house means so much to me. That's why I invested in renovating it . . ."

Regina stifles an eye roll. Even I have to admit, Esme does bring up the renovations a lot.

Esme continues. "Because this is our family home. Mom's pride and joy. She was so proud that her grandfather had the foresight to pick such a beautiful property. How it's our own little corner of the world. No one else can build here. Like it was meant for us. Our own piece of magic." She dramatically looks us each in the eye. "Mom's biggest wish was for the three of us sisters to continue the tradition. That's why she gave us the house and had her estate pay the taxes for the next fifty years for us, as long as we all come every August. Alan, our family attorney and dad's best friend, who we adore, made sure everything was set up for us." She frowns. "But I do worry that my sisters aren't making much of an effort. Piper, I know you have the baby, but the house was a disaster this afternoon, with dirt and pool water splashed all over the new floor. And falling asleep watching the kids?" She shakes her head. Now it's Regina's turn. "And Regina, Lana makes a mess and you never pick up a thing or tell her to. You haven't made any effort to help. You're lounging around all day."

"I went to the fair today with you all," she retorts.

"And you looked at your phone the whole time," Esme says. Then she looks at us expectantly.

"I'll work on pitching in more." Regina almost chokes on the words as they come out.

"Thank you," Esme says.

I guess it's my turn to apologize, even though Esme seems like she's being awfully selfish to bring this up in front of the whole group. Is she trying to humiliate me?

"Sorry, Esme. It won't happen again."

No one else seems to register it, but Paul gives me a sympathetic nod. He can probably tell by my blazing cheeks that I'm embarrassed. He speaks up, mercifully changing the subject. "Speaking of the fair. How many rounds did it take you to win those huge toys, Greg?" Paul asks him with a grin.

"Eh. A few." Greg shifts his shoulders.

Next to me, I feel Regina recoil. Now she's squirming as if she has to physically stop herself from speaking. I think she's upset she wasn't able to get Lana a big toy, too.

"You know those games are rigged, right?" Paul says jovially. He launches into a tale about the behind-the-scenes secrets of the carnival, with everyone listening intently and laughing at his punch lines. Paul's so good at making easy conversation. He does it at the front of the house at the restaurant, and in the kitchen with the staff.

"That explains it then," Esme says smoothly. "Greg used to be a pitcher in high school. He was offered a baseball scholarship but decided to go Harvard for medicine."

"Esme." Greg shoots her a look. "You don't always have to do that."

"Do what?" she says, lifting her wine glass to her mouth.

"You're always so concerned about appearances."

She bristles. "That's not true."

Greg turns to Bryce and Paul. "This is the woman who by the end of our first week dating started planning our wedding venue."

She huffs. "I've told you that the nicest venues book out two years in advance. I simply inquired to them about the waitlist. You were the one who mentioned getting married early on," she reminds him.

"You took one word and ran to the altar, didn't you?" He laughs, giving the men a knowing look.

Esme's face remains a mask, but I can see the vein in her neck.

Paul chimes in, "Our wedding venue was a no brainer, and the catering, too," he says, referencing our wedding reception at his restaurant.

"We had to settle for the second-best chef in town," I say, remembering the night fondly. "I had to remind Paul he wasn't allowed to cook for our wedding, or else he might've spent the whole night in the kitchen." No one but me laughs at that, they just sort of nod politely with a quick glance in my direction. I know I'm at the end of the table, but it feels like I'm not part of the conversation.

"Let's bring out the steaks." Paul gets up and heads to the kitchen to get the meat.

Esme abruptly stands up. "You know what. I think I've lost my appetite," she says. "All this heat." She narrows her eyes at me. "I trust you can clean up after dinner while I rest upstairs?" She carries her salad plate over to the trash compactor and empties the contents into the bin before placing her plate in the sink. Then she turns and pads up the stairs without another word.

Once she's gone, I get up. I clear her wineglass from the head of the table. And then I sit in her place, where there's finally space for me.

CHAPTER

17

Regina

I'M SPRAWLED ON the couch watching a *Jaws* marathon. My body is comfortably tucked into the cushions with a cashmere wrap encircling my legs, and I popped a few THC gummies to really help me chill. I finally feel myself relax as I watch the opening scene on the beach unfold on the screen.

The stairs creak and I look up to see Esme coming down. My alone time is disrupted. I'd thought I'd finally be able to watch a show that's not on the Disney channel. Bryce and Greg are upstairs reading the girls a bedtime story, and Piper, Paul, and Preston are up in their bedroom doing God knows what. I'm nursing a margarita that is definitely not my first. I started at dinner—which got better after Esme left—and had to make another pitcher a little while ago.

Now that my movie is interrupted, I'm feeling pretty annoyed. Esme saunters in and stands over me, her white pleated shorts highlighting her tanned, toned legs. There's not a hair out of place on her head. And that expression on her face, like she's found exactly what she expected, gets me steamed.

But I need Esme. I need her to buy us out of the house. I have to play nice.

"Hey. Heading somewhere?" I say to her, and it comes out more accusatory than I'd planned it.

She picks up her purse on the end table and slips on her shoes. "This house is a mess," she says, scanning the living room, kitchen, and dining area. "I'm upstairs for a couple of hours, and this is what I find? Didn't we just discuss this?" Her small mouth is downturned in a deep frown. She begins picking up the living area first, remnants of board games, toys, coloring sheets and crayons, discarded beer cans, empty glasses, towels, and various fishing gear strewn about. Glancing around, I realize it does indeed look messy compared to its pristine condition when we arrived yesterday.

"There's ten of us here sharing the house. It's going to get untidy," I say to her.

Suddenly her movements become jerkier. She takes the toys and slams them into a corner basket. She gathers cups and bottles and chucks them into the sink with such force that I hear the sound of glass breaking.

"I don't suppose you're going to lift a finger, huh, Reg?" she says sarcastically. "Would you like me to pay you to help clean up?"

A burst of irritation runs through me. "Where do you get off?" I say, shaking my head. "I guess that's a 'no' to buying us out? Huh?"

She continues cleaning, and doesn't answer.

"Fuck's sake, it really is a 'no.' You can't even say it to my face." Now my voice is rising and sounds shrill to my own ears.

"I should have known you'd never help me. So high and mighty."

"Have another margarita," Esme sneers at me, pushing past with her shoulder.

I look down at my large blue margarita glass. Don't mind if I do.

The sound of shouting and breaking glass has apparently alerted Piper, who peers around the top of the stairs, regarding us as if she's witnessed a crime.

"What are you guys doing?" she shout-whispers, taking the steps down. "It's nine at night! The baby finally—*finally*—just fell asleep. You guys are hollering and banging around," she says, putting her finger to her mouth in a desperate signal for us to be quiet.

I wince. "Sorry," I say, feeling selfish. "Want a margarita?" I ask her, walking over to the pitcher I've made.

"No," she scowls. "I have a baby to care for. And I never drink. You know that."

Oh, that's right. Last night she said she doesn't drink anymore, something about motherhood and not liking the way it makes her feel. Well, maybe she should drink. She's awfully wound up. Rather than tell her that, I put my glass down and make a show of cleaning the plates off the dinner table. Without Esme here to oversee cleanup, the table is strewn with remnants from our dinner.

I pile the plates high in one hand, balancing them and feeling proud of how many I can stack. Just then, a fork gets stuck under a plate as I place it on top of the pile, and it all comes crashing down to the floor, chunks of steak trimmings and bits of green salad strewn everywhere. Luckily the plates don't break. But it's a mess.

Esme, who is back in the kitchen, shoots daggers at me with her eyes and Piper looks as if she'll lunge at me.

"I'll clean it up," I say, looking for a broom.

Piper comes over with a roll of towels and starts scooping up the food while I gather the plates again. Maybe I'll take two trips this time.

When the floor is cleaned up, I pour a third—or is it a fourth?—margarita for myself and hand one to Esme.

She places it on the coffee table without taking a sip, and continues cleaning.

When the three of us have made progress—the floors gleam, the clutter is gone, and the dishwasher is loaded—Esme checks her watch, then finally takes a sip of her margarita and perches on the couch anxiously.

Piper sits down next to her and I take a seat on the sectional across from them. I pick up the remote to tune back in to *Jaws*.

"Guys," Esme says, "there's a situation that's bothering me. I saw something weird at the grocery store today." She looks stressed, in fact, more ruffled than I've ever seen her.

"What?" Piper says, sounding worried

"I swear I saw Alexis," she says.

Piper's face goes white.

"That's impossible," I say, gnawing at a loose nail on my finger. "What makes you think it was her? Did you talk to her?"

"No," Esme says. "I couldn't catch up to her at the store, and then she was just gone."

Piper leans forward. "That's like what happened to me. I found her doll, and then I heard her voice on the monitor, talking to Preston. But she wasn't here."

Esme looks startled. "That's right, you did say that. But she couldn't have been in the house?"

I think about the sound in the woods today. I dismiss it—it was some animal, albeit large to make so much noise. I won't feed into this nonsense. "After what happened last time Alexis was here, there's no way she'd show her face," I say. "And she wouldn't just come into the house, that would be crazy."

"I hope not," Esme says. She sips her drink and leans her head back, closing her eyes, her hand to her temple. "So, neither of you have heard from her or spoken to her directly? Are you sure?"

Piper shakes her head, as do I.

"No," I say. "I think you're overreacting."

"I hope you're right, for once," Esme says under her breath.

Suddenly, the idea of staying here another two weeks with my sisters feels unbearable.

When I'm with them, I feel like an angry teenager again. I'm never as good as Esme, and Piper always makes me feel guilty for one thing or another. And Piper is such a pushover, never standing up to Esme, so desperate for her approval. Not to mention such a stick-in-the-mud. They both act like I'm so awful. But they don't know how to lighten up and let loose.

Now all this talk of Alexis. It dawns on me that I always feel bad about myself around them.

I think back to my conversation with Bryce. He's right that we need the money, that's what we came here for. I have to ignore my feelings and let it go. Who cares if I feel crummy? Suck it up.

I clear my throat. "Esme, I'm sorry I got pissed earlier. I shouldn't have yelled like that. But have you had time to consider what we talked about? The house?"

Piper's ears perk up. "What about the house?" she asks, always wanting to be included.

Esme answers for me. "Reg and Bryce want Greg and me to buy out their portion of the house." Then she laughs, as if it's hilarious.

"It's not funny. Bryce and I are going through a lot. We really need the cash. And you love this house."

"Do we look like we're made of money?" she says. "Is that all anyone sees when they look at us? Dollar signs?" She glares at me.

"Of course not. But you do have significantly more than either of us do." I look to Piper for solidarity, but her expression remains impassive. She doesn't like to take sides or be involved in conflict. I can see her retreating into her shell like a turtle.

Esme scoffs at me. "So, we should be punished? Because my husband works his ass off as a neurosurgeon, is hardly home, and because I invested my inheritance wisely, we should have to support you our whole lives? You and every other person who wants a handout?"

"Well, you got more to invest than us, didn't you?" I say, thinking about how Esme, the firstborn, the darling of our family, had an eye-watering sum given to her by our parents in a living trust when she reached the age of twenty. A living trust that neither Piper nor I received. "Plus, I'm not asking for a handout. I'm asking you to purchase something—my portion of the house is worth money. It's a transaction."

"A transaction that solely benefits you!" she says.

I've had enough of this. I drain most of what's left in my glass, then I stumble when I try to get up and unfortunately splash blue margarita onto the cream sectional. Esme's eyes light up with rage. She mutters something else as she walks, once again, toward the kitchen for the paper towel roll and to get cleaning spray.

I stand up, too. "What's that?" I ask. "Why don't you say what you have to say to my face?"

She rounds on me and throws the paper towel roll at my arms, which I'm unprepared for, so it bounces and lands on the floor between us. "Clean it yourself," she says. "And I said, it's always something with you. You're a ticking time bomb. No one knows what will set you off, but it's only a matter of time before you explode."

"Is anyone allowed to make a mistake around here? You're like the fun police, Esme. All that money and not an ounce of amusement. Not sure I'd trade places with you, after all. Maybe that's why your husband cheats on you." I immediately regret my words.

Esme looks as if she's been slapped. She walks toward the front door, grabs her purse and keys, flings open the door, and flees out into the night.

Piper stares at me, the stain on the couch, and shakes her head. "That was low, Regina, even for you."

She grabs the baby monitor and looks like she's getting ready to head upstairs.

I'm being abandoned. Both of them hate me. "Go be with your baby. God knows you need all the practice you can get caring for him. Some people aren't natural mothers, you know?"

She turns around, her eyes watery. "You have real issues, Regina. Seriously. You should get that checked out. Your anger."

I feel trapped by this house. Their rejection stings. I grab my phone, my glass, and the margarita pitcher, and escape outside to the darkness of the back porch.

The porch lights are off, and the only lighting is the inground lights of the pool and hot tub. Steam radiates off the hot tub, evaporating into the night. I walk over and put my feet into the hot water. Even though the night air is still warm, the sting of the water feels good.

I pour myself the last of the margarita mixture and drink it down, considering what needs to happen.

It's clear that no one is going to help me. Esme doesn't care and won't help. My husband is the one who got us into this mess. So it falls to me to come up with a solution. Lana needs me to come through for her.

I take out my phone and scroll to the number I've missed several calls from over the past few weeks. I've never responded to them, and deleted her messages. I knew it was *her* all along.

But I'm backed into a corner here. There's no choice. I need to call her back and hear her out. Maybe we can work together to achieve our common goals.

Without thinking of the consequences—or the reasons it's a terrible idea to call her—I hit the call button.

CHAPTER

18

Esme

THE BOARDWALK IN front of the Bergamont Resort at nine-thirty PM is fairly crowded. It's the end of the season, and people are packing in the last balmy nights of summer. Couples stroll past the open-air vendors hand in hand; others leave the waterfront restaurants and head back to their hotel. The area is lit by lampposts dotted along the boardwalk and the glow of the hotel. The air is filled with the fragrance of restaurant food cooking and fresh ice cream.

B stands for Brigit. When I reviewed her application to be nanny to Brielle and Gracey last summer, I'd been impressed. She had studied French abroad in Paris and was fluent. She played piano and had performed with the Connecticut Symphony. Piano and French were the two primary tutoring skills I needed in a nanny. When I'd looked at Brigit's social media profiles, I'd been slightly taken aback. The bikini photos and short skirt selfies hit my stomach in a funny way. But she was the most qualified applicant. Besides, didn't all young people dress this way now, and post for all the world to see?

I should have listened to my instincts. Should have taken the less qualified, non-fluent-in-French nanny. But I had gone ahead with the interview. Brigit was well-spoken, energetic. The girls instantly liked her, and I hired her to start in the fall.

Maybe if I hadn't, I wouldn't be about to confront her for having an affair with my husband.

She's standing by the dock, her long brown hair billowing around from a gentle breeze coming off the lake. Her slim body is clothed in a very short skirt and too high heels; there's that lewd taste in clothing that I ignored so blithely.

The sudden urge to push her into the water overcomes me. I pause, imagining running full steam ahead, our bodies going over the railing and me dragging her beneath the dark water. I'd hold her head under until her lungs filled with water and her lifeless body stopped thrashing.

Instead, I tap her on the shoulder. She spins around, and the look of shock at seeing me is priceless.

"Expecting my husband?" I ask her.

She takes a step back, almost tripping, and steadies herself on the rail. "Mrs. Wimberly. What are you doing here?" She looks around wildly, as if expecting my husband to come and rescue her from the situation. Normally when the two of them meet for their rendezvous, he makes sure I'm nowhere near and will have no chance to see them meeting together. She clearly wasn't expecting me, but my husband. Alone.

"He's not coming," I say. "It was me who texted you from his phone."

She's horrified, and her shock quickly turns to tears, and for a moment I almost—*almost*—feel bad for her. But not for long. The crocodile tears are probably part of her act. This girl is responsible for destroying my marriage.

So is Greg, yes. But he'll get his. First things first.

"You can cut the theatrics," I say, my eyes narrowing and my stance widening. "Do you remember the two little girls I trusted you to care for and instruct?" I ask.

She nods, wiping her tears away and resigning herself to the fact that her sniveling won't get her out of this.

"Those two young children were entrusted to you. By me. I hired you to look after them. To nurture them. I paid you well. I treated you well. Like part of our family. We brought you on vacation with us to Bermuda. Invited you to school recitals and to go to see the Nutcracker in New York City with us. And what did you do? You took my trust." I hold out a shaking finger at her. "You took my trust and you screwed my husband." My emotions threaten to boil over, waves of anger alternating with grief.

I don't care if it's displaced. I'm furious at Greg, but goddamn it, I'm mad at her, too. I thought I was a mentor to her, someone she looked up to. I thought she actually cared about us.

"You were a good actress," I say, "because you fooled us all. But it's over now."

"I'm sorry." The sound of her high-pitched voice makes me want to retch.

"I don't give a damn." I hear the note of mania in my voice and realize I need to get this over with before I go too far. I reach for my purse. "How much do you want?"

"What?" she says.

I pull out my checkbook. "How . . . much . . . money . . ." I draw each word out. "How much money do you want to get the hell out of our lives, and never come back?"

She looks at my checkbook and my pen, and back up at me, and there it is. Her expression changes. A hard, calculating gleam in her eyes takes over.

I can't help but roll my eyes. "Spit it out."

"I—I don't know," she says. "How much were you thinking?"

I know she can play hardball. When we were negotiating her hourly rate to be our nanny, she got top dollar out of me. Maybe that was another red flag I should have heeded.

"Five thousand," I say.

She doesn't flinch. "Twenty," she says. "I know how much you guys make."

The blood that has been boiling under my skin starts to erupt. I jab the pen into my hand, steeling myself not to lose my cool. Not here. Not like this.

"That's insane. A young girl like yourself, you can make a fresh start and easily get a new job and a new, age-appropriate boyfriend, with a sum of eight thousand," I state.

"Fifteen," she says with a sneer on her face, like she's doing me a favor.

"Ten," I say. "Final offer. Otherwise, you walk away with nothing. Greg doesn't want you, and now that I've found him out, your little trips will be ending."

At the mention of Greg, she looks protective, the green-eyed monster of jealousy surging from her.

I start to put my checkbook and my pen back in my bag. "Suit yourself."

"Ten," she says. "And you won't see me again."

I lean on the wooden dock fence railing and scribble the check. I rip it off and hold it out to her. She snatches it quickly, checking the numbers and details to make sure it's legitimate.

"The check is good, Brigit." I'm about to leave when the urge to impart wisdom overcomes me, as it tends to do. "You know, you could have been so much more than this," I say. "I hope in the future, you know you can be better."

She looks me up and down, clasping the check happily in her red-nailed hand, and smiles like the cat who got the cream. Then she turns on her tawdry heels and walks away without another word.

CHAPTER

19

Piper

WHEN I OPEN my eyes, it's pitch black, middle of the night. It was the crying that woke me. The baby must be hungry. I peer into his crib, my eyes adjusting to the darkness, and see his eyes closed, his breathing slow and steady.

The crying must have been in my dream.

I start to get back into bed, but out of the corner of my eye, I see a dark figure. I blink hard, but it's still there. Unmoving.

I wait, willing the dark shape to shift, move, go away. But it stands, motionless, until suddenly it's moving toward me.

I open my mouth to scream, but no sound comes out. Wetness is all around me. The dark shape is hugging me, dripping wet, cold.

"Aunt Piper." Her voice is familiar.

"What happened?" I ask Lana, squinting my eyes in the dark. I peek over at Preston, relieved his sleeping shape is there, unbothered. "You're soaking wet."

Her small frame is shivering. "I . . . I . . . I can't—"

"You can't what?"

"I can't tell you."

I pull a throw blanket from the bed and wrap it around her.

"Let's get you changed," I say quietly.

"No," panic rises in her voice. "She's out there."

"Who?" The hallway is dark. I pause, listening for sounds.

"The woman from the lake," she says.

"Who's that?"

She doesn't answer.

"Let's go get your mom, and get you changed," I whisper, glancing again at Preston, who hasn't stirred, and Paul, who remains blissfully snoring in our bed.

I lead her down the dark hallway. My eyes have adjusted to the dark, and when I open Regina's door, I see she's not in her bed, either. I can make out the shape of Bryce's head. I look in the bathroom. Regina's not there, either.

I motion for Lana to follow me, and we tiptoe to the other end of the hallway to the bedroom she's sharing with the twins. I breathe a sigh of relief when I see Gracey and Brielle sleeping, their hands and hair tangled next to one another.

I grab a pair of pajamas for Lana and indicate for her to follow me. Downstairs, all is dark. I flick on a lamp. I use a towel to dry off Lana, whose pale face looks frightened. I help her change into clean, dry pajamas, and the color starts to return to her cheeks a bit.

"Wait here," I say. "Don't move."

I grab my flashlight and creep down the stairs. Lana mentioned a woman by the lake, so I step out the front door and observe the water. All is still.

When I return upstairs, Lana is waiting for me. I give her a hug.

"Everything is okay. You're safe. Do you want a sip of water?" I ask. She nods her head yes.

I give her a glass of water from the refrigerator dispenser, and she gulps it down.

"Tell me what happened, Lana. Why were you all wet?" She looks guiltily at me. She doesn't speak.

"Are you okay? Are you hurt?" I ask, unsure what else to do.

She nods.

"Who is the woman from the lake?" I ask her again.

"I'm tired. Can I go back to bed?"

"Sure, sweetie."

I walk her back upstairs and tuck her into the bunk bed next to her sleeping cousins. I sit and wait a few minutes by her bedside until her breathing becomes regular.

Worry festers in the pit of my stomach. Rather than try to go back to sleep, I head back downstairs. I creak open the front door, but all I see is the blackness, with the sound of cicadas filling the night air. I spot Regina and Bryce's car still parked in the front. Could she be out there, this woman from the lake? I step outside and look again.

I decide to wait for her on the couch. I go back upstairs and grab the baby monitor. Paul is in the room with Preston, but he sleeps like a rock, so I need to have the monitor with me in case Press wakes up fussing or crying. Maybe tonight he'll sleep longer than his usual four hours. I do the math in my head. He's already been asleep for three, so at best I have another hour or two before he will want to eat again. I feel panicked at the idea that my precious sleep time has been cut into, and then further worry about Lana. Why was she soaking wet? She didn't smell like chlorine, so I don't think she was in the pool.

Surely, she couldn't have gone to the lake by herself in the dead of night? Then what else?

Dark worries swirl around my head, images haunting me. I try to push them away.

I lie on the couch, the monitor in one hand, my eyes on the door. And wait.

CHAPTER

20

Regina

WHEN I WAKE up, I'm startled to find that I'm on a patio lounger, a towel thrown over me for a blanket.

I scratch at my ankle, noting that I have numerous angry welts from mosquito bites. But that's the least of my problems. I rack my brain, forcing myself to remember what happened last night. I retrace my steps. All I had wanted to do was watch *Jaws* after a long day in the heat with Lana and the twins and crying Preston and crazy Piper and awful Esme. But I was interrupted from my *Jaws* respite. The fight with Esme and Piper ensued. I spilled the margarita on the damn couch. Who buys a white couch? Then I recall coming out here with the margarita pitcher. I got in the hot tub. Made that phone call—

The phone call. *Shit.* The phone conversation comes back to me.

No, no, no. *Why did I call her?*

I get up from the lounge chair and look up at the house. All is quiet and still inside. I check my phone and see it's still early, five in the morning.

Opening the glass slider as quietly as possible, I step inside. On the couch, I see Piper's light brown hair splayed out as she sleeps on her side.

I tiptoe up to my room and close the door quietly. Inside the dim room, Bryce stirs. I stand still. I really don't feel like explaining to him why I passed out on the lounge chair outside. When his breathing returns to normal, I creep over to the bed.

Slowly, inch by inch, I lift off the comforter, and slip under the covers. I hold my breath, waiting, and he doesn't stir.

I can't believe what a mess this trip has turned into. Regret teems through every brain cell, and I spend the next hour berating myself for all I've done wrong. It's all my fault. I drank too much. I fought with Esme and Piper. Words came out of my mouth that I didn't mean. Then the phone call . . . Shame burns in my stomach.

Finally, Bryce stirs. I pretend to wake up, too. The knot in my stomach grows tighter. I need to tell him that the money's not coming.

"Morning, babe," I say.

"Morning," he says, yawning and sitting up.

"Before we go downstairs, I have to tell you. I talked to Esme again. She's not going to buy us out."

He looks over at me with his puffy eyes and disheveled hair. Even at this early morning hour, he manages to wake up enough to process this bad news.

"Really? Are you sure?"

I nod. "Very."

"What happened?"

"I tried to tell you. My sister sucks. She doesn't want to help. She has no reason to. It doesn't benefit her, and she doesn't care if we need the money."

"She doesn't care that we're going to lose the house?"

I hadn't told her that Bryce lost his job last year. That we thought he'd be picked up quickly at another sales position, but that it took ages for him to find a new company to work for. When he finally found a new job, the salary was half what he was making before. That the late nights and extra shifts I've been taking at the bar aren't helping.

Add to that the debt we already had, and we can't keep up with the bills. We got the notice from our mortgage company last month. We have to get current with our payments, or we'll go into foreclosure.

I know Esme won't care about any of that. *What about that trip you took to the Grand Canyon last year?* She'll ask. *How did you afford that? What about the new car you bought?* I can't bear to have her judging every purchase. How we spent our money recklessly, the debt we have, the bad decisions we made. *Why did you buy such a big house?* I remember she'd called us "house poor" when we'd bought it, telling us it was quite extravagant. I said it's good to have a house we can grow into. We'd make it work.

Only, we didn't.

The worst part is that I know how disappointed Lana's going to be. She loves the house. She's made good friends in the neighborhood and at school.

Moving will mean a new school for her. It will break her heart. I slam my fist on the crumpled bed sheets. *I'm such a fuckup.* Why can't we make it work, like every other family? Why are we the couple whose house goes into foreclosure and has to move their kid to a shitty new school district, away from her friends and her soccer team?

Meanwhile, Esme has more money than she knows what to do with. And it's not like she even earned it. Mom and Dad gave her a huge sum in a trust fund when she turned twenty. Money that Piper and I never got—she was always their favorite. She invested that money well, sure, she made good decisions. But she had a leg up I never had. And Greg makes a killing as a top neurosurgeon in their area. He also comes from money, the old kind that's generational. They can live like royalty on passive income alone without ever touching the principal.

Their twins go to a prestigious private school. The tuition for that alone could pay our entire mortgage.

It's not fair. None of it is fair.

Finally, I answer Bryce. "I didn't tell her the extent of it. But if she says she won't buy it, I doubt us losing the house will change her mind."

Bryce's eyes are dark, creased with worry. He must be thinking the same thing. We're fucked. "Maybe I can talk to Greg," he says.

"I thought of that, too," I say. "But he doesn't seem to handle their finances. And Esme already said no. Do you really think he'll go against her?"

"Let me talk to him, man to man. You sisters have too many issues that complicate everything. If Greg knows we need to be bought out, and understands our home is at risk, he'll help." He sounds so certain that I almost believe him.

"Okay," I say, biting my lip. "Go for it." I think of my nasty comments to Esme last night, and I know that I need to apologize to her first thing this morning. Probably to Piper, too.

Except I'll never tell them about the phone call I made last night. What I said, and what I did.

That was a mistake, one that I can't afford to admit.

CHAPTER

21

Piper

THE NEXT THING I know, I'm opening my eyes. It's bright—morning time. The three girls are rummaging in the kitchen in their pjs, hungry for breakfast. I sit up from my place on the couch where I fell asleep after helping Lana last night, and rub at the crick in my neck.

I see Regina come down the stairs in a long nightshirt.

"There you are," I say, rubbing my eyes. I look at the monitor, shocked that Preston hasn't woken me up yet for a feeding. He has to have been asleep for over seven hours now.

"Where were you?" I ask Regina as I get up.

She stares at me blankly with no reply.

I head up the stairs past her—I'll deal with her later—as my concern for my baby trumps every other concern.

Pulling open the bedroom door, I find he and Paul cuddled up, an empty bottle beside Paul, and both of them asleep on the bed.

I pick up Preston, hugging him tight, feeling the slight rise and fall of his chest, and then transfer him into his crib. He doesn't stir.

Paul's eyes flutter open. "Hey," he says. "What happened to your arm?" he asks, looking at the bandage I have on my forearm.

"Oh, that. I cut myself on that window glass that broke yesterday. I didn't even notice it right away. It's fine, it's nothing." I pull my sleeve down over it.

"It doesn't look like nothing."

I turn to Paul and wave him away. "It's fine. But the strangest thing happened last night," I say. He listens to my account of what happened with Lana without comment. "Isn't that weird?" I ask. "I'm going to ask Regina where she disappeared to last night. And see if Lana will tell me more now that it's daytime. Why was she soaking wet?"

He shrugs. "Maybe just drop it," he offers. I feel like this is an odd suggestion. Come to think of it, he's acting weird about the whole thing. He's not curious like me. It's as if he thinks I'm making a hassle. Maybe he doesn't want to cause any additional waves or tension in the house.

"Okay," I say. "You don't think we should involve the cops, maybe?"

"The cops? Why? Unless there's a crime, there's nothing for them to do." I nod and realize he's correct. I get up, leaving him with Preston to go downstairs to talk to Regina.

In the kitchen, Lana's at the counter eating a bowl of cereal. Regina is making coffee, and Bryce is looking through the fridge.

"Lana, honey, can you tell me why you were all wet last night?" I say to the child.

She pauses, her Cheerios on her spoon, but doesn't say anything. "What do you mean, Aunt Piper?" Her face has guilt written all over it, but her words are clear.

I say it again, slower. "Last night, you were soaking wet. I helped you change into dry pjs—the ones you're wearing now. You wanted your mom, but she wasn't in her bedroom." At this, Regina spins around.

"What are you talking about?" she asks.

Paul comes down the stairs, and I flip on the monitor in my hands, now that Preston is alone in the room.

"Lana. You were shivering cold. You said there was a woman in the lake. You said, 'She's out there.'"

Lana blinks and shakes her head, looking to her mom. "No, Mom," she says.

"Lana, we just want to make sure you're not hurt," I say, but she won't meet my eyes.

Regina says quietly to her, "Why don't you take your cereal and watch TV with your cousins." Lana nods, gets up and moves away.

"Piper, once in a while Lana still wets the bed," Regina says to me. "She gets embarrassed about it. Thanks for helping her change. I'll change the sheets today."

I shake my head. "You don't understand. It was more than that. She was soaking, like she'd been in the pool or the lake."

Regina shrugs, her sloppy bun bobbing on top of her head. "She drinks a lot of water. But I'll talk to her, okay?"

"It's just—last night . . ." I want to say more, but the words won't come out. I feel like I can't breathe. I put my hand to my chest, and I feel my hand shaking.

Paul, Regina, and Bryce all look at me.

"Piper, why don't you go back to bed?" Paul says. "It was a long night for you."

"No," I say, my face feeling hot. "I'm okay. You," I point to Regina, "were nowhere to be seen while I took care of your daughter. Why weren't you in your room last night?"

She puts her coffee cup down and sighs. "I don't know what you're talking about, Pipe. I must have gotten up to pee."

"Okay." I give up. I want to say more, but I don't want to cause a scene. Instead, I feel an overwhelming desire to get out of here. Drive away and not look back.

I go to grab my keys, thinking I'll head anywhere but here, just to clear my head. I stop when I realize Preston needs me. I can't abandon him. He was already with Paul all night. He'll be missing his mommy.

I'll just take him with me, then. I head up the stairs to get my baby. We'll head into town and get some much-needed distance and space from this house. And everyone in it.

CHAPTER

22

Before

Alexis

I'M AT THE small desk in my room, working on yet another picture. I scratch the pencil against the paper, shading the face of my mom. I pause, trying to get it just right. I'm worried I'll forget what she looks, so I've been drawing her. And it's better than sitting alone in this room staring at the ceiling. Since the ring ordeal, this past week at the lake house has been awful. Esme won't play with me. Whenever I try, she makes a face and tells me she doesn't want to get into trouble. Piper follows her around and keeps her eyes down. Regina will sometimes play with me, but she's so little, it's not much fun.

Just yesterday, Esme was brushing the long golden hair of a large doll while Piper had a baby doll in a little crib. "Can I play?" I asked them.

Esme made a face. "She's my special doll. No one else can touch her. You might ruin her. Or try to steal her."

Piper's eyes were wide, but she didn't say anything.

After a moment, Piper handed me one of her teddy bears. "You can have him if you want to play."

Esme snatched him away from Piper's hand. "That's mine, too," she said, turning her back to me.

I reached out and gave a sharp tug to Esme's long blond hair. She wailed and ran to tell her mother.

Aunt Audry grabbed my arm and dragged me to her bedroom closet, the lock clicking behind me. In my pocket, I took out a knife I'd been keeping handy. Just in case. I scratched into the wall one word: "Help."

My aunt hasn't said much to me, at all, this past week. She just eyes me suspiciously at meals. She probably saw the writing in the closet.

I've thought about telling her the truth. That Esme gave me the ring. That Esme lied and told me she'd found it. But I doubt my aunt would believe me anyway.

Uncle Frank is sort of nice to me, though. Slipping me treats and making sure I have pencils and paper for drawing, and books to read. I think he feels bad. Maybe he knows his daughter is a trickster. He's outnumbered by the women in his family. He doesn't say much, but at least I know I have a friendly face around.

We're leaving tomorrow. Back to their large home in Greenwich, Connecticut. Then I'll start a new school. My cousins tell me it's very strict there. You're expected to do your lessons and homework without being told twice.

The school I went to before, hardly anyone noticed if you didn't show up. And if you turned in an assignment, you were in the top of the class.

I put my pencil down and am about to go see what the girls are up to outside when I hear the front doorbell ring. I step into the hallway and stand at the stairwell, watching.

Aunt Audry opens the door. A woman in a brown skirt and matching brown suit jacket walks in, setting her briefcase on the floor. Her chunky heels clank against the hardwood, and I watch as my aunt offers her coffee.

My heart starts beating wildly. No one dresses like that in town or around the summer house. This woman is here on official business. I swallow hard and listen intently, not moving a muscle.

"Thank you for coming out here. We thought it best to do it here and avoid another transition back to the house."

The woman's voice is softer, and I have trouble making out her words as she speaks.

My aunt replies to her, "Indeed. Very upsetting. There's been the theft of one of my most prized rings, which I was fortunate to discover before it was too late."

My stomach flips. So this is about me.

"But really, it's that the girls don't feel safe. They feel threatened by her. She's unstable. There's no telling what she'll do. Some days she's happy, but she's always playing roughly. Other days she's sullen and withdrawn. She makes odd comments that frighten the girls. Esme says she can't sleep at night for fear of what Alexis might do to her."

The other woman murmurs quietly.

"Direct threats?" I hear Aunt Audry's voice answer, "I'm sure. The girls don't want to tattle on their cousin, but they've made it clear they're scared. She's pushed the girls down, caused a great deal of chaos and fighting."

My hands ball into a fist. She's telling it all wrong. The only time I get mad at Esme is if she's teasing me or her sisters to shreds. The awful things she says. I tell her to knock it off or else I'll make her. Someone has to stand up to Esme. Piper and Regina sure don't. Her mother thinks she's an angel that can do no wrong.

"I caught her with a knife," my aunt adds.

"A knife?" the woman sounds concerned.

"Yes. She was carving into the wall. But I worry she'll do more . . . You can see why the girls and I are frightened."

The woman takes out a folder from her briefcase and hands it to my aunt, along with a clipboard. The woman points to the bottom, and my aunt signs. She flips the page again, and signs.

My stomach gurgles and I shift. The floorboard underneath my foot groans. Both women look up.

"There she is now. No doubt eavesdropping. Alexis, you may as well come down, please," my aunt says to me.

I step down the stairs and approach them by the couch, my arms crossed. I'm thinking of the best way to explain that I didn't steal the ring, and that Esme is in fact the one giving me a hard time. Always bringing up how my mom is dead and how my dad was never around. How she's the only family I've got, and they don't want me, either.

"Alexis, this is Madeline Bryant from Social Services. She's going to help you find another family to live with. A family where you'll be happier."

My feet are frozen in place. I'm not sure how the words she's saying could possibly be correct.

When I'm able to speak, my voice sounds small and far away. "I have to leave?"

"Yes, dear," my aunt says matter-of-factly. "It will be for the best. You'll see."

The woman in the brown suit looks down and avoids my gaze. She shuffles the paperwork, inserts it into her carrying bag, and then clears her throat.

"I will help you pack your things, and drive you there, dear," she says, not unkindly.

I blink back tears of frustration. After my mom died, I thought being pulled from my apartment and neighborhood where I'd spent my whole life was the worst thing that could've happened. But the Howards are the only family I have left. Now, they're throwing me away.

I turn to go back up the stairs to pack. But not before giving my aunt one last hard look.

CHAPTER

23

Esme

THAT MORNING, IT'S back to business as usual. I clean up the mess from breakfast—cereal left scattered on the living room coffee table, a frying pan with scraps of eggs left on the burner. I scrub at the pan and dry it with a cloth. If I can get the house back to order, maybe my thoughts will also fall into order.

As I wipe the kitchen counter, I can't help but remember last night. Brigit, then fighting with Regina, her spilling her drink all over my new couch. The whole night feels like a bad dream. My hand fumbles as I empty the dishwasher. I grab a water bottle from the beverage cooler, twist off the cap and bring it to my lips, drinking from it, trying to stave off the headache I feel pounding at my temples.

There's a hastily scrawled note on the counter that I spot as I declutter the center island. Greg has written that he's taken the twins and Lana to the lake for fishing on the boat with Bryce. A second note says that Piper took the baby into town to shop while Paul went on a hike. I don't know where Regina is, but thankfully I don't see her anywhere around.

To think I confided in her about Greg's affair with the nanny. She couldn't care less. She was only talking to me so she could ask for money.

What else did I expect, though? Her whole life, she's always looked to me to bail her out. First it was Mom coming to her rescue, and now the job has fallen to me. When will she grow up and take care of herself?

I fold the blanket on the couch and arrange the pillows as I fume, recalling Regina's disgusting behavior last night. If she thinks throwing Greg's affair back in my face is the way to get me to help her, she's mistaken.

I jump as I hear the front door open behind me.

Brielle enters the house, her small frame dwarfed by the large oak door. Her face is drained of all color. She runs up to me and buries her head in my leg, wrapping her arms around me.

I bend down, looking her in the eye. "What's wrong?"

"Mommy, there was something scary in the lake. She . . . she wasn't moving."

Her wide eyes search mine, looking for guidance.

My mind jumps to the worst place.

"Where's your sister? And cousin? Where's Dad?" I glance behind her at the open door to the house, but don't see anyone behind her.

"At the lake. Daddy's calling for help. I ran here. I was scared." She buries her head again.

I hug her tight. "Is everyone safe?"

"Yeah," she nods her head. "They're okay, with Daddy."

I wrap her hand in mine and pull her toward the door. “Let’s go find them.” Grabbing my phone off the table, I jam it in my back pocket.

Outside is bright and humid. The lake in the distance is still. The boat must be farther down on the lake, past where the tall trees obstruct the view.

“Show me where they are,” I say. She heads right, down the path toward the boathouse. The dust kicks up and my feet, in sandals, are quickly coated in grime. The trail leads first to our boathouse, where they would have launched the deck boat not more than an hour ago.

It’s still morning time, and Esme slept in and saw the note. But knowing what time her kids would sleep until, she has a vague window of time when she can assume they’d have left. Maybe the earliest she imagines Greg could get them out of bed, fed and load up the boat, they wouldn’t have left until 8:30 am or later, assuming it’s 9:30 now.

“This way,” she says, her small hand tugging at mine.

The path continues and eventually curves around to a pebble shore.

As we approach the clearing, I see several things at once. Our boat is anchored in the water just offshore. Greg is on his phone at the water’s edge. He’s speaking frantically, while holding Gracey’s hand, and trying to comfort Lana, who’s shaking uncontrollably.

My stomach lurches because as I take in the scene, I can’t help but see what I’d hoped wouldn’t be there.

A lifeless body. White flesh. Pulled up on the beach. A woman’s body, lying on her stomach.

Time seems to stand still as I look. I know exactly who she is. My knees threaten to buckle under me.

I notice Bryce just then as he jumps off the boat, wades over to the body, and mercifully places a towel over her. “What’s going on?” I say, my voice cracked and dry.

"We found her floating," Bryce chokes on the words, "in the water. We pulled her in. It's clear she's . . . She's gone."

"You just found her? In the middle of the lake?"

"When we launched the boat, the girls spotted something in the lake toward the shore here. We drove closer, not knowing what it was . . . that it was . . . you know." He's wild-eyed, looking all around.

I shake my head. Brielle's hand is still in mine. The children can't be here.

Forcing myself into action, I call out, "Girls, come with me."

The girls break away from Greg, and his eyes meet mine as he speaks on the phone. "I'm on the phone with the police," he says to me, and I nod.

Wrapping my arms around Lana and the twins, I hurry them back to the path. "Let's go. Daddy's calling for help. We don't need to be here."

As we round the corner, I pull the girls closer to me.

"Mommy, that lady," Gracey says to me, head nuzzled in my leg. "She looked like Brigit. Is that her?"

"I don't know, honey, I don't think so." I shake my head.

"Why wasn't she moving?" Her voice wavers, about to break. "Is she dead?"

"Please, don't be upset. Try to put it out of your mind. Help is on the way."

I pat her back and try to keep the girls moving toward the house.

I risk a final glance back at the lake, at the lifeless form. In that instant, I know that my life, as it was before, is irrevocably changed.

The police will come. They'll ask what I did last night. My alibi. If I had any problems with the deceased.

My breath catches. I hug the girls tighter. I need to steel myself for what's coming.

CHAPTER

24

Before

Regina

WE'RE AT THE public pool in town, just to get out of the house, and I'm already regretting it. It's hot and crowded.

"Why don't you jump in?" Esme asks, tying her blond hair up in a ponytail then beginning to apply suntan lotion.

I check my CD player, making sure my earbuds are plugged in, and shake my head. "I'm okay. That pool is full of kiddie pee," I say, and push play.

Esme shrugs and continues applying her lotion. Alexis and Piper return from the snack stand holding sodas.

It's still weird for me to see Alexis.

Since she went to live with another family almost eight years ago after Piper cut her hand, I'd sort of forgotten about her. We never visited her. I'd heard that she went to live with a foster family, and then at a group home, and then with another foster family. Something about how she kept getting into trouble and getting moved again. But a few weeks ago, Mom and Dad sat us down.

"Girls, now that Esme's off to college in the fall and it could be the last summer we all spend together at the summer house, your cousin Alexis is going to join us for our holiday this year." Mom had been very matter-of-fact.

Esme had been pissed. "Mom, no. We don't even know her. Why?"

My dad had stepped in. "She's been writing letters to us regularly. Her new foster family thinks it's important for her to spend time with us. Apparently, she talks about us often." He looked uncomfortable and stopped.

"It's important to her. It's only a few weeks," Mom said, and it sounded as if she was convincing herself. She gave Dad a look and he nodded.

Piper looked down at her hands, at the small scar from when she broke the mirror. I wondered if she feels responsible for Alexis leaving? It's not her fault. From what I remember, it was just too crazy having her in the house. Esme and Mom especially didn't get along with her. I think Esme was jealous, and maybe Mom was, too. I decided it's best to give her another shot, maybe she's not so bad.

But the past few days have been super awkward. Esme does her best to ignore Alexis. Piper seems afraid of her and barley talks. I feel kind of bad for her, but I don't really have anything in common with her. If anything, she and Esme have more in common. At least, they kind of look alike—both are really pretty, though Esme's hair is a lighter blond, and she's smaller. But they style their hair parted to the side, and both wear their jeans low on their waists, showing their belly buttons.

Alexis sets down her drink on the ground next to my chair and spreads her towel on the chair next to me.

Piper takes off her T-shirt and crosses her arms self-consciously over her one-piece suit. "I'm going to hop in," she says.

"Right behind you," Esme says, standing up and tossing her bottle of suntan lotion on the chair, the smell of coconut and vanilla filling the air.

I turn up my music and try to ignore the sun. I close my eyes, but after a few minutes I feel a shadow block the sun.

I open my eyes. There's a guy standing over me.

"*Load* blew," he says.

I take out my earbuds. "What?"

"*Load* blew." He points to my T-shirt. "I love them, too, but their new album blows."

I look down at my Metallica shirt. "Yeah," I say. "Still good, though."

He sits on the chair next to me. "Where are you girls from?"

He has a kind of cute smile and I like his spikey hair, so rather than turning over to ignore him, like I usually would, I answer. "We have a summer house here."

"Well, if you're looking for something fun to do tonight, we're having a bonfire down at the lake. Beers, music. It'll be a good time. All local kids." He flashes a smile. "But you'll be good if you're with me."

"Maybe," I say. The chance that my parents would let me go is slim. Even with Esme as a chaperone, they're pretty strict.

"We'll be there," Alexis says, leaning over.

"Cool. Let me get your number," he says to me.

* * *

Later than night, we tell a white lie to my parents. "We're going to get some snacks and hang out at the burger place in town," we say. My parents nod, blissfully unaware.

"I'll drive," Alexis says, taking the keys to my mom's minivan from me. I get into the passenger's seat, and Piper sits in the back. Esme has refused the whole idea, telling me she doesn't want to hang out with sixteen-year-old local losers.

Piper looks scared when I glance back at her in the side mirror. This is the first time I've taken her to hang out at a party scene.

She hadn't wanted to come, but Alexis had insisted. "Don't be lame. Come on," she'd said.

When we get to the parking lot where Ben, the guy from the pool, had told me to park and meet him so we could walk to the party, Piper looks like she's going to lose it.

Alexis turns around in the driver's seat and opens her purse. From her bag, she takes out a small bottle. She opens the cap and pours two white pills into her hand.

"Here, take this." She holds one out to Piper.

"What is it?" she asks.

"Just to relax you. Trust me. You'll have so much fun. Want one, Regina?"

I shake my head no and look to Piper. She reaches out and without another word, swallows the pill. She opens a bottle of water that Mom always has stashed in the car and washes it down.

Alexis lets out a whoop. "Piper, stealth mode party champ," she says. She swallows her own pill and washes it down with a strong-smelling liquid from a bottle in her bag.

She passes the bottle to me, and I take a swig. And gasp. My throat burning.

Outside, it's dark, but Ben finds us and gives me a quick hug. He smells like cologne and his T-shirt is soft against my skin.

"You made it," he says, giving me a squeeze. "I didn't think you'd come."

"Yeah, my older sister gave me a hard time, wouldn't come with. Said we shouldn't hang out with the locals."

At this Ben, turns and gives me a quizzical look. "Why?"

"Just that we're from different circles. She's dumb, who cares? No one's good enough for her," I say, wishing I hadn't mentioned it.

We walk down to the water, following the sound of music. It's a pretty chill scene, with a group of about eight guys and two girls. They all go to the town high school with Ben. He's sixteen, a year older than me, and says he just got his dad's truck.

There's a firepit going, and music is playing. Ben passes me a can of beer and asks me to sit by him on a folding chair.

The night seems to be going well, and as time passes, Ben is slowly putting the moves on me. I let it happen. He wraps his arm around my shoulder. Then he places his hand on my leg.

When he turns to kiss me, I let him.

After a while of kissing, I pull away. I look across and my heart drops when I see Piper. There's a guy with his arms wrapped around her and he looks to be way older, like nineteen or twenty to her sixteen. My mind kicks into overdrive and I realize this was a bad idea.

I push Ben away and head for Piper. I pull her arm and break her free from the older dude. "Let's go," I say.

That's when I look at her eyes and realize she's totally out of it.

"Who are you?" she says, and now she's starting to scare me. "Why does your face look like that?"

"Piper, come on," I say, tugging her away from the group. I spot Alexis and call to her, "Alexis, we gotta go. Now!"

Alexis turns to me and rolls her eyes. "Chill," she says, and at that moment I could punch her.

I move closer to her, bringing Piper with me. "Now. She's really out of it."

Alexis protests, but finally agrees to go.

Ben calls after me as we walk up the embankment, but there's no time to explain.

When we get back in the car, Piper is really worrying me. She can walk, but she seems aimless and would wander off if I didn't lead her in the right direction. The darkness is disorienting, but she's not right at all.

I help her into the backseat and shut the door. I tell Alexis to give me the keys, which she tosses at me. "Whatever," she says.

As I turn on the headlights and start to reverse, I hear Piper in the back. "Stop!" she calls, and then, "Please don't hurt me."

When I turn my head, she's talking to herself and putting her hands out, as if she's fighting someone off.

My heart is beating hard and I hurry to get her home, telling her, "It's okay, Piper. You're safe. We're almost home."

When I pull into the driveway, the lights of our house are off. I help Piper out of the car and into the house then up the stairs to her bedroom.

I take my clothes off and am about to get into bed when I smell smoke. I sniff at my hair, thinking how strong the bonfire smell is. But then I realize, with horror, that it's too strong to be from my hair. It's real smoke, and it's coming from inside the house.

I rush out of my room and see smoke coming from Piper's room. I open the door and see a small blaze in the middle of her floor. She's wide-eyed and just staring at it.

"Come on!" I yell, and I tug at her, ripping her away before the flames get so close they'll burn her, and go to wake my parents for help.

CHAPTER

25

Piper

EVEN THOUGH LAST night was a sleepless one, I realized I couldn't stay in the house a moment longer, restless as I felt. So I'd quickly gotten changed and ready, and I've taken Preston into town this morning to get a breather and try to clear my head after the Lana ordeal last night. Greg and Bryce were taking the twins and Lana fishing. Paul wanted to go hike, and had hoped I'd come. He has a front hiking pack he puts Preston in so we can bring him with us. But I said I needed a little retail therapy, and Paul gave me a kiss and told me to enjoy. Said he'd try the mountain bike out on the trail.

The main street in town brings back a wave of nostalgia. My favorite corner shop had rolls and rolls of stickers, and Mom would let me pick as many reams of stickers as I could carry. Then we'd walk over to the arcade and play games.

I remember bumper cars and Skee-Ball, mini golf. And we'd finish the day off with a giant ice cream cone from Big Ed's ice cream hut. Nothing was sweeter than double chocolate cream in a waffle cone. We'd sit on a bench until we licked every last drop and finished the entire cone.

I tickle Preston on his cheek. "When you get bigger, will you play mini golf and Skee-Ball with me, Press? Momma will buy you a big ice cream scoop afterward. Will you like cookies and cream like Daddy? Or double chocolate like Momma?"

His blue eyes crinkle and his mouth folds into a smile. Smiling is new for him since we've been at the lake house. It seems at least one of us is enjoying the trip.

I lift his car seat out of the backseat tether and attach it to the stroller that I've unfolded from my trunk. Paul had said I didn't need it, but see, Paul, how I'm using it now? I'll never go anywhere without a stroller.

I've dressed baby Preston in a white cotton shirt that clips at the bottom to prevent it from riding up, and paired it with soft muslin shorts and a gray linen sun hat. I pull the muslin canopy over the top half of his stroller to protect him from the sun. He kicks his legs up. "Soon you'll be running around here, Pressy," I say. "But for now you're content in your stroller. Want to come window shop with Mommy?"

In my mommy and me baby group, the instructor has said numerous times that the more we speak to our babies, the better. It helps their language development and helps their vocabulary, just by being exposed to a greater number of words. Therefore, at any point in the day, on the long days and evenings I'm on my own with him, I can be heard chatting away to him. I'm sure this is another point that my sisters would say proves I'm losing my mind. But I know I'm doing it for his best interest.

Plus, they say babies love the sound of their mother's voice. He heard me all nine months in the womb, and it's still his favorite voice, according to my group instructor.

"Mommy might buy a new tote," I say, as I head toward the shops. I peer in the window at the closest store, and see it doesn't open until ten. It's still only nine, so I'll have to walk around until the shops open. Maybe grab a coffee and pastry.

I remind myself this is my vacation. Vacations are supposed to be relaxing. Enjoyable. I try to relax my shoulders, pushing Preston along, willing myself to ignore the tiredness tugging at my eyes. Sleeping on the couch has left me with a stiff neck and bags under my eyes from fitful sleep.

The shop windows display their novelty items. There's an oil and vinegar store, a bathing suit and T-shirt shop with Lake George logo apparel, a toy store, and a children's clothing store that opens at nine thirty—I make a note to come back to it after it opens.

Every year we come, it seems that one or more of my childhood shops closes. In its place a new, overpriced store opens. I look across the street and thankfully can spot the giant statue that marks Big Ed's ice cream. I don't want to live in a world where Big Ed's is replaced by a chain, or a high-end creamery that serves liquid nitrogen ice cream.

I push Preston into Corner Café. Inside is cool and filled with the smell of freshly brewed coffee. I stand in line and Preston looks around happily.

At one of the tables I see two women in athletic outfits chatting. They look alike, and I wonder if they're sisters. I think of my own two sisters. Regina told me she doesn't think I'm a natural mother. While a few days ago this might have hurt me, something inside me is changing.

I'm starting to wonder if maybe I'm the sane one. Regina is the one drinking half a bottle of tequila nightly. She constantly looks upset and angry. She's having major financial trouble. And when her daughter needed her in the middle of the night, she wasn't there. It was me who was there to help Lana. Should I really be offended by what Regina thinks of me?

And Esme is selfish. Maybe I put her on a pedestal all this time. Older, prettier, my parents' favorite. But she doesn't have all the answers, either. Her marriage seems strained, at best.

Motherhood is teaching me a lot. Maybe I need to trust my own instincts a little more, and worry less about my sisters. I'm tired of caring so much.

What matters to me is Preston. And Paul. He's not a perfect husband, but he's a good man and a good father. That's what's important: my immediate family. If my sisters don't want to be kind and have me be a meaningful part of their lives, then it's sad, but what can I do?

Ever since I got here, I've had a bad feeling in the pit of my stomach. Maybe it's time to call it; to give up and let go of the dream that motherhood will bring us sisters closer.

All motherhood has done is highlight the disparity and discrepancy between us. I used to think it was because they were mothers. Wiser. More experienced. Busier.

But now I realize they're just selfish.

"Preston," I say, "Do you want to go home today? After shopping, we'll tell Daddy it's time to get back to our house. Back to your crib. Your toys. Our neighborhood."

He smiles and seems to agree, though to his credit, he seems to return my smile regardless of what I'm saying. I smooth my hand on his cheek.

After I order an iced latte and give Preston his bottle, we stroll around back to the stores I was eyeing. The street is dotted with quaint black lampposts and colorful hanging flower baskets. We pass the grocery store where Esme says she saw Alexis.

I used to feel only fear and guilt when I thought of Alexis. I've always thought she was out for revenge. After what happened, could I blame her?

But I'm starting to have an idea of how Alexis might have felt growing up. I wonder if I were to see her now, would I be able to relate to her better? We have more in common than I might have thought.

In the kids' clothing store, I find a trove of adorable outfits for Preston. I buy him several in his size, and some in nine months and twelve months so he can grow into them. I won't be at this store again for another year, at the soonest. The store clerk folds the adorable outfits: small sweaters and pants, T-shirts, collared shirts, and shorts in patterns made even cuter by their baby sizing. The clerk smiles, saying the choices are adorable.

I leave the store with a smile on my face. "Are you ready for a nap, my love?" I ask him in his stroller. His eyes are already drifting closed. I hope the transfer from the stroller into his car seat won't wake him. Luckily, by the time we get back to our car, he's fast asleep. I turn on the car and let the cool air blast, not wanting his little body to overheat.

As we drive around the lake back to the house, I resolve what needs to happen.

The summer house vacation has to be cut short this year. The broken glass, finding Lana wet in the wee hours of the night, the belittling comments from my sisters. It's just not working. Better to leave now, and maybe next year they'll show me more respect.

I'm tired of my sisters acting like they've all got it figured out, while insinuating I'm the one with a screw loose. It's not my fault the window broke, or that Lana came to me in the middle of the night. And when I heard Alexis's voice over the monitor, maybe that was lack of sleep. Or maybe she's back.

Esme thinks so. I don't know, and I don't care right now. I just want to go home.

Heading up the drive, I hear the sound of sirens. Way out here, that seems unusual. Rather than fading away, the piercing sound gets closer. So close that I worry it's going to wake Preston. Annoyance turns to fear as I see the lights appear in my rearview mirror. I pull over into the brush. There's not much room on the one-lane road to our house, and as the fire truck passes by me, I flinch, worried they're going to slam into the left side of my car.

They make it past safely, but my gut clenches with anxiety. We're the only house on this road. The emergency fire truck is headed straight for our summer house.

CHAPTER

26

Esme

WHEN WE GET to the house, after leaving Greg and Bryce at the lake with the body, Greg on the phone with the police, I help the girls inside. "Let's go upstairs and I'll turn on a movie," I tell them. I usher them upstairs and grab towels from the linen closet.

In their bedroom, I wrap a towel around each girl. Lana is shaking, so I find a dry pair of her shorts and a T-shirt and help her get changed. Brielle sits in her suit waiting for my help while Gracey gets changed into a pink dress. I change Brielle into a blue dress that matches her sister's pink one and sit them on the bed.

"Girls, I'm going to turn on the TV now. I want you to stay up here. I'll be right downstairs if you need me. But it's best you stay up here, unless it's an emergency. I'll bring snacks up."

"We get to eat in the bedroom?" Gracey says, awed at this break in the rules.

"For today, yes, love," I answer.

I give Lana a hug, and then Brielle and Gracey. "It's going to be okay, girls. There's nothing to worry about, all right?"

They nod, but their expressions are solemn. Their lives have thus far been blissfully sheltered and innocent. I can only imagine the upset and fear they're feeling.

"Mommy and Daddy, and your aunt and uncle, we're going to talk to the police. But everyone's safe. We're all going to be fine, I promise," I say, trying to sound convincing.

I go downstairs and rummage through the cabinets. I grab white cheddar cheese puff bags, which I absently note will make a mess, but I'm beyond caring. I grab granola bars and juice boxes, and haul it all back upstairs. The girls are on the bed, wrapped up in an animated movie. I set the snacks down on the TV console, and Lana gets up and tugs on my shorts.

"What happened to the lady in the lake?" she says, eyes wide.

"I don't know." This much is true.

"Wasn't that the same woman from yesterday? She lost her puppy. I wonder who will take care of the puppy?"

I bend down to Lana. "What did you say?"

"The puppy. We should go look for her."

"Sweetheart, I think you're confused."

My hands are starting to shake as I close the door. The reality of what I saw is setting in, and my whole body feels cold. I absently walk to my room to find a sweater, and pull on a gray cashmere crewneck over my head, shivering as I do so.

That's when I see it. Greg's phone, lying on the side table. I pick it up and punch in the passcode, and then flick through his open tabs until I get to his messages.

There's nothing from B. In fact, when I type in her name to see if there's any old message threads, her name, B, is no longer saved under his contacts. He must've deleted her contact information. I don't have the clarity of mind to think through why or how he would've come to delete her as a contact, but I note it, and set down his phone again.

I move out of my bedroom and practically run into Regina in the hallway, coming out of her bedroom. Her eyes have dark shadows under them and her face is creased in worry.

"What's going on out there?" she asks.

I peek over the stairs, and through the front windows I can see our driveway and road are lit up with flashes of blue and red. There are four emergency vehicles: a firetruck, an ambulance, and two police cars.

I whirl back to Regina and pull her into my bedroom, closing the door behind us.

"You want the money, Regina?"

She shakes her head, confused. "What? The money? Yes. Why are there ambulances here?"

"If you want the money, it's yours." I can't shake the cold numbness seeping into my body, and I feel my teeth start to chatter. "But if you want it, you have to say I was with you last night. The whole night. I was here, home, with you and Greg and Bryce and the girls."

"But you left pretty late last night," she says, rubbing her eyes, trying to focus. She looks at me, baffled.

"I know, Regina, I just drove around to get some space. You're missing the point." I shake my head in frustration. "I will buy your part of the house so you will have the money you need, but you must cover for me. Say I was here with you last night. Don't say that I was gone after we fought."

She blinks slowly. I picked the wrong sister to try to bribe. Does she not get it? Is she so hung over that it's not registering?

Then again, Piper is a goody-goody. It'll be harder to convince her to tell a lie. She must still be out shopping. I'll have to catch her when she gets home, so we're all on the same page.

Maybe I'm being paranoid, but I've watched enough police procedural dramas to know that there's a dead woman in our lake, and it's not good that my time was unaccounted for last night. Maybe it was an accident. Maybe she went for an early morning swim and drowned. But it didn't feel that way. It felt like someone did this to her. She wasn't dressed for a swim. And the fact that not only did I go out to meet Brigit late last night, but the purpose of our meeting? Not good.

When I came home last night, the house was dark. Greg was already asleep. I slipped into our bed and he didn't even stir.

The image of the lifeless body is stuck in my head, and I can't shake the icy coldness all over my body. This whole situation is a catastrophe.

Back to Regina, I say, "Don't tell the police I was out last night. Just say I was here all night. Easy. And we'll purchase your part of the house first thing next week. I'll write you a check today. Got it?"

Realization starts to dawn on her. "Really?" She nods. "Of course. You got it." She motions to outside the bedroom. "Why are they here, Es? Is everyone okay?"

"Our family is fine. Lana, Bryce, all of us are fine. But," my voice shakes as I speak, "the girls and Bryce and Greg, when they were on the boat. They found a body."

"A body!" she says, her eyes widening.

"A dead body."

CHAPTER

27

Regina

"WHAT THE HELL?" I say, looking at my sister. They've found a dead person in the lake. My head is pounding, and I wonder if I'm still asleep and in the midst of a nightmare. An awful feeling of guilt and worry sinks in my gut. "Who?"

She hesitates. Her blue eyes avoid mine. "I'm not sure who it is."

She looks like she's lying. Coupled with the fact that she's prepared to suddenly buy my share of the house, it looks like she's in some deep shit. I suspect she knows exactly who it is. But her secret is safe with me. If she's in jail, I may not get the money. Probably legal fees fighting for her freedom would drain her account, or freeze her funds at the very least. Esme isn't the kind to take a plea bargain.

She snaps her fingers. "Regina, hey. Come on. Get it together. Do you understand? Tell the police I was home all night. Make sure Bryce knows, too. I'll talk to Piper. Just make sure you tell the police I was home all night. We were all together at the house. Got it?"

I nod. I understand. Lie. Get the money. But who's in the lake? I have to know. I have to make sure I'm not the one who's going to need legal fees for an attorney.

I think back to the phone call I made last night. Was there anything else? The rest of the night gets fuzzier after that. The heat of the hot tub, all those margaritas. I feel asleep after the phone call, right?

"You're sure it's a woman?" I ask.

She nods and gulps. "I could see that much." Esme's face is ashen.

"Okay. We should go down there. See what's going on. Where's Lana?"

"She and the twins are in their bedroom watching a movie. With snacks and drinks. I told them to stay put."

I run my fingers through my hair. "Oh my god. The girls found the body? They saw it?"

"Yes, but not for long. Brielle came back to get me, and I hurried to get them out of there."

"Thank you," I say. Suddenly I'm more scared than I can remember being. I reach out and give my sister a hug.

Her small body is trembling, but she wraps her arm around me and hugs me back.

"We have to go out there. See what's going on. Talk to the police," I say.

She nods.

We go downstairs and see the lights still flashing, filling the living room with an eerie glow.

With Esme right behind me, I open the front door and immediately see two officers walking toward us. One radios something to another voice on the end of a walkie-talkie, and I stare with my mouth open as they approach.

"You live here, ma'am?" the first officer asks me. He's young. So young that I imagine he must be a rookie. At the most, in his second year.

"I do. We do," I say, looking at Esme for help. But her usual take charge attitude seems to have vanished.

"May we come in?" The other officer is speaking, and I recognize him instantly. It's Ben, the cop who came to the house yesterday. He's the same guy from the night of the fire Piper started so many years ago. My eyes snap back to the younger officer to avoid Ben's gaze that's directed at me.

"Yes," I say, opening the door for them. "My sister just told me. I can't believe it, it's so awful . . ." my voice trails off. Everything I say seems too loud. And wrong.

"What's happening out there?" Esme asks, her eyes focused on the window. We're all standing inside the entryway. We don't invite the officers to sit.

"The EMTs have determined that the person found in the lake by . . ." Ben says, and checks his clipboard for the name, "Greg—"

Esme interrupts. "That's my husband. He called after they—he and the girls and Bryce—they found a body in the lake while taking the boat out."

"Yes. The EMT determined that the person is deceased. The other officers are securing the area while we wait for a forensics team to arrive. In the meantime, Officer Barnes and I will take statements from everyone individually."

Ben looks at his colleague. "Barnes, take her into another room and get her statement, while I take hers." Ben nods to Esme.

Officer Barnes nods at him in acknowledgment, and I let out a sigh of relief that Ben won't be interviewing me. Ben continues, "Afterward, we'll need to interview the children, since they were witnesses to the initial event."

"Is that really necessary?" Esme says, her frown deep.

"I'm afraid it is. We need to get all the information from every pertinent party. It won't be a long process."

He motions to the couch and for Esme to sit. "Shall we sit here?"

Then he looks up at Barnes and me, still standing by. "You two can go to the kitchen for your interview." His look lingers on me for a moment, and I move quickly away before he can speak further.

I walk to the kitchen island barstools and Barnes follows behind me. We sit at the center island, our chairs facing toward the back pool patio and away from Esme and the other officer.

"My name is Vince Barnes." He slides a laminated card over to me. "I'm going to be asking you a series of questions about this morning and the events that led up to the call here today."

I gulp. My mouth feels dry, and I absently think I should get a glass of water.

Barnes has a silver case that contains a pad of paper, and he clicks on a blue ballpoint pen. He asks my name, and as I spell it for him, I notice his handwriting is almost entirely in caps, like an elementary child's might be.

"Okay, Regina. Tell me your whereabouts this morning when the body was discovered. Were you also on the boat?"

"No," I say, smoothing back my uncombed hair. "I was upstairs. I went back to bed to rest this morning, after getting the girls breakfast and changed into their suits." I don't want to sound like a lazy slob. No need to mention my morning-after headache. Or the edible cannabis gummy I took last night. "My husband, Bryce, wanted to take them on the lake. Fishing. With their Uncle Greg."

He nods and makes notes in his blocky penmanship.

"And it was your husband's idea to go fishing?" he says.

"Yes. It's his idea every day to go fishing." My weak attempt at a joke garners no response from him. He nods and his pen starts moving again.

"Where were you when the body was found?" he asks.

"I'm not exactly sure," I say. "In my room, probably. I came out of my room and saw the police lights, and that's all I know. I'm not sure how long ago they found it. Esme told me. Do you know who it is?" I ask him tentatively. My thoughts feel out of sorts. I'm confused about the timeline, and every word I utter seems like it's wrong.

"We'll work on identifying the victim once the coroner takes the body," he says.

"Victim?" I say. "Like, victim of . . ." I can't bring myself to say what I'm thinking. The M word.

"Homicide. Yes. We investigate all possibilities until the evidence can suggest facts about what happened."

"Oh," I murmur. That sinking, icy feeling of anxiety kicks back in.

"So, you did not view the body?" he asks.

"No. I've been here."

"Do you have any idea who it could be? Are there any guests missing?"

"Everyone's here except Piper. My other sister. But Esme said she left a note saying she went to town with her baby. My sister, Esme, she saw the body. She didn't know who it was. She would've recognized if it was our sister."

"Can I get a full list of who is occupying this summer home?" he asks.

I list off our three families and each member of our families, spelling out the names for him. "There's no one else around here. We're the only home for miles in either direction. I guess she could've come from another part of the lake . . ."

He looks up at me, his eyes flashing with the slightest hint of suspicion, and then he simply nods.

"Anyone in the family having problems with another individual that you are aware of?"

I feel myself start to perspire. These questions seem awfully intense for ten in the morning. I swallow. But it's a possible murder investigation. Of course he's asking serious questions.

I think about the money Esme promised. I think of her confession that Greg was cheating. Guiltily, I think of my phone call last night. My fight with my sisters. There are a few people who would want to harm us. We want to harm each other most of the time, too.

"No one I can think of," I lie.

He makes a note of this.

He asks what date we all arrived here, if there were any other occupants staying in the home prior to us. Then he says, "Walk me through your steps the past few days. Give as many details as possible. It may seem insignificant to you, but it may prove helpful to us."

I uncross my legs and recross them. "Yesterday morning I went fishing with my husband. I made lunch with my sister Esme here at the house. Then we all spent the afternoon here swimming. Paul made dinner at the house for everyone, and then after the kids were tucked in, I watched *Jaws*." This isn't strictly a lie; I did try to watch *Jaws*. I just don't mention the fighting or storming off or passing out after the hot tub outside on a lounge chair.

"And this morning," he prompts me.

"This morning, like I said, I made breakfast for the girls." I nod to the discarded half- eaten breakfast plates piled in the sink. "And then I went back to sleep. I knew my daughter was with my husband."

He finishes his notes and looks back up at me. He seems satisfied with my answers. And when I think the interview is over, he clears his throat.

"What about you and—" he checks his notes, "Your husband, Bryce. Any martial problems, stressors?"

I instantly feel defensive. That's none of his business. But then I take in his uniform. The gun at his belt. The walkie-talkie he's turned down. I guess it is his business. He's just doing his job.

"None," I say simply. It may be his job, but it doesn't mean I have to disclose every little detail. I'm sure our financial problems would be of no interest whatsoever to him. Now he can get back to doing the real work of finding out who is responsible for the dead body lying outside our home.

CHAPTER

28

Piper

MY THROAT FEELS constricted. I pull my car off to the farthest side of the driveway, away from the ambulance, fire truck, and police SUVs. I watch Bryce greet the paramedics, and they quickly follow him down the path toward the lake. I see no sign of my own husband or any of the others.

I jump out of the car, grab my bag, and open the back door to get Preston out of the car seat. He stirs as I lift him, but there's no time to sit in the car with the air conditioning on while he naps. He has to come with me.

Holding him close to my chest, I trail behind the three paramedics, who are carrying large black cases of equipment with them, as they follow Bryce. When I round the corner to the clearing, I see the boat anchored off the shore, and Greg standing on the beach. My eyes immediately shoot to the woman's pale body lying on the ground. Face down. She's dressed in a black outfit, a short sundress, maybe. She has long chestnut hair, tangled and covering her face.

The paramedics run to her, kneel down, and turn her over to take her pulse.

I gasp, covering my mouth with my hand, as I watch her large eyes staring up at the sky, glassy and empty. I can't speak. I can't breathe. I know her. That's her. . . .

That's Alexis.

I hold Preston closer to me, thankful he's asleep, as my entire body starts to shake. I'm quivering so hard that I worry I'll drop him.

I need to get him out of here. Away from this.

I walk over to Bryce, and Greg joins us. Where is Paul? We stay clear of the paramedics, who are performing resuscitation efforts that look to be unsuccessful.

"What happened?" I ask. My voice sounds far off, as if someone else is speaking.

Greg is pale. For a surgeon, he looks more shaken than Bryce. "We took the boat out," he says. "Lana spotted her. We drove over, and when we saw it was a person, and she wasn't moving, I jumped in and pulled her to shore."

"Can they save her?" I ask, looking at the body as they work on her, then quickly averting my eyes.

Greg shakes his head. "I don't think so."

"How can this be happening?" I ask him. "You know who that is, right?"

Both men are quiet.

"That's our cousin, Alexis," I tell them.

Bryce stares at me. "Is it really?"

I nod, but Greg steps closer in. "I don't think that's Alexis." He clears his throat. "I could be wrong, but I don't think that's her." He lowers his voice. "When a body is submerged in water, and death sets in . . . it changes its appearance."

He thinks just because he's a doctor and I'm not, that he has all the answers. But she was my cousin.

The paramedic who has been performing CPR stands up and takes out his walkie-talkie. "Dispatch, we have a DOA and are going to need to dispatch a coroner and an investigative officer to secure the scene. Signs of possible struggle with the victim. Over."

Two uniformed officers round the corner. One starts taping off the area with yellow and black tape. Another uniformed man approaches us.

"You're the ones who called in the deceased?" he asks. He's young but professional.

"Yes," Greg says. "We found her, brought her to shore, and called for help." I note that he didn't try to perform CPR. He's a doctor. Why didn't he try to save her like the paramedic is doing?

The officer says, "We're need you all to go back to the residence and wait there so we can take a statement from each of you. We need to clear everyone out now and secure the area."

We're shuffled away. I feel like I should say more, do more. That's my cousin. Instead, I walk away, back to the house, holding onto Preston for dear life.

As we round the corner, I see Paul on his way out to find us, worry creasing his brow. Bryce explains the situation to him. His face pales in shock.

He wraps his arms around Preston and me. "It's our cousin, Alexis." I bury my head in his shoulder.

From the corner of my eye, I see Greg shaking his head no.

"Let's get you inside," Paul says. "We can sort things out."

CHAPTER

29

Before

Alexis

THE DAY IS gray as I pull up to the graveyard. The funeral procession is on a grassy hill, mourners dressed in black.

The Howard sisters must have forgotten my invitation, but not to worry. I'm here. I don't think I'll approach the grieving sisters. Not quite yet.

I watch as the casket is lowered. A priest presides over the ceremony, and I cross myself and say my own prayer.

Afterward, they walk slowly back to their cars. I get into my own, not wanting to be seen, not yet. Though I don't have to worry. They're in their own world of grief. No one is looking at me.

I follow them back to the familiar street, though it's been many years since I've been here. Even longer since the last time I saw my family. My stomach knots at the memory.

The night of the bonfire, when Piper started the fire at the summer house. I remember Uncle Frank dousing the flames with the fire extinguisher. They took Piper to the hospital, then transferred her to a mental health facility. Apparently, she kept hearing voices and seeing things long after the drug wore off.

"The drug that you gave her," Aunt Audry had practically spit at me. And her cold stare. I could feel her hate radiating out of her the whole car ride home, barely a word would she speak to me.

I sat here at their house on the front steps, waiting for my foster family to pick me up, only to be told that after the incident, they didn't want me back. It was back to the group home for me, until I'd age out at eighteen, two long years away.

I'm not a vulnerable teenager anymore, though. In fact, I'm a grown woman. Not only can they *not* get rid of me now, but it's also time I'm given what is mine.

I'm a rightful member of this family, whether Aunt Audry Howard wanted to acknowledge me or not. She may have shirked her duties to care for me when I was most vulnerable. But she's not going to deny me what's mine in her death—a piece of their small fortune.

I turn the wipers on as I sit in my car, watching the sisters walk up to their parents' home, dressed in sensible black stockings and heels. Why should they inherit all of this wealth? Why should it be so easy for them, when I've had so little for so long?

If my aunt had had even an ounce of caring or sense of responsibility, she wouldn't have turned me out when I was ten.

It's only now that I'm an adult that I can see how awful what she did to me was. Sending me—her only sister's daughter—to foster home after foster home, with group homes in between. She can't imagine the horror I endured there. The cruelty. The neglect.

I swing open my car door. Audry is gone now, and I'm not afraid of ghosts. There are three sisters inside that house who can begin to make things right.

The foyer is full of people milling around, and my presence goes unnoticed. I slide the door closed. Memories flood my brain. It's been almost twenty years, but the place remains largely unchanged. High ceilings, tile in the foyer, wainscoting on the walls against blue paint.

Growing up, when I'd come to visit with my mom, I was always in awe when we'd come here. I felt like a princess in a castle. But moving here after my mom died had felt very different. I knew I wasn't welcome. The large house felt suddenly overwhelming. The endless hallways and bedrooms made my loneliness feel even bigger.

Every August we would go to the family summer home for a two-week vacation. Then I was cast out of the family, and this was no longer my home.

I head into the formal living room, where there are platters of food spread across the buffet table. The guests are of every age; several people look to be in their eighties and nineties, punctuated by younger kids and teens, and everyone in between.

Then I spot her. Esme is making a beeline toward me with a look of confusion and growing displeasure.

"Alexis?" she says, her voice tight. "Is that you?"

"I didn't get an invitation to the funeral, but I wouldn't miss the repast for the world," I say. It really did rub me the wrong way that I didn't get notified of my aunt's death. I'm family, after all. Were they ashamed of how they'd treated me? Didn't want a reminder of the Howards' ugly past at Saint Audry's funeral?

"Please, don't make a scene," she says through clenched teeth.

"Who's making a scene? I'm just standing here. You look pretty amped up, though."

She looks at the floor and collects herself. "Please, help yourself to the food and drink. Then be on your way. We want this to be a nice event for people who loved Mom to come together and mourn."

I glance back at the food. "I'm not here for the overpriced hors d'oeuvres," I say. "But I did want to talk to you about a matter concerning Audry's assets."

Her eyes widen. She looks around. "Not here. Let's not do this here. Anyway, I don't think there's anything to discuss."

"The way I see it, there is. I'm entitled to one-quarter of her assets. I'm sure your dad would have left something to me, had he gone last."

At the mention of her dad, Esme gets very still and her face becomes pinched, red. "I want you out of my house. Now." She moves a step closer to me, trying to usher me to the door. A few people nearby halt their conversations and stare at us.

I stand my ground. I knew it wouldn't be easy, getting what's mine. I don't have a legal team or the resources to fight her—she knows that—but I refuse to budge. I have something she doesn't have—grit.

"I'm not going anywhere," I say, raising my voice to match hers. "In fact, I think I'll stand right here until you're ready to discuss what's mine. Because the way I see it, my mother left me in Audry's care when she died. Audry and Frank were made my legal guardians. If they had done what's right—cared for me, like they agreed to do—I'd have been an heir. So, we're going to make it right. We'll be splitting the family fortune *four* ways instead of three. It's such a large sum. You'll still have plenty."

"You're not blood. She wasn't your mom," she says, staring at me incredulously, as if I'm not getting it.

"It's not my fault they gave me up, like the selfish cowards they were! Audry was a mean and hateful bitch," my voice rings out, and I hear gasps from the mourners who are watching our exchange in horror.

"Get out," Esme yells, and she steps forward, so close that I think she'll push me. "*Get. Out.*" She's shaking.

Her husband, Greg, comes in from the other room. He registers recognition. We've met before and he knows exactly who I am.

"Ladies," he says, his voice low. "Let's all take a minute. Alexis, why don't you come with me. Let's catch up in the other room." His eyes look pleading, and I decide to relent. I've made my point for today.

"Fine," I say. "But I'll be back. I won't leave until I get what I deserve. Your mom may be an evil bitch, but you could right her wrongs."

Esme's face is florid and her small body is rigid with anger. "You will regret this," she says. "Mark my words. You will pay, not me. Now get out." She turns and flees the room. Greg gently takes my arm and walks me toward the foyer and into his parlor down the hall. He leads me in and closes the door behind me.

CHAPTER

30

Esme

THE DARK-HAIRED OFFICER in front of me jots down the last of his notes, and then hands me his card. "I'm officer Ben Sherman, and this is my contact information. We'll be in touch in the coming days as the investigation unfolds. If you think of anything else, don't hesitate to call me."

"Absolutely. Thank you," I say, tucking his card into my wallet. Out of the corner of my eye, I see Regina finishing up her own interview, getting up from the kitchen island and coming our way. She looks as rattled as I feel.

"So what's next?" I ask Officer Sherman, wrapping my arms around myself, hoping he doesn't notice that I'm shivering. "What do we do?"

"Well," he says, "don't disturb the area where the body was found. There likely will be divers and further investigations out there collecting data. Keep yourself and your children away from the area."

I bite my lip. "I'm thinking it would probably be best to leave. We were planning on staying here another week, but after this . . . I can't imagine my daughters will want to stay here. None of us will."

He shakes his head. "You'll need to stay put until the lead investigator gives you the okay to leave. We may need to re-interview you or gather more information as there are new developments. It may be several days."

My face falls at this news. I want nothing more than to get as far away from this place as humanly possible.

I steady my breathing, focusing on taking air in and out.

Just then, Piper walks in. She's carrying Preston, who is crying. She looks at me with concern.

"Esme," she says. "Did you see—?" I nod, trying to indicate with my eyes that we should wait to discuss until the officers are gone.

"Let me help you with the baby," I say, reaching for him. She lets me take him in my arms. "Is he hungry?" I ask.

She nods, and I tilt my head, indicating we should go to the kitchen. "We need to take care of this one," I say over Preston's cries, excusing myself from the officer and moving away to the kitchen. He keeps his distance, having no interest in the crying, I assume.

"Esme," Piper says, as she fills water into a pot and turns on the stove to heat the bottle. "I can't believe it . . . I can't believe it. Alexis. She's dead."

I stop dead in my tracks.

"What did you say?" My voice is low and urgent.

"Alexis. Our cousin. I told you she was here. Now she's dead. I saw her. Her white, lifeless face."

The bottle is ready. Piper takes Preston back from me, his face red from wailing, and mercifully he latches onto his bottle. His cries are replaced by a sucking noise.

"What are you talking about?" I ask. I try to keep my voice low, aware of the officers milling about in our foyer. I turn my back to them. "That's *not* Alexis."

"Yes, it is. I saw her," she says, and she looks angry now. "It was awful. Just lying there." She blinks, hard. "Every time I close my eyes, I see it." She rocks Preston.

"Piper, I don't know what you think you saw, but I saw her, too. The dead body. It wasn't Alexis. I promise you." I blink, now also seeing the woman's sprawled-out body in my mind's eye. Her face wasn't turned toward me, but I'm certain I know who it was. And it's not Alexis.

Maybe it would be better if it were Alexis. But it's not.

Piper looks like she's about to faint. "Sit, sit." I usher her, still holding Preston, into the chair.

I glance at the officers. "My sister is very shaken up. Can we have a moment?"

The officers nod and move toward the door. I open it, holding it for them. I close the door behind them and head back to Piper's side.

"Piper? Are you okay?"

Her eyes look glassy and far off. She's looking down at Preston, and I'm not sure she's listening to me.

I go to the kitchen and grab a glass, fill it with ice and water. "Here" I say, holding it out to her. "Drink this."

I hold Preston's bottle for her while she takes a sip. "There, there. Good," I say, setting down the glass and sitting across from her.

Regina joins us. "What did you see out there, Piper?" she asks. The dark circles under her eyes make them look sunken, as if worry has aged her ten years.

"I saw Alexis. Our cousin? Have you two forgotten about her? About what we all did to her? Now she's dead."

Regina looks to me, and I shake my head. "I would have recognized her if it were Alexis. It's not." I bend down to Piper. "We need to put on a united front, Piper. Regardless of who it is out there."

Her eyes meet mine now. "Why?"

"Our house is in a remote spot. We found the body. It's all circumstantial, but it looks like one of us was involved with a crime. We need to be united in protecting our family from this. I wouldn't want you, or Paul, none of us should be implicated." That seems to get her attention. She's listening.

"Okay," she says.

"Say that we were all together last night. Don't mention that I ever left—that will only distract and confuse the investigation. Be sure to tell Paul as well."

"Fine, I will."

"Good. Don't mention that we fought last night. Do you understand?"

Piper lifts Preston up and pats his back. A small burp sounds from his tiny body. She returns him back to the crook of her arm, and he resumes eating his milk. "Okay," she says. "I can do that. We're family, we stick together. I don't want to cause problems or make matters worse. But I know that was Alexis out there. It's going to come out. What we did to her." Her skin is pale with two pink spots burning on her cheeks.

"We're all in shock right now. It's easy to see things that aren't there."

"Maybe," Piper says. "Then who?"

Regina joins us, her eyebrows creased in concern. Both she and Regina look to me. "I don't know. We'll find out soon, I'm sure. In the meantime, we don't give them any reason to entangle our family in this mess. If they're treating this woman's death as a homicide, we need to tread carefully." A thought occurs to me. "Greg and I need to get on the phone with our attorney. I'll let you guys know what Alan says."

They nod.

Regina looks antsy. "Are we agreed?" I ask her.

"Yes," she says. "I just feel like I might be sick."

CHAPTER

31

Regina

THE SOUND OF the flushing toilet hurts my head, and I watch the contents of my now empty stomach twirl down the bowl.

I keep replaying the phone call I had last night with Alexis over and over again. It feels like a bad dream. I pound my head lightly against the wall, cursing my own stupidity.

How am I always putting myself in bad spots? I thought being broke and losing our house was as bad as it could get. But now? Alexis is dead, and I'm probably the last person who talked to her. I'm the reason she was here.

I bang my head again.

Think. *Think.* What precisely happened? What exactly did I say?

I remember drinking the last of the margarita, the THC gummy in full effect, the steam of the hot tub making me feel dizzy and reckless.

Dialing her number, I'd felt numb. Invincible.

"Hello, Regina," she said, her voice calm and unfazed. "This is unexpected."

"Alexis," I said. "I'm at the house."

"The summer house?"

"Yes. My sisters and their families are here, too. We're all here for the annual August vacation, remember? But we're not one big fucking happy family. Esme, especially. Such a bitch. I want you to come here. Come and stay as my guest. If I have to be here, at least you can come and keep me company."

"You want me to come, as your guest?" her voice was smooth as she spoke.

"Yes." I swallowed down the last of my blue margarita, and the glass tipped over as I set it down, but luckily it didn't shatter. I dangled my legs over the edge of the hot tub, splashing the hot water around. "It's my house." *And since Esme won't buy my share from me*, I thought, *I can have whatever guest I want.* "You'll be my guest."

"You know how your sister feels about me."

"Fuck her," I said.

"Well, actually," Alexis said something, but I was looking at the stars and I wasn't sure I heard her.

"What was that?" I said. "Sorry."

"I said, I'm staying at the Bergamont Resort. I'm here. In town."

I hadn't answered, maybe shocked that she was in town. A little creeped out.

"Wow," I said. "Why? You knew we'd be here. Were you planning a visit?" I had asked, ignoring the sneaking suspicion that this call was a very bad idea.

"Sure. I was going to call you, actually."

"Oh, right, so you just decided—" I was about to ask her more questions. But then I pictured Esme's face when Alexis walked in the door. That'd show her. In fact, every year I'll invite Alexis. Maybe a few friends from college. The rowdy ones who would drive Esme crazy. That'd really show her. "Great." I said instead. "That makes it easy. Come by tomorrow in the morning. Bring your bag. You can stay in the guest room downstairs." My chest puffed up and swelled with pride at my amazing plan.

"Are you sure, Regina?" Her voice sounded peculiar, but I wasn't sure why. I ignored any warning signs I was getting. I didn't care that she sounded odd. I just wanted her here. To see Esme's reaction.

"I'm sure, Alexis. Geez. Better yet, come over now, why don't you? Grab your stuff, and come have a drink with me. I'm out by the pool, under the stars. Let's make it a party."

"It's midnight."

"Just get your bag and come. I won't take no for an answer," I remember saying, and then punching my phone's end button.

The thought of the conversation makes my stomach clench again, but there's nothing left to empty into the toilet. I'm not sure if it's the margaritas, or the steely fear that's making me nauseous.

Alexis and I have never been close, but I don't want her dead. Could she really be dead? If so, I don't want to be held responsible for her death. I was the last person to talk to her. I'm the one who told her to come here.

I have to think of a plan.

I'll cover for Esme, but who will cover for me? How can I cover my tracks? Like a lightning bolt going off, I realize my phone is the key.

I grab it from my back pocket and look at the history. Sure enough, my last call to Alexis is right there in black and white. I delete my entire call log, and all my texts, for good measure. There.

I log into my social media accounts. Not that I ever post, but I look at any activity from last night, to double-check I didn't post anything about Alexis coming, or send her any DMs. After scrolling through my history log and messages, I decide I'm in the clear.

What else can I do to protect myself? I didn't mention anything to the cop about talking to Alexis. Or the money trouble we were in. Or the fight with Esme—funny how she's going to buy the house from me just so I can say what I would've said anyway. I wasn't going to tell him anything that would make me look suspicious or tied to Alexis.

There is hope, though. Esme is sure the body isn't Alexis. While Piper is sure it is.

I hold out my phone. I should just call Alexis. My finger hovers over her name and number, ready to press the call button. If she answers, it would all be better. The woman in the lake is someone else, not related to our family. Alexis would answer and make all this go away. This horrible, wretched feeling in the pit of my stomach that's eating me alive.

She'll answer in her snarky manner, telling me I'm crazy for having worried. She may not be the best swimmer, but she's tough. No one would get the best of her.

But I have a horrible suspicion she won't answer. Part of me is sure she's who they found in the lake.

I fell asleep last night outside on the lounger. If Alexis had come and found me asleep, she would have woken me up. But maybe not. So what did she do? Did she go into the house? Let herself into the spare room?

I must go check.

Unlocking the bathroom door, I turn left and head down the hallway. The downstairs has been redone, thanks to Esme, and this whole section is an addition, with the rec room and guest bedroom-office. When we first got here and Esme showed me around, she was very proud of the addition and made note that if anyone needed a private place to answer work calls, this would be ideal. I walk in the room and see the bed is made. The office desk is clear. When I open the closet door, it's empty, with just a few lone hangers on the rail. I close the door, scanning the room for signs of life, but it's clear there's been no guest here.

That's when I spot it. In the corner of the room, a sticky note attached to a key card. Scrambling to pick it up, I see blue pen ink. The letterhead is from the Bergamont Resort. On the paper, in blue scrawled handwriting, is a phone number and room number. I turn it over. Nothing else. I tuck the key and piece of paper into my pocket, unsure if I should call the number, but thinking I better wait.

Who would have left this here? I know it's not from Esme. She never leaves anything out of place. This must have been from Alexis. She said she was staying at the Bergamont. Damn. Could that really be her in the lake? A lump in my throat is forming.

The driveway. I need to check it.

If Alexis came here last night, she had to drive, right? I remember something about her, way back in the past, not driving. Something about losing her license. But surely now she has a car, right? How else would she get here? I move back into the hallway and through the back patio doors. I'll go around back to avoid the officers and crime scene.

Coming around the side of the house, I walk through the pathway that's cleared and opens to the three-car garage and paved driveway out front. I peek my head around. The ambulance and fire truck have left, but the two police SUVs remain, and there's another patrol car now. But I don't see any other vehicles parked in front, other than Piper's. Just to be sure, I open the side door to the garage.

My family's car and Esme's are here, but the third space is empty save for a few mountain bikes. So there's no car that would belong to her. Though she could have taken a taxi or car service.

Or maybe the key card belonged to Greg. He may have been up here earlier this year, staying at the Bergamont Resort, and coming to the house to oversee the renovations. Maybe the phone number was for a contractor, or a friend at the resort? Maybe this piece of paper doesn't mean Alexis was here.

Please, let her not have been at the house. Please, let Alexis not be the body in the lake.

CHAPTER

32

Piper

PAUL WALKS THROUGH the front door and comes to my side, kneeling and giving me a hug.

"You all right?" he asks.

"We're fine." I love him fiercely, and I almost melt with gratitude to have him by my side right now.

"What did the police say out there?" I ask. I'd watched from the window as the officer with the dark hair talked to Paul, jotting down notes and motioning to the lake.

"He just asked me some questions, tried to get a sense of what happened this morning, if we saw anything suspicious." He shakes his head. "I can't believe they found a body practically in our front yard. Terrible the girls had to see that."

"It's Alexis, Paul, our cousin. I'm telling you it was her."

"I think you need to talk to the officer next," he says.

"Yeah. I've had my hands full with Preston. I will, now, if you take him."

We move to the window and watch as a large paneled van pulls up. A man with white scrubs exits the vehicle, accompanied by another technician in white. They pull out a stretcher from the back of the van. After consulting with an officer, they head in the direction of the lake.

"Do you want to go speak to them?" he asks.

"Maybe now isn't the best time. I don't want to get in the way. They said earlier they'll make the rounds to interview everyone."

"There's time," he says, rubbing my back. "You can talk to them after they examine the body."

"I'm scared, Paul," I say. "They said it looks like a homicide. I don't feel safe here. There's someone out there. I want to leave."

He places a protective arm around me. "It'll be okay. We're all here together. No one can hurt us. When we know more, we can leave."

We stare out the window, waiting.

Eventually, one of the techs is visible again. This time, with the help of an officer, he's carrying the stretcher, the weight of a body now filling the shape of the stretcher. A white sheet covers Alexis as they load her into the back of the van and close the double doors behind her.

Seeing the body carted off that way propels me to action. Handing Preston to Paul, I take a deep breath. I remember a therapist of mine once told me I have an avoidant personality style. I deal with my emotions, or problems, by pushing them down. She said that doesn't work, though, because eventually those emotions come up to the surface. Eventually, it all bursts out and explodes.

I decide I can't run from this.

I step outside and ask the officer to speak with him. Once he begins to interview me, I answer his questions in a haze. I tell him that I saw her and I think the body might be that of our cousin Alexis, but I can't be sure since I haven't seen her in years. That sets off a whole maelstrom of questions. *Who is she? Why was she here? Was she staying with you? When's the last time you saw her? What's your relationship like? Has anyone else seen her recently?* I answer as best I can. He writes her contact information down carefully and thanks me for my help

When it seems he's finished and turns to go, I stop him. "Do you know who did this? Do you have any leads?"

He shakes his dark head. "We're investigating all possibilities at this time."

I go back into the house and take Preston from Paul's arms. I hold him close to me. More than ever, I can't let him out of my sight. There's a murderer out there, and he's targeting our house. Our family.

There's also a deep sadness within me. I haven't seen Alexis for years, but she was my cousin. Seeing her lifeless body is one of the worst experiences I've ever had. What a sad, awful way to go. Did she struggle? Did she drown? Or was she already dead before she was tossed into the water? No one deserves that.

Was there more I could have done to save her? From the moment we got here I had thought I heard her, felt her lurking around. Maybe if I'd taken action, rather than being scared, I could have prevented this. I should have called her. Or called the police after the bedroom window broke. Something.

As the sun sets, the police cars leave, one by one. The dark-haired officer knocks at the door and tells us they'll be returning in the morning.

Regina and Bryce are in the rec room playing cards with the girls. Esme heads back into the kitchen to work on dinner. I decide to join her. I put on my baby wrap and snuggle Preston inside so when I walk, I'm literally wearing him. I don't trust him to be in the crib even with a monitor, not even with Paul. Preston can sleep on me. He likes cuddling anyway.

Esme is slicing tomatoes for a caprese salad. "Ouch," she cries out. "I sliced my finger." She wraps the tip of her finger in a paper towel, red blotting the white sheet.

"I'll get you a bandage," I say, heading out of the kitchen to get it from my bag.

When I get back, Greg has joined her in the kitchen, their bent heads together. As I approach, they break apart, but the look on Greg's face is unmistakable—guilt.

"Thanks," Esme says, stepping away from him and grabbing the adhesive bandage.

"What are we going to do, guys? I'm scared."

"I've put in a call to our attorney, Alan," Greg supplies in response. "He'll get the pulse on the situation. Then advise us how to proceed."

I look at him strangely. "But what about staying here? Tonight? I don't feel safe. Someone's out there. They think someone murdered that woman. And remember Lana last night? She was all wet and talking about a lady in the lake."

Greg and Esme exchange a look.

"There's no danger, Piper. We're safe here. We're all together," Greg assures me.

"Piper." Esme finishes wrapping the bandage around her finger, then reaches for her purse. "I've got some of these pills. I think you should take one. It will help you sleep. I'm worried about you."

"You should be worried about the person who murdered Alexis," I say.

Another look crosses between the two of them.

"I know it's all upsetting; I'm scared, too." Esme places the small round pill in the palm of my hand. "Take it."

C H A P T E R

33

Before

Alexis

GREG CLOSES THE office door behind him, shutting out the sound of the mourners who are no doubt discussing the scene that just unfolded between Esme and me.

"What's going on?" Greg asks, standing with his arms crossed.

"Your wife didn't have the decency to invite me to Audry's funeral. But I wouldn't miss this for the world," I say. Suddenly, beyond my control, my lip starts to quiver and my eyes well up. "Did your wife tell you what Audry did?"

He nods. "I'm sorry." He says it with sincerity. "It must have been a very difficult life for you. I can see why you're upset."

I'm afraid if I speak again, I'll start to cry. I remain silent for a time. Greg walks over to a crystal decanter and pours some brown liquid into a rocks glass. Then pours one for himself. He hands me the glass. I drink it in one gulp, the liquid burning away the tears.

I nod. "Thanks." I exhale. "Look. I just want my portion of the inheritance. That's the least they can do. It's rightfully mine."

He winces, looking at me thoughtfully. "I'm not sure that's true."

"If they had kept me, and raised me as one of their own, as my mother wished—and Audry agreed to—you don't think they would have given me an inheritance?"

"Maybe not. People are funny about money and bloodlines."

"There's that word again. Blood. I am blood. My mother was Audry's sister."

"Sisters, yes, but from what I heard they were never close," he corrects me.

"Still sisters. Which makes me blood."

"People are hesitant to part with their money, Alexis," he says. He's not being unreasonable, and somehow it deflates me. My anger is quickly turning to sadness. I need to get out of here.

"Look, I'm sorry I ruined the party. I'll go. But you should know; I'm going to find a way to get my money."

He puts his hand out, reaching out for my shoulder, stopping me.

"Wait," he says. "Maybe we can work something out. You and I." He looks into my eyes, and at first I'm not sure what he means.

I squint at him. "How so?"

"I could find a way to give you some money," he says. "For the hardship you've endured. To help you get on your feet." His eyes appraise my outfit, assessing my worn shoes and discount handbag. "Help you move on from this ordeal."

He takes out a piece of paper with Audry's initials on it and scrawls numbers down then hands it to me, enclosing it in my hand. "Take this. Get in touch with me after the funeral. No more exchanges with Esme. She's got a lot on her plate. She has the funeral, and then cleaning out the house and getting it ready to sell. It's an emotional time. Leave peacefully, that's my condition."

This is a man who is used to getting what he wants. He knows he's made me an offer I can't refuse; one that I won't refuse.

I nod and turn, wordlessly closing the door and getting as far away from that house as I can.

CHAPTER

34

Esme

It's morning time, the day after the body was discovered outside our home, the third day of what was supposed to be a nice family vacation. When I open the front door, I see the first state police SUV pulling into our driveway. Then little by little and more and more clearly, I hear a helicopter buzzing overhead and circling the lake, and I close the door. I'm not ready for the circus to begin where it left off yesterday.

Greg comes up behind me, encircles my waist with his hands. We made love last night, the first time in a few weeks. It's brought us together, this death. This horror. I see the bags under his eyes, the worry in his expression.

I'm strangely protective of him, even though it defies all reason. He created this mess. Yet all I want is for our family to remain intact.

His phone buzzes. "Oh, that's the attorney, calling me back," he says, loosening his hold on me and answering.

"Alan, finally," he speaks into the phone. "Yes . . . It is. Very upsetting. Thanks for your call back." He pauses, listening. "That's outrageous." He starts pacing. "We're not staying here. No, that's too long. I have patients I need to get back to . . . I have surgeries scheduled. Absurd." He pauses again, and then he stops outright. His face pales. "Well, Alan, I need you to do more. We need to get out of here."

We were supposed to be here another week and a half. Even when he was having an affair with Brigit, he had planned on taking a week with her at the Cape, I remember reading in their text exchange. So he doesn't have patients. He's lying; he must be desperate to leave.

He disconnects, shoving his phone in his pocket. When I reach for him, he swats my hand away in annoyance.

"What did he say?" I ask.

He shakes his head. "Alan knows the sheriff in the next town over. He's got the inside line on the investigation. They don't have a positive ID on the body but should tomorrow. Right now, they're saying they've got skin under the nails of the dead woman; she put up a fight. The body was recovered before the water washed away all the forensic evidence. So, they're testing the skin for DNA, and results should be ready within a week. For now, he said stay put. We're going to be here for a while as he straightens things out."

"Should we talk about what really happened that night?" I ask him.

"What do you mean?" he snaps back.

"We both know who they pulled from that lake. And it's not Alexis."

He gulps and turns his head toward the stairs. "Say nothing. To anyone. You hear me? We'll be fine." He pulls me closer.

"We just have to stick together. Alan will advise us. Until then, not a word to anyone. We've been at the house, and that's it. No mention of the Bergamont. No mention of *her*."

I nod.

I half expect his phone to start beeping, interrupting us as it always does when I try to talk to my husband. But then I remember.

She won't be texting him anymore.

C H A P T E R

35

Before

Alexis

I APPLY THE FIRST flick of paint onto the canvas, a small stroke, and then another. My brush moves before I know where it will go. I change colors and mix, finding the right blend of cobalt blue, and then ivory and cream, creating an image. A silhouette of a woman. My hand moves the brush, each stroke getting the figure closer to what it's meant to be.

When the knock at my door sounds out, the banging echoes in my walk-up Brooklyn studio apartment. Even with the white noise of the traffic outside, the knock is sharp and loud.

I set the brush down then run my fingers through my hair. A glance in the mirror shows me that my white cotton tank is splattered with paint, but my cotton pants are relatively unscathed. My hair is wrapped up in a high bun, off my neck in this heat. My air conditioning window unit is cranked at capacity, working overtime, but barely cooling off the flat as the muggy summer temperature soars outside.

When I open the door, the man standing in front of me looks as out of place as he probably feels.

"Hey," I say to him. "I wasn't sure you'd come."

"I'm a man of my word," Greg says, stepping inside. He glances at my kitchen, my unmade bed, the painting that's positioned by the window overlooking the street and high rise opposite this building. It's an artsy, up-and-coming area, dotted with coffee shops, indie bookstores, vintage record stores, and consignment shops. Even so, I can barely afford the rent here, but I work extra shifts to make it work. The light is perfect for painting, and the city below makes me feel at home. It reminds me of the apartment I grew up in with my mom. The sounds of cars honking at night, peals of laughter, shouts of anger, the smell of food cooking, they serve as reassurance that I'm not alone in the world.

"Or is it because you knew I'd track you down, and you wanted to avoid another scene with me and your wife?"

He chuckles. "That, too." He struts in my studio, his large frame filling the space. He stands in front of my canvas. I watch his eyes move to the wall, where my paintings are hung, and the floor where they're stacked. He reaches out, looks through the stacks.

"You're talented." He states it not as a compliment, but as a fact.

I always wondered what I could have become. If I'd had a family to nurture my talent and send me to art school. If Audry had fulfilled her responsibility, rather than cast me aside.

"Thanks. Are you into art?"

He puts his hands in his pockets and shrugs. "Not much time for art. Long hours at the hospital. The twins' nannies keep leaving, and Esme's interviewing private schools for kindergarten . . ."

At the mention of Esme, I feel my stomach clench.

"Only the best for Esme," I say, my voice hollow.

"So is this your occupation?" he asks, regarding my latest canvas. "Artist?"

"It doesn't pay the bills, no. Barista, dog walker, odd jobs. I was working at a bank—" I stop myself.

I feel his eyes on me briefly. Suddenly I'm very aware of how my white tank shows the curve of my breasts, how my flat stomach peeks out from my loose-fitting pants. I catch my reflection in the mirror: flushed cheeks, paint on my fingertips.

"May I sit?" he asks.

There's my bed, a small loveseat, and two bar stools at the small island that separates my sleeping quarters from my modest kitchen. I nod to one of the stools.

I stand opposite him, across the counter from where he sits.

"So the bank didn't work out?" he asks.

"No. I was fired. The boss was an asshole. He—" I stop myself. He's like every guy, isn't he? But despite myself, I find myself spilling it out to Greg. "My boss tried to take advantage of me, and when I stopped him, he found a reason to get rid of me."

"You're better off out of that situation."

"Tell my bank account that," I say.

He takes out the check. Lays it on the counter and slides it toward me. "Maybe this will help."

He smiles, nodding that I should take it when I hesitate. Looking down at the number written on the check, I feel numb. As much as I know I'm deserving of this—more, even—it's less satisfying when it comes from him instead of my cousins.

"You don't look very happy," he says. "Not large enough?"

"No," I say. "It's fine. I just expected it to feel different. This money will change my life. But somehow, I just feel empty."

"You've had a hard time of it, haven't you?" He looks around, then back to me. "No family to look after you. So talented, but never having the formal training or space to dedicate to your craft. But still, you persevere. You're a fighter. You came lobbying for what, some would say, is your right to inherit, while others would say it's not. But you've got guts." He hesitates. "Can I ask you something personal?"

"Sure," I shrug.

"How are you still single? A beautiful woman like yourself, living alone like this . . ."

I laugh. "I haven't found the right guy, I guess." I leave out the part about not trusting anyone. About having my heart broken so deeply that something within me decided I'd never put myself through that again.

The only reason I'm letting Greg in, now, is that he's unavailable. He's married. To my cousin. Besides, having him here feels comforting. He's the first person to seem to care about me in longer than I can remember. He's handsome, too, there's no denying it.

He nods. He reaches out his hand, briefly letting his fingers pass over mine.

"I think things are going to turn around for you," he says, nodding at the check. "This can be a new beginning for you. You can open up your own art studio. Invest in your own business. The world is your oyster."

"Let's not get carried away," I say. "It's not that much. In fact, I'm pretty sure this just scratches the surface of the inheritance Audry and Frank must've left behind."

"You're sharp," he says, letting out a laugh. He places a hand on his stomach over his button-down shirt. "I'm starving. Where's somewhere good around here to eat?"

"Depends on what you like."

"What's your favorite?" He leans in.

"Thai or Italian. You can't go wrong with Gino's or Royal Thai."

"Why don't you join me?" He tosses the request out casually.

"Right now?"

"Sure," he says. "I need to eat, you need to eat. Show me where's good. My treat."

That's how it started. By the end of the night, I'd notice his gaze lingering on me. He'd find a reason to reach over and touch my arm, briefly. A zing of electricity between us.

He insisted on walking me back to my apartment, stating it wasn't safe for me alone. Shoulder to shoulder, our arms rubbing against one another. An intimacy I hadn't felt for years.

"I'm alone here all the time," I insist at the door to my building, telling him not to bother walking me up.

"Just because you do something all the time, doesn't make it right."

I relent. We walk up the stairs to the door to my apartment. With each step, despair overcomes me. He's leaving. To go back to Esme. Hot anger fills my belly. Greg's an amazing man. What did Esme do to deserve him? She has beauty, money, adorable twins—and a perfect husband.

I pull him into me, my lips finding his. He hesitates, but then I feel him relent, letting my mouth move over his—

And just like that, it's over. He pulls away and looks down.

"I can't," he says. "You're stunning. I've enjoyed our time together . . . But I can't."

"It's fine," I lie, and close the door behind me without saying goodbye.

I go turn into my apartment, alone again.

An hour later I receive a text from him saying he can't stop thinking about me, and asking when he can see me again.

CHAPTER

36

Regina

When I wake up in the morning, the day after the body was found in the lake, I'm momentarily confused. There's a small foot digging into me. I look over and see Lana's sleeping body curled up next to me, and next to her is Bryce.

I'm annoyed to be woken up by her cold foot pummeling my side, but then it all comes back to me. The body. Lana was afraid to sleep alone. She was shivering last night. I wrapped her up and said of course she could sleep with us. Who needs a good night's sleep? It beats the lounge chair outside, that's for sure.

The money. That's right. I remember that Greg and Esme have agreed to buy us out of the house. We'll be okay. We don't have to move.

But then I remember why. The body in the lake. My phone call to Alexis. Guilty me.

There's a humming coming from outside that sounds like a windmill churning. I slip out from under the covers and cross the room, peeking out of the blinds. There's a helicopter overhead, and a police car already in the driveway. I blink, closing the blinds against the brightness of the early morning sunrise. I'm regretting all the wine I had last night. No rest for the wicked.

I cross the room to go to the shared hallway bathroom and close the door behind me. Turning on the faucet, I splash water on my face. There are three things I need to do today. First, I need to get the check from Esme and Greg before they change their mind. Or go to jail. Then, I need to call the phone number on the Bergamont stationary. And then I need to pack up my bags, my family, and get the hell out of here.

Patting my face dry, then taking out my toothbrush, I begin a quick routine to start my morning. I want to crawl back into bed. I still feel off from the margaritas two nights ago, plus more of Paul's Napa Valley wine last night. Moreover, I want to get out of this house. But will the police think we're guilty if we leave?

Once I'm ready, I cross back through the dark bedroom. Lana is sleeping peacefully, and by peacefully, I mean that she's now kicking Bryce and encroaching on his sleeping space. But both of them are undisturbed by the helicopter noise that was overhead, and has now passed.

After I change into a fresh pair of shorts and a tank top, I tiptoe across the room and out into the hallway, closing the door behind me.

At the same time, Piper comes out of her room, baby Preston in her arms. "You survived the night," I say.

"You shouldn't make light of it," she scowls. "A woman is dead."

I shrug. "Sorry," I say. "How's the little guy?"

Preston is snuggled in her arm like a little prince. He's a cute baby, that's for sure. I hope he doesn't inherit his mom's loopy disposition.

"He must sense all this anxiety and stress, because he had a long night. He's hungry now, and needs his bottle," she says as we make our way down the stairs. Greg and Esme are in the living room.

"Morning," Greg greets us.

"Have they said anything?" I ask, nodding to the police car outside.

"Not yet," he says. "The guy from yesterday, Officer Sherman, got out of the car, went to the lake where it's taped off, then back into his cruiser."

I nod. Officer Ben again; he sure has been here working nonstop.

"Did you get a chance to write that check?" I say quietly to Esme. But instead Greg nods knowingly. "Esme and I discussed it, and we're in agreement."

He writes down a number on a piece of paper and hands it to me. "Does this sound like a fair number?" he asks.

"It does," I say, peering at the paper and then back up at him. His face looks strained, and his eyelids are baggy. He looks like a different man from his usual confident, tanned, bright-eyed self.

"I'll write you the check now. Just remember what that means," Esme whispers, glancing at Piper in the kitchen.

"I will." I say, annoyed. I'm not a fool. "I'm going to get some coffee, pack, and once Bryce and Lana are awake, we'll be heading out."

Esme and Greg frown at me, and even Piper glances up from feeding Preston.

"You can't leave," Esme says. "None of us can."

"Um, no. Why?" I say with a sinking feeling.

"The officers said that until they know more about what happened, we need to stay put. Our lawyer has advised us we need to be here."

"For how long?"

"A couple weeks, as planned. Or longer."

My shoulders tense. I've always hated being told what to do. When a teacher would tell me not to talk, I'd write notes instead. When I was supposed to be doing homework, I'd slip out and walk to the neighbor's house. Someone telling me what to do makes my skin crawl. That's why even though I don't love my job at the bar, I stay. I can pretty much do what I want. I get to pick my shifts, and there's a regular clientele I can chat with if I want. When I make a joke, they laugh. It's easy to know the right thing to say so my tips are big at the end of the night.

Not only do I not like this lake house, but also now I'm being told I literally have no choice but to stay here.

That's not going to work.

I fling open the front door and walk up to the police cruiser. I rap on the door. Sure enough, it's Officer Ben Sherman who rolls down his window. Just my luck.

"Good morning, Mrs. Dune," he says.

It throws me off that he remembers my married name. That's not good. Is it because he's suspicious of me? Does he know about Alexis and me? It's unnerving that he seems to remember our past connection so well, from that night years ago.

I recall him saying he was going through a tough divorce when we ran into him the other morning. I shake the thought away that his attention is being misdirected at me, and my family. I suppose he has to be here for the investigation. But it feels personal, somehow.

I lift up my chin. "Hey. So, my family and I really need to be leaving today," I say, and even as the words come out, I can see his expression harden.

"It's our recommendation that all parties stay on the premises while the investigation is under way. We may need your cooperation, or follow-up details, and it's easier if you're here."

Exasperated, I push forward. "You can call us for anything you need. You have my contact information."

"This is a criminal investigation. You are not entitled, by law, to vacate the premises while the investigation is ongoing. Perhaps you'd like to come down to the station? If you'd be more comfortable there?"

"No, no. Here will be fine."

I slink back to the house. Lana's woken up and padded down the stairs. I move to the kitchen and pull out cereal and milk for her.

"Where're Brielle and Gracey?" she asks.

"They're in the game room. You can go play after you eat."

"What did the officer say?" Esme asks, coming up to me and pulling a mug of coffee from the cabinet

"No bueno," I say. "He said I can come down to the station and wait there if it's better."

Her eyes are wide. "Seriously?" She casts a worried glance at Greg. "These officers seem certain our family has something to do with the woman's death."

"There's something you should know," I say. "That officer—I know him, from before. He was there at the bonfire the night Piper had the incident."

"Oh, my Lord." She bites her lip.

"He's kinda creepy," I say.

"Really?" she says. "How so?"

"Lana, here's your cereal, babe," I call to her, putting it on the counter. Turning back to Esme, I say, "It's probably fine. Just the way he looks at me. We kissed that night, years ago . . . That shouldn't matter, but I don't know. It just sucks that now I'm trapped in this house, while he circles us like a hawk."

Esme frowns. "He did tell you he'd put you in jail if you leave," she says, whispering the word "jail" so Lana won't hear. "Seems extreme."

"My point exactly," I say. "But while we're stuck here, I'm going to need that check." I look at her expectantly.

She shrugs and reaches for her purse, and scrawls the check quickly then hands it to me. "I'll need you to sign the deed over to me," she says. "I'll have our attorney draw up the forms."

"I'll sign whatever you need me to. Thank you," I say, and mean it. Check in hand, I march off upstairs. I open the blinds, causing Bryce to blink against the light.

"What the—" he says.

"Get up. I got the check from Esme. We gotta head to the bank."

"Okay. What's the rush? Let me get some breakfast and coffee."

"Just hurry, okay? I want to deposit this before they change their mind. And get some space from this crime scene investigation. It's not good for Lana. We'll go to the bank and then spend the day in town."

"All right," he says, heading to the bathroom.

I sit on the bed. The check is burning a hole in my pocket. Then I have an idea. I take out my phone. On my mobile app, I try to deposit the check online. "Damn," I say under my breath. The check amount is too high; the bank won't allow an online deposit. It directs me to please visit my local branch.

It's a Tuesday. The bank should be open by nine. We'll stop on the way to take Lana out. I'm so close to having my problems solved, I almost can't bear to wait any longer. I can't let this slip through my hands. I've sacrificed too much for this not to work. Staring at my phone, I remember the keycard and piece of paper with the phone number written on it. If I could help solve this case, I could get creeper Ben off my butt and we could leave and start straightening everything out at home. I type in the number and hold the phone to my ear.

The line rings and rings. After five rings, a voice mail picks up. "You've reached the voice mail of Brigit. Send me a text instead of leaving a message. Byeee."

I hang up the phone. I have no idea who Brigit is, or why her number is here. She sounds young, and dimwitted if I'm being honest. She ends all her words with a question at the end. Byeee? Like she's unsure if she's saying bye or not.

Bryce has turned on the shower, and I can't wait anymore. I'll go to the bank by myself and stop at Bergamont on the way back. Look up Alexis, see if she's still checked in. Maybe knock on the door that belongs to this keycard. See if this Brigit is still there and why she was at our house . . . Well, Esme and Piper's house, technically, once I cash this check.

I straighten my back, feeling good about my plan, and even better about the check I'm about to deposit.

CHAPTER

37

Piper

THE PILL I took last night, at Esme's insistence, has made me groggy. Preston slept fairly well, but he still woke up hungry at four AM and wide awake.

I got him back to sleep and placed him back in his crib an hour ago, and have spent the past hour tossing and turning, trying to get back to sleep. That's when I hear the sound of a banging door, and shouting.

Peeking my head out the door, I see Regina.

I close our bedroom door behind us, monitor in hand. "Can you keep it down? I just got Pressy back to sleep."

She looks back at me. "Sorry," she says with a shrug. "Bryce is in the shower. Will you tell him I went to town to run some errands? Lana's in the playroom."

"Sure." I walk down the stairs with her.

I could use some space from Regina, especially after what she said last night about me as a mother. This house already feels like a pressure cooker, with the woman's body found in the lake, and Regina adds fuel to any fire. I've learned more about her this trip that lets me know she's not trustworthy. She's criticized me as a mother, when she in fact has been acting out of control and is apparently in deep financial trouble. She probably realized Esme and I aren't going to bail her out; we're of no use to her now, so she's putting in zero effort. Or worse—it crosses my mind that she might have something to do with the dead body turning up.

Paul appears at the stairs, giving me a kiss on the cheek as he passes by. He pours himself a mug of steaming coffee.

"Eggs and bacon?" he asks me, reaching for a pan, and then opening the fridge to rustle out the egg carton.

I watch him work, grateful he's taking care of breakfast. Preparing food for me has always been one way he shows his affection. It's his love language, as my former therapist would say.

With Regina gone, the house is unusually quiet; I'd call it peaceful if it weren't for the constant presence of the police in front of the house. Esme and Greg are out by the pool, Esme with a book, Greg on the phone, while the girls are keeping themselves occupied.

Paul sets my plate down on the counter, and I thank him and pick up my fork. My appetite has returned; last night I was too upset to eat anything. But at the sight of these eggs and bacon, I can hear my stomach growl and I dig in hungrily.

After food and coffee, I look down at the monitor. The green light is on, indicating the battery is working. The clock reads 9:05 AM, and a twinge of doubt crosses my mind. It's late for Preston to be sleeping. He last ate at 4:00 AM, which puts him overdue for his bottle.

"I'm going to head out and speak to the officer," Paul says. "Then maybe we'll go into town, head to the store for a change of scenery?" We both know it's hard for my mental state to be here right now.

"Sounds good. I'll see if Esme needs anything, then I'll get Pressy ready to go."

I slide open the glass door and head to the pool. Esme's sunning herself and reading.

"Paul and I are headed to town with Press. Need anything from the store? It's Regina's night to cook, but . . ." I shrug.

"Maybe you should get some premade dishes, just in case," she says with a knowing nod.

"Sure thing. Knowing Paul, he'll cook us up a few nice dishes if we're in a pinch. We'll get some supplies. Did you hear anything from your attorney?" I ask.

"Alan said to cooperate with the authorities, give them space to do their thing, and not leave town. Otherwise it's a waiting game."

"Paul's out there talking to them now. I'll let you know if he learns any news."

I walk back to the house, and head up the stairs to get Preston. I see Bryce in the hallway.

"Morning," I say. "Regina said to tell you she went into town. Lana's in the game room with the twins."

He nods and smiles. "Great, thanks."

When I open the door to our bedroom, though, my stomach drops. Preston isn't in his crib. Even though I feel like the wind has been knocked out of me, I will not allow myself to panic. I run down the stairs and scan the family room: no Preston.

I run to the back door and rip it open. "Have you seen Preston? He's not in his crib." I feel Esme and Greg's eyes on me, and they both shake their head no.

I let out a long breath. I run back into the house, and through the window I see Paul standing next to a patrol car chatting with an officer. Another patrol car has arrived in the past few minutes, and I see a light-haired officer getting out of his vehicle.

Rushing out the door, I call out to Paul. I catch up to him, and he flashes me a look of confusion. "I'm asking the officer here what's happening."

"Preston—he's not in his crib. Do you have him?" Though I can plainly see his arms are empty.

He shakes his head. "One of your sisters must have him."

I shake my head. "Regina's gone, and I just asked Greg and Esme," I say, but I'm talking to the wind. Paul's attention is back on the officer.

Frustration mounting, I head back into the house. Maybe one of the twins took him. He must be with the girls.

My heart rate is climbing with every step. Back inside, I see Esme coming inside.

"Is Preston with Paul?" she asks, and I shake my head no.

"The twins must have the baby," I say. Esme follows behind me as I walk down the hallway to the rec room.

To my dismay I find the two of them playing a video game, but no Preston. I scan the room anyway, desperate for an answer to where my baby is. He can't walk. Someone had to have removed him from the crib.

"Girls, have you seen Preston?"

They both shake their head no.

"Where's Lana?" I ask them.

"She was just here," Brielle says with a shrug, turning back to her game.

I spin on my heels and leave as Esme follows behind me. We check the guest room downstairs—empty.

"I'm sure he's here. This is just a misunderstanding," Esme says, her voice calm, as she follows up the stairs.

"Then help me find him," I command.

I check the twins and Lana's room—empty. I look in his crib again, thinking I must have been mistaken, but my gut clenches when I see it's still empty!

He's not in Greg and Esme's room, either, and I feel panic clawing at my throat.

We run back downstairs, and I scan the room looking for a reasonable explanation.

I open the garage door off the kitchen, desperately looking for an explanation that makes sense of where Preston is.

Inside the garage, I see Esme's car, Paul's mountain bike, and an empty space where Regina's car was.

Something within me snaps. Everything I've learned about Regina on this trip, the way she's acting so suspicious since they discovered the body, her guilty expression, her out-of-control outbursts. Why was she in such a hurry to go into town just now? Is it because she has my son?

She's implied this whole trip I'm not a fit mother. She's in huge money trouble. She's been acting so oddly—could she have been planning on taking Preston this whole time? Would she hold him for ransom from me?

It's always Regina. Every problem starts and ends with her. She caused all of this.

"Esme, call Regina," I command. "She left, she must've taken him."

"Regina doesn't have Preston." She shakes her head.

"Please," I say, searching her face. "Please just call!"

"Okay, okay," Esme says. She pulls out her phone and calls.

Her voice is soothing. "She's not answering, but she wouldn't take Preston without telling you. We'll find him."

"Call her again. It must be her! Why would she do this to me?" The room feels like it's spinning.

I rush back into the house, and head to the couch. I flip over the cushions. "Is he in here? Babies can get trapped in cushions," I say, remembering the advice in the pamphlet from the hospital that said to never fall asleep with your baby in your arms on a couch. Someone must have had him on the couch and he's in there.

Digging through each of the cushions, I find the couch empty.

We spend the next half hour searching the house. Paul joins the search, finally understanding our baby is missing. Preston's not anywhere to be found. Our search leaves us empty handed.

My baby is gone.

CHAPTER

38

Regina

I OPEN THE GARAGE door and back my car out. In my rear-view mirror, I see there's only one police officer still here at the house in the driveway, and it's not Ben. The young, light-haired officer is standing between me and the road to get out of here. He peers into my window as I pull around.

Just when I think I'll make it, he motions for me to stop and roll down the window.

"Morning. And where are you headed?" he asks, peering in.

"Just into town for some shopping. Grab some lunch. I won't be long."

He nods. "I'd make it a point to be back by this afternoon. There's more we need to cover; all of you will be required to be there."

I don't like the sound of that at all.

"Sure thing, sir," I say, and roll my window back up. I hit the gas to go.

With every passing tree I drive by, I feel lighter and lighter. I'm flying away, free as a bird.

I pull into the bank parking lot. It's a newer building, with glass walls and a modern look, as are most of the buildings in this area. The town has expanded since we used to come here. After I moved out and did a few years at the community college, I stopped coming for the August vacations. My mom and dad put up a fuss, but there wasn't much they could do about it. It's not like they were paying my bills. I was bartending at the hottest spot in town, and making tons of money. It didn't seem worth it to finish a degree when I didn't know what I wanted to do.

I push away the thought of my dad and mom. Dad died over five years ago, and I do miss him. Mom and I weren't as close, but I didn't want her to die or anything. It's depressing they're both gone.

Inside the bank, I approach the teller and she gives me the form to fill out to deposit a check. She takes my ID and the check and deposit slip back to another person, and I see them whispering and looking at me.

Finally she comes back and says something about having to report deposits this big to the IRS, but that it's standard. She gauges my reaction and I shrug, saying that's fine. I don't know if she's trying to imply that I'm doing a shady transaction, but I don't really appreciate her tone. She eventually returns with a receipt.

"A deposit of this amount will take five to seven business days to clear and go into your account. You can expect it at that time."

"That long?" My heart sinks. I guess there's nothing to be done. I leave the bank and feel slightly better, but I'll feel better when the money is in my account and I can pay our mortgage balance.

The Bergamont is on the other side of town, and it takes another ten minutes before I arrive. I pull into the self-park area and walk another ten minutes to the entrance. The hotel entrance is pretty quiet, with only a few valets milling around. One greets me and asks if he can help me, and I shake my head no.

In the lobby foyer, a grand place designed to invoke a feeling of classic opulence meets rustic retreat, with paneled wood and gleaming surfaces, I make my way to the guest counter. A young man greets me, politely welcoming me to the Bergamont Resort: "What can I help you with this morning?"

"I'm hoping you can help me," I say, channeling my best Esme impression. She's a woman who gets what she wants. Others are always tripping over themselves to do things for her. "I was supposed to meet a guest this morning, but I can't get a hold of her. Could you call her room for me? Alexis Howard."

"What's her room number, ma'am?" he asks politely.

"I'm not sure. Could you search using her name?" I ask, adding, "Please."

"His fingers click on the keyboard and then he picks up a landline and dials a number. We wait, and eventually he hangs up. "I'm afraid there's no answer. Would you like me to leave a message for her at the front desk?"

"No, but could you give me her room number? I can go check on her later."

"Unfortunately, I'm not able to give out guests' room numbers. This is hotel policy."

He eyes me with a hint of doubt. News travels fast in this town, and he surely knows about the body that washed up. Today of all days, I'm sure he's on high alert for anything suspicious.

"Thank you so much," I say. "I'll just go back to my room and try her later." I hold up the keycard I found in our house to show him, and then turn to the elevators. I push the third floor button. When the elevator doors open to the hallway, the walls are papered in a neutral stripe and white wainscoting trims the ceilings, with glossy pictures of the lake and historic photos framing the walls. I walk down the endless corridors, winding this way and that way, until I come to the door number. This keycard had a phone number that belonged to someone named Brigit, so I'm not sure if I'm expecting Alexis or Brigit to answer the door. But it's worth a try to find out more.

Tentatively, I knock. When there's no answer, I knock harder. Still no response.

I press the keycard into the door. The light turns green and I hear a click. I push the door open, and pause.

"Hello?" I call out.

I take a step inside the room, and pause to listen. It's quiet. I peer around the corner and see a queen size bed, the comforters and pillows still made up.

"Hello?" I call again, just to be sure, but it seems I'm the only one in here. I let the door behind me close.

The room is filled with a cloying perfume scent, musky but sweet. There are several items of clothing discarded on the floor, and makeup strewn around the vanity mirror.

My eyes land on something and I stop short. There's a check on the wood table, one that looks very familiar. It's made out to Brigit Max, and the signature is from Esme Wimberly. For 10K.

Man. My sister is really doling out the dough. I wonder how much they're worth, considering the cash they've shelled out to this lady and me alone in the past few days.

A black leather purse catches my eye. I'm used to going through purses that patrons leave at the bar, but it occurs to me I'm breaking the law being in here, and I don't belong in here. Still, a quick peek won't hurt. I grab it and open the satchel, pulling out a wallet and a phone.

Where is this woman? I'm starting to get creeped out. Who leaves their wallet, phone, and a huge check on the table? Did she just go down to get some breakfast? Maybe a spa appointment where she didn't want to bring her personal items?

The clock reads 9:40. If she has to check out at 11:00, she'll be back soon. I need to be quick. I scroll her phone so I can figure out her mystery connection to our summer house; I found this phone number scrawled on a piece of paper there.

I swipe the screen to wake up the phone, but there's a password locking it. I do a double- take when I see the screensaver photo; my stomach drops.

It's a photo of a young woman, presumably this Brigit, with her arms wrapped tightly around none other than my brother-in-law Greg.

My mouth is practically on the floor. The hair color of the girl in this photo is the same as what Esme described as being washed up on the beach, chestnut brown.

It hits me that Brigit isn't in her room because she's the woman found in the lake. Being involved with Greg meant she was in danger, but didn't even know it. Silly girl. Esme could have found out and killed her. Or Greg silenced her?

Which would mean Alexis is alive. I feel a small amount of relief at this idea. Alexis is alive! I'm not responsible for luring Alexis to her death. Surely the setup would come out if it were Alexis in that lake.

I eye the phone in my hand. This is evidence. I grab the check and pocket it. If Esme was willing to pay for an alibi, I'd be set for life if I have evidence against her. Plus, I'll keep the police from discovering this in Brigit's room. I'm doing Esme a favor, really.

I pause as another realization hits me. If it's this Brigit woman in the lake, that's bad, too. I'm here, now, at her hotel. I came into her room. I'm sure there are cameras that will show I was here. Fool! Why do I always end up in trouble? Esme tells me it's always something with me. She's not wrong.

I'm implicating myself further by being here. I pull my hair out of my bun and smooth it down around my face, trying to cover my profile. I grab my sunglasses from my purse and slip them on. Then I grab a sunglass cleaning cloth from my purse and wipe down everything I touched in the room. I turn, and I get the hell out of there.

I look both ways down the hallway, and then close Brigit's door and make a beeline for the elevator. I press the elevator call button, and it feels like it's taking forever. I need to get out of here.

I just can't believe this. I knew Esme and Greg were having issues with their nanny and their marriage, but this is some next-level stuff.

Sure, this Brigit seems like a nasty piece of work, but I still feel a cold, hard lump of dread in my stomach. My heart is beating wildly as the repercussions of what I've seen, and done, sink in.

At the front desk, I see the same front desk clerk, who regards me with a look of suspicion. I ignore him, hoping to avoid answering any questions. If he asks, I'll just say I was looking for Alexis, but couldn't find her. But he simply watches me walk away without further questions.

Outside, it's starting to get busier now; a few people are riding bikes, others walk by with their morning coffees. I answer the valet again that no, I won't be needing his help. Then I walk quickly back to my car.

Once inside, I slam the door shut and let my breathing return to normal.

Now I just have to get back to the house and act like I don't know what Greg and Esme have done until I can figure out a plan. A plan to make this whole mess work in my favor.

CHAPTER

39

Before

Alexis

My phone is next to me. When it buzzes, a thrill of excitement runs through me. He's here.

I run to the front door of my new apartment, checking my appearance in the mirror on the way. I'm wearing a negligee with a robe over it. There's no need to put on clothes, that would be a waste. Plus, I love the soft fabric, the way it feels when he runs his hands over my body.

I glance at a local takeout menu on my kitchen counter, but dismiss it. I doubt we'll get to dinner anytime soon. Maybe afterward. It's hard to keep our hands off one another.

When I open the door, Greg is standing there holding a single rose and a bottle of champagne. He comes inside, our arms wrap around each other, his mouth finding mine greedily. After a few moments, I pull him into the bedroom.

My new apartment has a view over the city, and in the twilight, the dusky horizon looks like we're on par with it—we're in heaven on earth.

When I picked out my new, luxurious bedding, I'd secretly known we might end up in it together. Greg and I pretended it's not where it was headed, but we both knew, on some level. The chemistry was undeniable.

Kissing with our arms wrapped around each other, Greg stops and holds my face in his hands. Then he spins me around. "God, you look amazing." He burrows his face in my neck. "You smell amazing." He kisses my neck, lower and lower to the cups of my breast. "You taste amazing."

"I've missed you." I feel his body tense momentarily, and I worry I've broken the spell. It's unspoken that this affair will not end his marriage. I can't have all of him. And I shouldn't ask.

Or should I? Maybe tonight I will broach the subject.

To get him back in the mood, I push him onto the bed. I move down his body and unzip his pants. That does the trick. He pulls me up to him. I want him so badly I can almost taste my desire. It's these moments—this intimacy—that I know we're meant to be together.

Afterward, my head rests on his chest. He strokes my hair lovingly.

"You're amazing, do you know that?" he says.

I take a deep breath and go for it. "You make me feel . . . I love you."

"I love you, too."

I savor his words, turning them over in my mind, repeating them, reveling in the glow of being loved.

Propping my head up on my hand, I look up at him. "Do you ever wish . . ." I start but don't finish my question.

"What's that?"

"Do you ever wish we could be together? More than this. Like, always?"

He doesn't hesitate. "Of course I do. You know that's what I'd want, if I had a choice."

"But you do. You could leave her."

He frowns and rubs his chin. "It's complicated. We've got the kids, the house. Our whole life is wrapped up together. I'm trapped. I'm not saying I like it, but it's not so easy to get out."

I sit up on the bed and slide my arms around my bare chest.

"You could, if you wanted to. I don't know how much longer I can do this. I love you so much. I can't take only having a piece of you." There. I've said it.

I hold my breath. I wait.

It's a lost cause. I put on my robe and move to get up. "I'm done, Greg. You should leave."

Finally, he speaks. "Wait. Just wait. Sit down. Okay?" He reaches out, runs his hand up and down my back. "I'll do it. I'll leave her."

I spin around and throw my arms around him, laying on top of him with my chin on his chest. "Really?"

"Really," he says with a smile. "But it's going to take a few months. A marriage, kids, it needs to be done delicately. The right way. I need to get things in order."

My heart is full. Looking out at the twinkling stars and city lights, his strong arms around me, is bliss. Never in my life, not since my mom died, have I felt like I'm right where I belong.

This is what I've been waiting for. For years, I haven't let my guard down; I chose solitude. But all this time, I was just waiting for the right man.

* * *

"I bought something special to wear for you, babe. XO," I type on the messenger app. Even as I press send, a mixture of humiliation and desperation permeate through the message.

Greg hasn't answered my texts, at least not the way he used to. I can feel him slipping away. It's been seven months of bliss, but I can tell. He's changed. A subtle shift. I'm trying to keep the magic, to recapture that blissful feeling of us against the world; I'm grasping at air.

A bubble appears. He's read my message. He sends back a heart emoji and fire emoji. I wait. But that's it. He hasn't asked to make a plan. No follow up. Just placating me. Stringing me along.

I wait another fifteen minutes. I roam around my apartment. I pick up a paintbrush. I should paint something. Get my emotion out on the canvas.

But I can't focus. All I can think about is him. I throw the paintbrush down. Why is he doing this to me? Is he ending things?

My fingers tremble, and I know as I send the message how pathetic it must sound. But maybe not. Maybe he just needs to know I want him. "Are you going to come over? Maybe dinner at the Thai place? There's a cozy corner booth with our name on it."

There's the bubble. He's read it. He's typing. Then it stops. Nothing.

No response.

The humiliation I feel is now tinged with anger. A fiery anger. Who is he to do this to me? To strip me down of all of my defenses, and then leave me waiting, bare and vulnerable? Begging to entice him. Does he know what he's doing? Does he feel my pain?

No. He feels just fine. His life goes on. He's got his wife and his kids and his money and his career and the vacation house and his fucking pride. He's intact.

I flip open my laptop and sit on my new couch. I log onto social media and click on Greg's page. He's not a big online guy, so the only posts I see of him are ones Esme has tagged him in.

I don't follow Esme on social media, nor does she follow me, but her account isn't private. I click on her page and scroll to the first post. It's of their twins, holding onto huge stuffed animals, wearing matching dresses and knee socks, with only a blue and pink bow to differentiate the two. The post reads, "Brielle and Gracey are the sweetest girls. Double the hugs, double the giggles. We're looking for a new full-time nanny for these angels. Please contact me with your résumé and references!"

I shake my head. The girls are cute, I'll give her that. But how annoying is Esme? I scroll to the next picture and instantly feel sick. It's of Greg and Esme, dressed to the nines, water glistening in the background, with his hand firmly around her waist as she leans adoringly into him. "Happy 9th anniversary!! What an adventure our life has been. I'm a lucky girl to have you—my best friend, my hero, the world needs you as a renowned neurosurgeon, my better half and a wonderful father to our precious children. Love you."

I slam my laptop closed. I pick it up and am about to throw it through the window. I'd like to smash it to pieces. To feel the glass shatter. Watch the laptop plummet to the sidewalk. Maybe I'll dive off the building, too.

But then he'll get what he wants. I'll be a distant memory, a ghost, and . . . she'll win.

No.

I sit back down and open my laptop again. I scroll back to Esme's first post. She's looking for a nanny. Again.

A nanny, who will be in their home, get close to the girls and close to Esme. Close to Greg, too. Someone they explicitly trust.

I could dye my hair. Wear glasses. Apply for the job.

Too obvious. Even though we don't keep in touch and she's only seen me once in the past fifteen years, Esme would know me a mile away.

But what if I sent in a Trojan horse?

I click into a new browser. It would have to be someone with low scruples. Someone who is concerned with money above all else.

I type in the name of the agency Esme directed applicants to apply through. I sign up for the service, and then I click through the young girls, making notes. I'm going to host some interviews of my own.

It's time to make Greg—Esme—very, very sorry for what they've done to me.

CHAPTER

40

Esme

Time seems to be slowed, every minute ticking by without finding Preston making Piper more and more hysterical.

Piper is wild-eyed. "Where is he?" she says to me and Paul. "Where is my baby?"

"We'll find him, I promise," I say, trying to soothe her worry. Bryce and Greg have joined us, too. "Keep calling Regina, please," I snap at him. He nods.

Piper pushes past me into the living area. She's opening all the cabinets. "Would the girls have hidden him in here? Or in the game room?"

"They've been playing down here the whole morning, right?" Paul says, his face pale.

"Yeah," I say. "I don't think they would have, but we'll check again." I'm starting to become really concerned, but I try to keep my voice calm for Piper's sake. "Paul, Bryce, please check the game room and get the girls in here so we can ask them again."

They nod and rush off.

Piper and I search upstairs again, to no avail. "This can't be happening," she says.

"Piper," I turn to her. "There's got to be an explanation for this. We'll find him. Promise."

Her eyes are glassy and look past me, searching. I feel her trembling next to me. I squeeze her hand, wishing I could offer her more comfort.

I look down and see Piper clutching the monitor. "He was in the crib last you saw him, right?" I ask her. She nods her head yes.

"And you didn't hear anything on the monitor?"

She shakes her head, and looks down at it. "The green light means it's on. If he made even a peep when they took him, the red light would go on and I'd have heard him. Unless I missed it . . ."

"Is there a camera on it?"

She shakes her head helplessly. If the past two days have taught me anything, it's that we need a security system at the house. It hardly seemed necessary before, considering we're the only house out here. But clearly it would have been useful not once, but twice, now.

"We have to find an officer and tell them he's missing," she says.

I hate to involve the police, but at this point I'm running out of ideas. "Okay, let's just think for a minute." We rush down the stairs and stand in the living area. Piper opens the front door, her eyes frantically scanning over the yard, down the driveway, and out to the lake.

"Come inside." I pull her arm, closing the door.

Just then Gracey and Brielle appear with Paul and Bryce. The girls are holding stuffed toys and arguing.

"Girls, are you certain you haven't seen baby Preston? This is important. He's missing."

They shake their heads no. "No, we told you.We haven't seen him all morning," Brielle says.

Piper sits on a couch and is hugging her arms around herself.

Bryce looks around and narrows his eyes. "Where's Lana?" he says to the twins.

Brielle shrugs, and Gracey says, "I don't know." I recognize that look. She's guilty of something.

"Gracey," I say. "Come right here. Where is Lana?"

"I don't know! We were playing with our stuffed animals, and she tried to take ours—"

"Mine," Brielle interjects. "She tried to take my animal, and I said no."

"And I didn't want her to have mine, either," Gracey says. "I told her to go get her own."

"And?"

"And she ran off," Gracey says, looking at the floor.

"How long ago was that?" I ask. They look at me uncertainly and shake their heads.

I clench my jaw. Lana and Preston are both gone. Is it possible that Regina took them both without telling us, and we didn't notice?

"Bryce, she isn't answering her phone?"

He shakes his head.

"Would she have taken Lana and Preston?" I ask him.

"I was in the shower, and when I came out you said she went to town, and Lana was in the room playing." He shrugs. His unhelpfulness is particularly frustrating at this moment, and I have a glimmer of pity for what Regina must feel like being married to him.

"Would she have reason to want Preston with her?" It seems crazy, but it's the only explanation I can think of. Piper was right, Regina must have him. But she'd need a car seat. "Piper, I'm going to go check your car to see if she took your car seat. Maybe she told us she was taking him, and we didn't hear her." I look at Bryce. "Please keep trying to get a hold of her."

I turn to go and as I do, I glance out at the pool. My mouth drops open and I rush to the slider.

Flinging the door open, I cry out, "Lana!"

She's coming up the deck steps from the backyard. She almost loses her balance, because in her arms, wrapped in his blue blanket, is Preston.

"Piper," I call back in the house. "He's here!"

I hurry to meet Lana so the baby doesn't fall into the pool, and sweep him up in my arms. Piper runs out of the house and takes him from me.

"Preston." She clutches him and checks him all over to make sure he's okay. As she does so, a note flutters to the ground from his blanket.

"What on earth, Lana?" My anger instantly goes down a notch when I see her expression. Her eyes are welling with tears.

"What's this?" Piper looks at the note. It's just one word. "WATCHING," it reads. "Is this some sort of joke?" she says.

Lana shakes her head, and two large tears spill over.

"Let's go inside," I say, ushering them in. The twins are inside, suddenly very quiet and still. "Greg, will you take them outside, please?"

He nods. "Brielle, Gracey, let's go out front."

We all gather on the couch. Bryce sits down on the other side of Lana, and Piper and Paul are next to me, holding onto Preston for dear life. Piper has an expression of joy and misery on her face, and she's doing her best to contain her emotions.

I turn to Lana. "You're not in trouble, but you need to tell us exactly what happened."

"Brielle and Gracey were being mean. They never want to play with me. They always say it's their game and I can't be part of it."

This rings true. The twins have been known to be exclusive. I'd thought it was going well with Lana, but after few days with her, the novelty wore off and they're back to wanting just each other.

"Okay, what happened then?" I ask her.

"I went to play on the boulders in the backyard. I like to see how far I can jump off. And then, I thought it would be more fun to play with Cousin Preston. To have a friend."

Piper's body stiffens. "He's so little, Lana. Why didn't you ask an adult to help you if you wanted to hold him?"

Lana shrugs. "Everyone was busy. So I went and got him." She looks down. "I just held him and then laid him on the grass while I played. But when I heard you call for Preston, I brought him right back." She adds quickly and looks at Piper, "I'm sorry, Aunt Piper. It was bad to do."

"You shouldn't have done that, Lana," Bryce says to his daughter. "You can never do that again." He looks to Piper and me. "I should have been watching her more closely."

Piper shows Paul the note with "WATCHING" scrawled on it. "Lana, where did this come from?" Paul asks gently, holding it up.

"I don't know—I didn't put it there. I promise." She begins to cry, and I hug her to my shoulder.

"I need to feed my baby," Piper says, excusing herself to get by us. She doesn't look any of us in the eye. She stops and turns around, leaning down to Lana. "It's okay, Lana. It was a mistake. It's over now. Don't cry, sweetie."

I can hear in her voice it's hard for Piper to say this, but clearly the girl is distraught. She seems comforted by Piper's words.

I get up and follow Piper, while Bryce comforts Lana.

"You okay?"

"He's safe, that's what matters," Piper says quickly. Her eyes are wide. "She didn't mean any harm," she says, but there's hesitation in her voice.

"Of course not."

"Maybe you should speak to the twins," Piper says slowly, giving Preston his bottle. "Ask them about the note? Would they have put her up to this? Maybe Lana is covering for them?" she says pointedly. "It could have been their idea to take him out of the crib. Gracey is always asking to hold him."

"Could be," I say to appease her. "I'll talk to them."

"Good," Piper says, her eyes focused on Preston. "And Esme?"

"Yes?"

"Ask them to be kind to Lana. Include her."

I don't like how my girls are being blamed for Lana's misbehavior, but now is not the time to point that out to Piper. "Sure."

I hear the front door open and Greg enters, our girls trailing behind him, subdued by the drama that's occurred.

"Esme, we need to talk," Greg says, pulling me away from Piper.

"Can it wait? I need to talk to the girls."

"Now, Esme." He gives me a look. "Let's go upstairs."

I nod to Piper.

Upstairs, Greg closes our bedroom door behind us and sits on the bed. "Esme . . . things are about to get worse."

"What do you mean?"

"I spoke to the officer out there. I explained to them I'm a surgeon. That I'm on the board of a charity that donates to a lot of benevolent societies. To let them know I'm one of the good guys. On their side. To see if they'd give me any insider info."

"Did they?"

"They're working on a search warrant. For the house. And for buccal swabs."

"Buccal what?"

A flash of irritation. "Swabs to your cheek. To check your DNA."

Even though I'm not a surgeon and have no medical background, Greg somehow expects me to know all these technical terms. "Who are they swabbing?" I cross my arms.

"Us. All of us."

"I don't understand."

"We're suspects, Esme." His skin is pale, and he swallows. "They haven't said that, of course. They say it's just standard procedure to rule out the only people near the lake where the body was found. But make no mistake; they wouldn't be doing this if there weren't real suspicions."

"They haven't even identified the body yet. How are we the suspects?"

"I don't know, Esme, we just are," he says, running his hands through his hair.

"You have to call Alan again. Tell him to drive up here—we need him."

He nods. "I will. No way I'm doing those swabs, but they'll try to get us to. Though, it's not like we have anything to hide."

Over the past ten years, I've come to know Greg's tells. When he lies, his right eye squints. Just a small amount.

His right eye squints now.

"What are you not telling me?" I say, standing up, leaning into him.

His eye squints again.

"Greg." I lean my face close to his. "What are you not telling me?"

"Nothing. Let's just wait until Alan gets here," he says, and has the nerve to sound like I'm annoying him. Hounding him. "There's no need to panic."

I look at my husband and see Greg for what he's always been: the petulant child who never grew up. His mother coddled him. His wealth and privilege never taught him to have a strong moral compass, his biggest lesson being to look out for himself and to never feel discomfort of any kind.

"I've put up with a lot in our marriage," I say to him in a hushed voice, barely a whisper. "The cheating. The disrespect. But this is a murder investigation. We have to talk to each other."

He stands up. "This conversation is over. I was just trying to give you a heads-up. Every conversation turns into you attacking me. I'll call Alan now and have him come down. He'll sort it."

A little fire erupts inside. "No. You don't get to shut me down. Why don't you get out of the house? Go somewhere else. Go stay at *the Cape*," I say pointedly.

He has the audacity to roll his eyes. "Just take off, Esme? The cops won't let anyone leave," he insists.

I ball my fists. "Then go away. Go out to the pool, or to the rec room or office. Out of my sight," I say. "I'm taking the girls into town."

I feel like if I don't get out of this house, I will explode. I burst out of our bedroom and down the stairs.

I glance angrily at the new floors, the expensive kitchen marble and tile, and I hate it. I hate it all and I never want to see it again.

"Girls, let's get dressed," I say. "We're leaving."

CHAPTER

41

Before

Alexis

SHE SITS ACROSS from me at the coffee shop. Short skirt, and silky, pin-straight hair. Early twenties.

So far, she seems perfect for the job. I had to scroll through dozens of potential candidate profiles posted on Esme's nanny site. I'd narrowed it down to a handful of girls who would fit what I'm looking for, résumé and appearance-wise. The first two I interviewed had looked aghast and run out of the coffee shop when I'd mentioned extra money under the table, and the unusual setup I was proposing.

"And you speak French?" I know Esme will find this almost irresistible. She frequently posts about their trips to France and her determination to have both girls be fluent in a second language, since "starting at an early age is key for fluency."

"I do speak French, oui." She sits very still and straight. "My mother is from Nouvelle-Aquitaine. My parents moved back there after I graduated high school."

"Any other family nearby?"

"Not really."

I nod. "Look, what I'm proposing is different from any other nanny positions you may have had before. Unless . . . have you had a fling with a wealthy, older man before?" I ask.

She bites her full lip. "Once. Sort of. It was with my friend's dad. We had a situation. But that's over now."

"And you're not in college or anything?"

"Nah." Her eyes look dead inside. "I've got a following going on socials. Soon I'll reach influencer status and get brand deals. But for now, I need to fund my wardrobe."

Oh, wow. She's serious. Girl has a plan, I'll give her that. And the lacking moral scruples part certainly fits.

"Well, someone like Greg, the husband, can really take care of you. Make your life easy. Support you, buy you whatever you wish. And the mother of the girls, Esme, you'll be interviewing with, will love that you're fluent in French. Don't mention your socials or influencer goals. Keep it very basic and simple when you interview."

"I can do basic," she says, and I can see how this wouldn't be a far stretch for her.

"And the husband." I swallow. I set aside my feelings for Greg. "Once you're in, find ways to be alone with him. Tell him your car is broken and you need a ride home. Start slow. I'll guide you. He's an attractive man," I say, "so it shouldn't be hard to feign interest."

Her eyes brighten a fraction. "I looked them up on social media. He's a total zaddy."

"A what?"

"A zaddy. A fire older guy with swagger."

"Ah." There's a burning in my chest that I ignore. "See? Easy."

We agree on a payment for her interview with them, and a larger weekly payment schedule if she secures the job. "Let's meet after the interview," I say. "Break a leg."

The next week, I get a call from her. "I'm in," she says, her voice scratchy and bored.

"Well done, Brigit." She'll be wanting her hire bonus from me. "Let's meet. I'll give you your cash and we can discuss next steps."

The following two months, we meet regularly. Brigit was smarter than her initial appearance led me to believe. She easily obtained the data I asked for: copies of bills, personal information she squirreled away from their home office. And Greg, sadly, was easily persuaded to begin a dalliance with her.

It hurt. The lies he told me—that I was the first and only extramarital affair, that I was special—he told her, too. I see now how easy it is for him. He plays the same game with her that he played with me. Pretending to be torn—he's a loyal husband—pretending it's his first time cheating, but that Brigit is just so special, he can't help himself any longer.

And I hear from Brigit all about Esme. Her controlling ways. But then something else too.

"She's trying to be, like, my best friend. Or my mother. Always giving me advice. Asking about my future goals. She says I have my whole life ahead of me. She even said they'd help find a way for me to get a degree in education. Adjust my schedule, help set up tuition."

"Really?" I say, the envy seeping into my veins.

"Yah. She thinks I'm like her. She's like living vicariously. She invited me to the ballet with the girls in December. Her treat."

"Sounds like she really likes you." I push aside my jealousy. "That's good. It makes it easier to trick her."

Revenge isn't always easy. Sometimes it hurts to accomplish a goal.

CHAPTER

42

Esme

I READ THE GIRLS a bedtime story then kiss their heads, still damp from their bathtime. It's been a long day, and I feel my eyes drifting; I could fall asleep right here and now.

But I need to talk with Greg. So, untucking myself from the girl's limbs as they softly breathe in and out, I get out of their bed.

When the girls and I got back from town today, they were exhausted and hungry. I made dinner for everyone. I knocked on Piper's door to let her know dinner was ready. She said to leave it there and Paul would come down for it. It seems that Piper and Paul are planning to stay in their room, only coming down for food and water, if even that.

Regina, Bryce, and Lana have been fairly quiet, too, sticking to themselves since Lana took Preston today. We're all tiptoeing around each other. I haven't had a chance to talk with Regina, but when I passed her in the hallway, she gave me a funny look. She's up to something, as always, but I don't have the energy to find out what. Not yet.

First, Greg. I want to keep ignoring him. To banish him. But I realize I can't. He's the father of my children, and we need to get through this together. Maybe when this ordeal is over, I will finally file for divorce. But now is not the time for that.

It's dark outside and Greg's watching a baseball game on the TV. I look at my husband. I allow myself the ungenerous thought that is always there, but I never let myself think: that it was a mistake to marry him. That the core of who he is, his very essence, is rotten.

He looks so perfect on the outside. So much so that I believed the facade. But I'd get glimpses of a rotten core, decayed and selfish and greedy. I hoped it was fleeting. After all, even the best of us have bad moments. Dark thoughts, bad behaviors.

But now I see his flaws outweigh his good. The good, in his case—being a good dad, a good provider, being handsome—it doesn't make up for the bad. It doesn't erase his selfish nature. He may be the weak link that will destroy our family.

He glances at me, then back to the game. "Grab me a beer, hon?" he says over his shoulder.

I could tell him where to shove his beer. But I won't. My mother would have been aghast at that language use.

Instead, I go to the fridge, grab an IPA and pop the top off the bottle, and bring it to him.

I sit on the opposite side of the couch.

"Did you speak to Alan? Is he coming here?"

"He said we need to appear cooperative, but do not let them search the house or take any physical evidence. He said to insist on a search warrant, and if they have that, insist on our lawyer being present to execute it. Buy us some time. Essentially, he said we're innocent, but it's crucial we stay quiet. Don't answer complicated questions. That can only get us into trouble. If they question you about anything, tell them you've been advised to only talk with your lawyer present."

"That makes sense. Did Alan say if they know who the body is, for sure?"

"If they do, they haven't shared the identity. Alan said he'll call with any updates. He's on call 24/7 for us until he can get up here, hopefully tomorrow or the next day."

"Will the police be able to search our house?"

"Alan says they're getting a court order, yes, to search the house. It's just a matter of time."

"Why? Why would they do that? They don't even have a victim. Just because we're the only house here, and because you guys tried to rescue that woman? We're being targeted."

He looks deep into my eyes. We both know there's more to it.

"I agree it doesn't seem fair. But Alan seems sure this will pass. Even if they are allowed to search the house, the police won't discover any evidence here, and they'll continue with an investigation focusing on other leads."

On the table next to Greg, his phone starts buzzing.

"It's Alan." He mutes the game and picks up. "Yes." He listens intently. "What? Are you sure?" Another pause. "I can't believe this. Yes, I will. So what does this mean for us? Esme and me?"

He pauses, and the answer from Alan causes his shoulders to slump. "All right. We'll be in touch tomorrow. Bye."

"What did he say?"

"They identified the dead woman. He just got word from the coroner."

"Who is it?"

And when he answers, my world shatters into tiny, broken pieces.

CHAPTER

43

Before

Alexis

BRIGIT IS LATE to our meeting. Which is normal for her, but now it's verging on twenty-five minutes. I have her money, so you'd think that would be incentive enough. Apparently not.

These past few weeks, she's been hard to get in contact with. Her lack of communication caused me to question what she was up to. I've followed her in cabs a few times to hotels. I had to see it with my own eyes. That Greg really was meeting up with her. Indeed, only the best hotels for them, I noted, comparing how we only ever stayed in my apartment and ate local takeout.

* * *

Finally, she comes breezing in the doorway. No apology.

"Glad you could make it," I say and take another sip of my coffee.

"Do you have the money?" She looks at me blankly.

"I do." I pull the envelope out. But before I slide it over to her, I need some answers. "I want an update. You've been hard to reach lately."

She folds her hands, her red nails shiny at the end of her slim fingers. "Things are going to change. He's going to leave her. So this," she motions to herself and me, "won't be necessary anymore."

I laugh. "Brigit," I say, leaning in. "Brigit. Really? You believe him?" I know that youth is naive, but in what world does she think that she and Greg will be together? I refuse to remember my own naivety when he made me the same promise. Equally as unlikely. At least I was closer to his age. "You're barely twenty."

She sets her bag—a new, expensive designer one, I note—on the table. "Can I just get what I'm owed? I got you what you asked for, well, part of it."

It's true that she took the explicit photos I'd asked for, with Greg clearly identifiable.

But she hasn't given me everything I need, not yet.

"We're headed on vacation in two weeks," she says. "He's going to their summer house, the one in the Adirondacks, next week. That's when he's telling his wife it's over. Then we'll go away, just the two of us, for a whole week to celebrate. Maybe he'll have a ring for me."

My heart rate speeds up. I consider what this means. I'll have to move up my timeline. But this could work.

"Next week, you say?"

"Yes. He's got his family vacation, all his wife's sisters have to go every year to the summer house. It's so lame, right?"

It stings. It shouldn't, but it does. They all gather every year to celebrate and luxuriate. A family tradition. Splashing in the clear water, the blue sky overhead, surrounded by glorious nature. Audry would put something like that in her will. Of course I would never be included.

"The house is redone, at least, it's fabulous," she gushes. "You should see the pictures Esme showed me. It's gorgeous. Esme took the girls up there to oversee the last of the renovations, and Greg and I had a whole week to ourselves." She unfolds her hands. "When he and I are officially together, we'll go there for long weekends whenever we want."

"Is that so?"

"Course. No one else uses it. Esme told me that her sister Regina doesn't like going. They aren't very close. In fact, Esme told me she only talks to Regina during those two weeks when they're forced together."

"Really? What else did Esme say about Regina? Did she say why they don't talk?"

"She only said that Regina is a mess. Always flakey. Always broke. Her husband's out of work and they're living in this huge house. Falling behind on payments."

So Regina is the outcast. Very interesting.

"But didn't Regina get money when her parents died?" I ask, more to myself than anyone.

She shrugs. "I dunno. Anyway, I don't blame Esme for not wanting to be around her mooch of a sister. Esme's not so bad. She'll be upset at first, when she finds out about Greg and me. But I think after it sinks in, we'll still be friends."

Brigit truly knows nothing about my cousin.

Brigit may think Esme's her friend, but she's not. Esme puts up with Brigit now because she's a paid minion, someone she can control and mold and reign over. But an equal? With a right to stay in the summer house? The girlfriend of her ex-husband? I almost laugh out loud. Never.

But these are not things Brigit needs to understand now.

"I'm happy it's worked out for you," I say, sliding her the money. "Good luck, Brigit."

CHAPTER

44

Piper

I'M LYING IN bed, propped up with pillows and huddled under the down comforter, when Paul and I hear Esme's voice at our bedroom door. Dinner's ready.

"Do you want me to go get a plate and bring it back up here for you?" Paul asks.

"I'd rather you make the food."

"You don't trust her? You think, what, she'd poison us?"

"Maybe."

I'm done being worried if I sound irrational. Because, despite what everyone in this family keeps telling me, everything is not okay.

I learned a technique from my therapist, the one before last. She was the best. She said when my thoughts started to spiral, to fact-check them. See if they were grounded in reality. I conduct this exercise, and run down the list.

My baby was taken today by Lana and returned with a note that read "WATCHING."

A dead woman was found by my family in our lake.

Her death is being treated as a homicide by police.

I heard our cousin Alexis's voice at the lake house this week.

Esme saw Alexis in the grocery store.

The window to my bedroom was broken, and it wasn't me who did it.

Regina has been acting even more volatile and suspicious than ever.

Regina disappeared in the middle of the night with no explanation and her daughter showed up soaking wet, afraid of a woman in the lake.

Regina took off like a bat out of hell today, at the exact time my baby was taken.

Esme and Greg are acting guilty.

Esme is a slithery one. She holds her cards so close, never letting down her facade. But something is off about her. And Greg. It's an undercurrent of entitlement. But I can't put my finger on it. I can't point to any facts about them. They're too smart for that.

So those are the facts, and the facts point to a simple conclusion. I think that one, or both, of my sisters is hiding something. They know what happened on the lake last night, and are trying to distract me from catching them.

It's funny how I started this trip with a simple wish. To be loved and embraced by my sisters. To join the esteemed order of motherhood and be initiated into their pact.

When I thought I'd lost Preston, it all became clear to me. The only thing that matters is my son, and my husband. My nuclear family. Everyone else is the cherry on top.

I think, maybe, having toxic people around me makes me unwell. I remember my therapist, the one second to last, used to say I'm an empath. People who are empaths are like sponges. They pick up others' feelings, like a sponge, soaking them in.

I think that coming here to the summer house, I've picked up some crazy, toxic vibes and my sponge has soaked it up. Everyone's telling me I'm crazy. But maybe they're the crazy ones. And I'm being gaslit to believe it's all me.

Well, that's not going to work anymore. I'm going to separate myself from the crazy. I'll just stay up here in this room, as long as I need to. Wrapped up in my blanket, safe from the outside world. Safe from whoever is watching me. Safe from my sisters.

Preston is asleep in my arms, on my lap. I bathed him tonight in the small baby tub we'd packed with us. I wrapped him in a warm towel, and changed him into his nighttime diaper and pajamas. I made a promise to him that I'll always be there for him. No matter what.

Moving the covers aside, I place him in his crib. He's fast asleep, having had his final bottle. He ate hungrily today, and his full belly and busy day made sleep overcome him.

"Paul?" I look over to his side of the bed where he's reading a book. He wears reading glasses now, and the dark frames make him look distinguished. He slips them off and looks at me.

"Can I ask you something?" I reach over, my hand on his leg.

"Sure."

"Do you think my sisters are capable of murder?"

His expression stays still. Then he shakes his head no. "Pipe, why would you ask that? Of course not."

"When Preston was missing today, the strongest sense of certainty overcame me: My sisters do not have my best interest at heart. They're hiding something, I'm just not sure what. But I do know one thing. I don't trust them. And they're responsible, in some way, for Preston being taken by Lana today."

He stretches his neck and considers. "Before, you thought maybe the twins put her up to it. I can't imagine why your sisters would do that. It's evil."

I sit up on my elbow, facing Paul. "I agree. I'm not sure if it's mind games. Or to create a distraction from the investigation. Maybe if I'm preoccupied and worried over Preston, I won't be asking questions of them? Esme and Greg are always whispering together and on the phone with Alan. Regina was sneaking around like a thief today right before Lana took Preston, and then refused to answer her phone." I sigh. "What do you think about leaving tomorrow?"

"I agree, I'd like to leave," he says, placing his hand over mine. "But you know as well as I do that the police won't allow that. We have to stick it out a while longer." He puts his glasses back on, shaking his head.

"All right. We just need to make it through another week or two. Then we can go." I squeeze his hand, and he nods.

CHAPTER

45

Before

Alexis

I SENT REGINA A message. Surprisingly, she answered right away and agreed to drive in from Greenwich and meet me here at the coffee shop. I had told her in the message that I had some updates about her inheritance. Which isn't true, of course, but I know she's having money issues.

We agreed to meet in the same coffee shop where up until yesterday, I'd been meeting with Brigit for our updates. It's only a few blocks from my new apartment. It has a cozy vibe, with funky, mismatched chairs and local artists' paintings on the walls. My paintings aren't displayed, not yet. I've been too preoccupied to work up the nerve to show the manager my work.

When Regina enters the coffee shop and waves at me, heading toward my table, twenty years fade away. I'm ten again, the summer after my mom died.

"Have a seat. I got you an iced coffee." I push the drink toward her.

She doesn't touch it. "I'm surprised to hear from you, Alexis. It's been years . . ." Her voice trails off, and maybe she's remembering, too. Not fondly.

She has the same dark hair, the same piercing eyes and sarcastic, impatient tone. It's odd how so much time can go by, yet so little changes. I wonder how I look to her?

As she appraises me, it's clear she is impatient to leave, or perhaps just anxious to hear what I have to say.

"I'll cut to the chase," I say. "I think we can help one another. I heard you're in a tough situation. Financially."

She balks. But I can see I've piqued her curiosity. "How do you know about my financial situation? And how can we help one another?"

"It doesn't matter how I know. I have my sources. Let me ask you this: Did your inheritance not set you up financially?"

A bitter look overtakes her. "Hardly. I got a third of their summer house." Again, a look of guilt passes over her face, considering what happened to me at their summer house. "But nothing else."

"The rest of your parents' estate and savings? What happened to that money?"

"Poof," she makes a motion with her hand. "Gone, I guess."

"Or Esme found a way to get it from them before they died. Setting up a tax-free irrevocable trust for her to transfer their assets to before death, is what I'd suspect."

Her eyes harden. "You think?"

"I'm positive." I have no idea, but she seems to think I have inside sources. And it's not something I'd put past Audry and Esme.

"Look how much you could use that money." I've seen her social posts. They're in a beautiful home in the suburbs, but

Brigit had said they're practically in foreclosure. "You work so hard. You deserve that money. Why should Esme have all the family wealth?"

She nods. "I agree. But what can I do?"

"Have her buy you out. Of your portion of the summer house."

Regina shakes her head. "There's no way she'll agree to that."

"Not at first, no." I do my best to give the impression that I'm more confident than I am. "But present the proposition to her. If she says no, leave the rest to me. I have a foolproof way to convince her."

"How?" Her suspicion is evident.

"That's between Esme and me."

She shakes her head and wrings her hands. "I don't know."

"Think about it. It's up to you."

"Why are you helping me?" she asks.

"Because I don't like Esme," I say truthfully.

"That's fair."

"Why don't you take some time? Think about it. You know how to reach me," I say coolly.

I hope she won't notice my bluff. I only have about a week to get Regina on board.

We say goodbye, and I head back to my apartment to wait.

* * *

Sure enough, three days later, Regina messaged me, asking me how much she should ask Esme to buy her share of the house for. I sent her some comps of similar vacation lake homes. I know Regina will be up there the following week; Brigit had confirmed that for me. Plus Esme had posted on her curated social profile all about getting ready for the annual trip to the summer house. It's all falling into place.

I booked my reservation for the Bergamont Resort.

My plan was being enacted, phase one.

The first step was that I needed Esme to discover Greg's affair with Brigit. I took the photos of him and Brigit in compromising positions, and backed them up to the cloud. Then I bought a burner phone. I texted the explicit photos of Greg and Brigit to Esme, pretending to be a concerned anonymous school mom who wanted to share the photos with her.

Esme lost it. She texted me a million times to the burner phone. Who was I? Where and how did I obtain these photos? How long had it been going on? Who else knew? What did I want from her?

I crafted my reply. "I'm a concerned friend. Coming from someone who's been through this before, you need to go to Brigit to be sure this doesn't happen again. Make sure she ends it. Don't trust Greg to be the one."

After that, I deleted the call log and trashed the phone.

The next phase of my plan was to get Brigit to the summer house in Lake George. I sent one final message to Brigit, encouraging her to surprise Greg at the Bergamont so he wouldn't back out on his plan to dump Esme and take Brigit to Cape Cod. She ignored my message. Which I thought meant she wouldn't come.

But something must have convinced Brigit to show up after all, because clicking on her profile, she posted that she's on her way out of town with a heart emoji. Sure enough, when I texted her, asking if we could meet one last time to discuss another job, she said she was busy, heading out to meet her man. Bingo.

Since I arrived at the Bergamont Resort yesterday, I have to say, I much prefer it to Esme's summer house. I open the closet where I've carefully arranged my clothes on hangers. I've upgraded my wardrobe with the money Greg gave me. I can appreciate the brand names and quality fabrics, and the tailored fit of my new clothes. But there's more, so much more, that Greg owes me.

Greg and Esme arrived at their summer house the prior day. Just across the lake. So close.

Phase three is next. The pieces are set.

I change into a top and shorts with strappy sandals. I carefully apply my makeup and style my new lighter blond hair, smoothing it with a styling iron to make it silky straight. With a final satisfied look in the mirror, I head to the bar.

Downstairs, I take a seat at the bar that overlooks the lake, a wall of windows providing a panoramic view. I order a sparkling water with fresh lemon. I take the first sip.

My feet aren't cold; quite the opposite. The closer I get to destroying Greg and Esme—blowing up their perfect life—the better I feel. So there's no doubt I will go through with this plan. It's a matter of watching and waiting for the exact right time.

Brigit should arrive any moment. Her first night of the reservation is tonight—I'd called the hotel, pretending to be her, verifying the dates of her stay.

Rather than wait until next week when she and Greg are alone together, this might be an even better time to execute my plan.

I take another sip and wait, keeping my eye on the elevator and the main staircase.

Another hour passes, and I decide I need some fuel.

"May I please have the lobster salad?" I order from the young bartender.

"Absolutely. Will anyone be joining you?" He's well-spoken and efficient, eager to please.

"I'm not sure when my friend will be here, so please put the order through now for me. And another sparkling water."

As I wait for my salad to arrive, the bar begins to get busier. Guests have arrived to check in or returned from their day trips canoeing or swimming. There are couples, a few families with older kids. I spot another single woman at the bar. She's older than me, with graying hair that she hasn't dyed. She's dressed expensively, and I can see her ring sparkle from across the bar. She reminds me a little of Audry, which is unnerving. Though it is impossible that it's her, I remind myself. She's dead.

Something about the woman is spooking me, though.

My salad finally arrives. As I take the first bite, my attention turns to the elevator doors opening. Out steps a woman with shiny brown hair, red nails, and a black mini dress.

She doesn't see me. Setting down my fork, I push out from my barstool and grab my purse. "I'll be back," I call to the barman.

When Brigit spots me approaching her in the lobby, her face drops.

"What are you doing here?" she says, looking around.

"I could ask you the same thing."

"Greg asked me to come . . ." She looks around. "Well, first he asked me. Then he told me not to come. But I was already on my way. So I insisted he meet me. Like you said, I don't want him backing out. We're so close."

"You did the right thing," I say. "And you look amazing."

She smiles knowingly. "Yeah, he'll like this dress."

"What's your plan? Are you meeting him here, or . . . ?"

"On the boardwalk at nine thirty." She looks at me as if she's been tricked into saying too much. "What did you say you're doing here, again?" Brigit doesn't know about my connection to Greg and Esme and their family. That would only complicate things.

"Just a trip with a friend, he'll be down any moment." I wink, the lie coming easily.

"Oh." She looks bored and eager to get away from me. "Well, bye."

"Brigit?" I say. "I have one last job proposition for you. A really easy one. Why don't we meet later tonight, here at the bar?"

"I'll be with Greg. It's not a good time."

"Well, text me if you change your mind. Have fun tonight with Greg. Good luck." I reach to give her a hug, and she stands stiffly as I wrap my arms around her.

Turning on my heels, I head back to the bar to finish my meal. From my vantage point, I watch as she takes selfies of herself by the water, posing in various positions. She's a beautiful young woman, that much is true. But her vacant and vapid attitude ruins it. I guess not for Greg, though.

I haven't seen Greg for a few months now. He slowly responded less and less to my messages, and I stopped sending them. I figured that for sure, by now, I'd hear back from him, but apparently, he's been so taken with Brigit, there's just no room in his cheating schedule for me.

After this week, I have a feeling that when I message him, he'll respond. I'm done being ignored. Thrown away. Greg will stand up and take notice of me.

I sign the bar check, charging it to my room, and smile.

CHAPTER

46

Esme

WE'RE SEATED IN the living room, the twins are still upstairs asleep, Piper and Paul in their room, and Regina and her family in their bedroom. When Greg hangs up the phone with Alan and speaks, his words confirm what I've known, deep down, to be true. "It's Brigit," he says. "Brigit's body was found in the lake."

For once, I'm speechless. There's nothing to say. I put my head in my hands and work not to be sick.

When I look up, to my dismay, Greg looks like an animal caught in a sharp trap. "What are we going to do?" His eyes dart around the house, as if the answer will appear on the walls.

"I don't know. It looks bad. Why was she up here?" I know the answer to this, and so does Greg.

But he won't say it. And neither will I.

He shrugs, and then his rambling becomes more and more high pitched with panic. "I'm the one who found her. They'll think . . . they'll think I had something to do with it. And that I didn't say who she was. That I was hiding it."

I look sharply at him. "Were you?"

"No! I didn't know. I wasn't sure it was her. She looked so different. I hoped it wasn't her. It all happened so fast."

"Remember, Alan told us not to say anything. To request a lawyer be present if they question us."

"They're going to question us! She was our nanny. She was—" He stops short of saying what else she was.

I add, "Former nanny." I'm so tired of the lying. "Is there anything connecting you to her? Any hard proof of the affair, other than the photos?"

"The photos?" he says, and now his expression turns from trapped to wild. The whites of his eyes are showing, and for the first time in our marriage, I wonder if he's taking drugs or medication.

"Yes. There were photos delivered to my phone. From an anonymous number." I hold up my hand. "I searched, and no, it's not traceable. The sender used a burner phone."

He stares at me in disbelief.

"A burner phone?"

He looks as if he may be sick.

"It must have been Brigit herself. Who else could have had access to those photos?" he says miserably.

"I'd considered that. It could be. But the source said they were a concerned mom at school. It didn't sound like Brigit, from the texts. Did you go out with her—in public? Do you remember anyone who saw you together?"

He shakes his head and runs his hands through his hair.

I think I know who is actually behind the photos—but I'm not ready to share my suspicion with Greg. I can't trust him. Not now.

"What did you do with the photos?" he asks.

"I deleted them, of course. I don't want to have those floating around. Imagine how it would affect the girls."

He comes to me now, kneeling at my side, and grasps my hands.

"Esme, you are the best wife a man could wish for. Thank you. Thank you for protecting me. Standing by me."

I give him an icy glare. "Don't be a fool. It wasn't for you. *You're* reprehensible. But the twins need a father. They adore you. Imagine what their life would be like if their father was a known philanderer with the nanny. Or in prison. Look what happened to Alexis after both her parents died."

At the mention of Alexis, he stiffens. I push him off me. "What about Alexis are you not telling me?" I say, balling my fists.

"Well," he looks down at his hands. "Since we're being honest. I did give her some money. To make her go away. After the funeral, I wanted her to leave you in peace, to leave our family in peace. You needed that. I did it for you."

His eye twitches. "What else?"

"Nothing. That's it."

I can't tell if he's lying. "So back to my question. Did anyone see you alone with Brigit?" The name catches in my throat.

"No. We were always careful." He has the nerve to look guilty. "We either went to her apartment, or once in a while a hotel in downtown Manhattan. The Waldorf."

"The Waldorf?" Revulsion makes my already sick stomach roll. "Does she have any roommates?

"No, she lives alone—lived. Lived alone."

Are those tears in his eyes? Is he crying for Brigit? I get up and walk toward the kitchen. I can't be around him right now. He trails behind me.

"Do you think it's possible someone is setting you up?" I look closely at his face, trying to read his reaction. "Is there anyone who would want to destroy you?"

He puts his palms up and shakes his head. "No."

"Tell me this, Greg. Will you be crying over Brigit when you're charged with her murder?"

"I'm not going to be charged, Esme. I'm a neurosurgeon. I would never—"

"Shut up," I hiss. "Do you know how dumb you sound? She was our nanny. You had an affair with her. She was found by our house on a remote lake. Of course you'll be charged—if we don't do something about it."

"That's all circumstantial. There's no evidence. I didn't do it." He blinks at me, and again I see the childish boy he once was, and never outgrew.

"We don't know that you won't be charged, evidence or not. Can you leave me alone? I need a minute to put all this together. To think," I say, my hands on the counter. He slinks away back to the living room couch.

The truth is, neither Greg, nor I, are completely innocent in this. A young woman is dead. If that isn't awful enough, we are being implicated in her death.

In this moment, I feel so alone. My husband is faithless. My sisters both abandoned me, maybe rightfully so. I don't have a single friend I could call who would truly be there for me in a dark time. The only two people on earth who are there for me are my girls, Brielle and Gracey. And they don't deserve this.

I have to think of a solution for their sake.

CHAPTER

47

Before

Alexis

It's almost nine thirty PM and I'm on the boardwalk outside the Bergamont. The moon is out tonight, its pale reflection dancing across the water. I've been following Brigit since she arrived this afternoon. So far her day has consisted of getting a pedicure, a bikini wax, and shopping.

The anticipation is thrumming through my veins, creating a heightened sense of expectancy. Things are about to get interesting. A sick fascination has overcome me. The idea of seeing her and Greg together is tantalizing. Will he be pleased to see her? Will he feed her the same exact lines he said to me?

I'm sitting on a bench on a raised area above the boardwalk, surrounded by a large planter bed filled with ferns and shrubs. I'm wearing my nice outfit so I'll fit in with the crowd here, and the lighter hair really seals the look. From my vantage point in the shadows above, I can see through the foliage down to Brigit standing on the dock, illuminated by the lights of the boardwalk and the glow from the hotel. So far she's just waiting, tapping on her phone.

When my phone starts buzzing, I almost jump, and my jaw drops open when I see who it is. Regina. Could she be here and have seen me? I glance to my left and right but don't see anyone in the dark garden area surrounding me.

I decide to pick up. I'm too curious to let it go. What could she want to warrant a phone call to me?

I answer quietly, keeping my voice calm and collected. "Hello, Regina," I say. "This is unexpected."

"Alexis." Her words are heavily slurred. "I'm at the house."

"Your summer house?" I ask, just to be sure.

"Yes. My sisters and their families are here, too. We're all here. But we're not one big fucking happy family. Esme, especially. Such a bitch. I want you to come here. Come and stay as my guest. If I have to be here, at least you can come and keep me company."

"You want me to come, as your guest?" I can hardly believe what I'm hearing. How easy she is making this for me.

Regina rambles on, clearly inebriated. She says something about me coming immediately. To party outside with her by the hot tub. That she won't take no for an answer.

Before I can tell her I'll be there soon, she hangs up. I slide my phone back into my pocket, and continue to wait, a small smile playing on my lips.

Then I sit up straight when I hear it: "Expecting my husband?" A woman's voice floats up clearly. It's Esme. I'd know that voice anywhere. Through the branches, I can see Esme's profile standing in front of Brigit.

"Mrs. Wimberly. What are you doing here?" It's Brigit's voice, filled with guilt and surprise with a touch of defensiveness. It makes me giddy.

"He's not coming," Esme says coolly. "It was me who texted you from his phone."

I wish I had popcorn for this exchange. This is exactly what I'd hoped would happen, but it's even better than I imagined it. Esme is falling right into my trap. She thinks she's so clever.

Then there's a pause, before Esme tells Brigit to cut the theatrical crying and save her fake tears. She launches into a spiel about how she trusted Brigit as a nanny, brought her into the family circle, and Brigit betrayed her in the worst way.

It sucks being betrayed by someone you think you can trust, doesn't it? I think, and almost say out loud.

Brigit apologies halfheartedly, which Esme declines to accept.

And then they start negotiating money to pay Brigit off. So that's Esme's angle. Brigit negotiates like a shark. Nerves of steel. She folds, though, when Esme calls her bluff. They agree to a sum of 10K. Brigit is really earning quite the nest egg through our family.

"The check is good, Brigit," Esme says, and then she continues, "You know, you could have been so much more than this. I hope in the future, you know you can be better."

Somehow this hurts me deep in my core. Esme's found a kernel of kindness, even for this woman who tried to destroy her marriage. Why could she never find it in her to give me a moment's kindness?

Then there's silence. I peer over to get a better view of what's happening—no more is said.

I watch Brigit turn on her heels and walk away from Esme, while Esme turns in the direction of the valet and front entrance. I stand up and race back into the hotel, through the lobby and out again through the revolving doors to the valet area, which is lit against the darkening night sky. I spot Esme. She's waiting for her car. Her face is a mask of calm.

I approach her, and when she sees me, it's her turn to be surprised. Her entire face falls into the look of reproach I'm used to seeing from her.

"What are you doing here?" she says, echoing what Brigit said to her moments earlier.

"I thought you might want to know who your friendly school mom is, the one who sent you the photos of Greg and Brigit."

"What?"

I smile, not unkindly. "Yes. Me. I got to know Brigit and encouraged their dalliance."

She takes a step back. "You're sick. You need help. You always have."

"Maybe so. But there's more. Brigit is going to fall on some hard times. Really bad. And I'll make sure that anything bad that happens to your nanny comes back on Greg."

Now she looks genuinely afraid. "What are you talking about?"

I shrug. Now I'm the one in power, and this mind game is mine to play. "I'm not sure what you mean. All I said was good luck finding a new nanny."

"You're crazy. I'll call the cops. You can't threaten us, or Brigit. Who do you think you are?"

"Call them. You're the one who paid her off. I wonder if maybe she should've filed a sexual harassment lawsuit, rather than accept a paltry 10K? I'll let her know she could have gotten so much more."

"How do you know about that?" she says, looking around at the valet and other patrons, paranoid. "You know what? You're nuts." She puts her hands up. "Just leave me and my family alone." She turns on her heels, walking away from me over to the sidewalk. I overhear her checking with the valet, who assures her they're on the way with her vehicle.

I could follow her. Tell her how maybe if she hadn't turned her back on me, things could have been different. We could have been family. Auntie Alexis. I would have been a great-aunt, treating the twins to special trips and visits to art museums. Esme and I could have spent all these years getting to know each other, rather than becoming strangers.

It didn't have to be this way.

If Audry hadn't been responsible for my mother's demise. Audry blamed Frank for their affair—their one-time dalliance that resulted in my birth, at the same time that Esme was born to Frank and Audry. Frank had two baby girls that year, not one. I was a blight on Frank and Audry's perfect story.

And she made my mom pay for it. Knowing my mom struggled with self-control, she made drugs and alcohol readily available to her. Audry sent her money when she needed a fix—not money for me, or for groceries, it always went to addiction.

Her visits, when she did come by, were to ridicule my mother. Insult her pathetic addiction, what a joke she'd become. Then she'd throw more pills at my mother and walk out.

I know my mother ingested the substances of her own will, but Audry killed her by making it clear there was no way out for her. No hope for redemption.

Audry's hate of my mom seeped from her right into Esme.

Since the age of ten, Esme has hated me. Audry told her the truth when my mom died. The first day I arrived at her house, Esme cornered me. She told me that my being born was a mistake, and I'd never be her sister, and she'd never bother her real sisters with the truth about me.

Esme hated me in the inexplicable way that becomes rooted and fixed in one's mind. Her hatred of me bred years of shame, questioning, and self-loathing in me. Why was I never good enough for her family? How could they just throw me away?

The little girl in me knows now that it doesn't matter. It was rigged. I was always going to be the loser, and she was always going to be the winner.

The only way to play a rigged game is to cheat. So here we go.

CHAPTER

48

Esme

GREG AND I have spent the past few hours silently lying in bed. The house is quiet, everyone else is asleep, but Greg and I are both wide awake.

I can hear him tossing and turning. Finally, he asks me, "You awake?"

"Yeah," I say.

He turns over on his side to face me.

"Esme, I'm sorry for earlier. The way I behaved. I panicked," he says, and his voice sounds more like the Greg I know. Confident. Assured.

He continues, "I need you to understand something. I'm prepared to take responsibility for this. I put myself in this situation. I told myself it was my high-stress job, and your being so busy with the girls and social affairs—but those are excuses.

I should never have cheated on you. It was wrong. I can't make excuses, because it's inexcusable."

I'm shocked at the words I'm hearing. In the dark, I can't see his expression. Maybe it's easier for him to say these things that way.

"I agree," I say. "I've always loved you. Been loyal to you. And this is how you show your loyalty?"

"Esme," he says. "I see it clearly now. The mistakes I've made. I would give anything to go back and do it all over again. And I promise, this will never happen again. If I get a second chance, I will never mistreat you or take you for granted again."

"Do you mean that?"

"I do. I'll spend the rest of my life proving it to you. You will see. There's nothing that matters more to me than you and the girls. I've been working too much. Letting my priorities get all mixed up. Moving forward, it's clear to me now. I was on the wrong path. But I'm back."

"I'm scared, Greg," I say, reaching out for him. All my anger has been deflated. I just need his support.

"I'm scared, too," he says, holding me close. "I'm sorry, Es. That I put our whole family in jeopardy."

"But you did." I keep my head on his chest, feeling his breathing. "And Brigit is dead. You're the one who found her. It doesn't look good."

"I'm aware. But you know I'd never do anything, right? I'd never hurt anyone. My whole life is dedicated to saving people. Helping them live. I could never take a life."

I do know this. Greg may be selfish and immature, and he has cheated. But he could never physically harm anyone. "I know you didn't murder her," I say.

I'm just not sure the police will see it that way.

"Greg, there's something I have to tell you, too," I say. "Alexis was here. Two nights ago."

I tell him about meeting with Brigit. How I paid her to leave him alone. And how Alexis confronted me outside of the hotel. How she said she was out to get Greg, and Brigit would fall on hard times.

I feel Greg stiffen underneath me, but he continues to hold me. "I wish you had told me."

"There's a lot that has gone unsaid between us," I say.

He strokes my hair. "I know. I understand why you wouldn't come to me right away. But you realize this changes everything?"

"How so?"

"We have to find Alexis. Tell the police about her threats."

"It's not so easy. What proof do we have?"

There's silence, as we both realize the answer is: none. We have no proof.

C H A P T E R

49

Regina

I STEP OUT OF the shower, wrapping a thick cotton towel around my hair and another around my chest. It feels like the longest day of my life. When I came home, the whole family attacked and yelled at me. Why didn't I answer my phone? Did I know Lana took Preston? She was crying about the twins leaving her out, and the entire family blamed me for the whole ordeal. All I could think about was getting Brigit's check into my bedroom to hide for safekeeping, but I had a lot of angry fingers wagging in my face.

Lana will sleep in our bed again tonight—it's clear the battle lines have been drawn and she won't be welcome sleeping in the twins' room. Once she's asleep, I'll tell Bryce about what I found today. We'll discuss how we can use it, maybe get ourselves set for the future.

After I'm dried off and dressed, I come out into our bedroom and find Lana and Bryce talking. It's clear by his expression that Bryce is upset. I sit down on the edge of the bed. "What's wrong?"

"Lana told me a very upsetting story. She said that two nights ago, she had a bad dream that woke her up in the middle of the night. She came looking for you, but didn't see you in our room. So she went downstairs, where she saw a woman. A stranger in our house. Lana had seen her the day before, out on the back trail, looking for her dog. Lana had gone with her, searching for her missing puppy."

I snap my head around to look at Lana. "Lana, is this true?"

Her face is pale, and she nods. I reach my hand around to her and clasp hers. "You should never go with strangers." I shake my head. "What did the woman look like? What did she say?" I have a sinking feeling in my gut.

"She was pretty. Light hair." She swallows. "She was outside. On the trail. She said she had a missing puppy and could I help her? So I did. But we didn't find her."

"And last night?" I ask her. "What did she say?"

Her face creases. "Um . . . She said you invited her over, that she was friends with you."

Alexis. I put my hand over my mouth, not making eye contact with Bryce. Alexis was at our house, luring my daughter with a puppy story? And then that night I invited her back here. I thought she never came, but clearly she did.

She's psychotic. I need to get a hold of her and tell her off.

Bryce continues. "Lana said the woman told her she wanted to show her a cool boat by the water, near the boathouse. She brought her outside to a small boat by the water. Lana noticed the woman had a knife in her belt and when she asked why, she said for protection in the wild but told her not to worry, it's fine, and that you'd told her to go with her. It was pitch black and Lana was shaking with fear, and the woman—"

"I never told her to take you, Lana, I'd never do that," I say helplessly.

She shakes her head. "I didn't know."

"So, the woman started to put her into the boat. She said she needed Lana to come help her puppy, who was sick. She said she knew you—Lana's mom—from childhood here. That you two were good friends as kids," Bryce finishes. He's visibly upset, and so is Lana. My stomach feels knotted into a tight, painful ball.

"I didn't want to go in the boat," Lana says to me.

Bryce continues, "The woman got very upset, and said she'd be speaking to her mother tomorrow."

"I was scared when I saw her knife. I jumped out of the boat. I ran back home," Lana says.

"Oh my God. I can't believe—how awful, my poor girl. Lana, I'm so sorry, baby."

"I thought it was a bad dream. But Aunt Piper asked me about it in the morning."

"Aunt Piper?" I ask. "She was there, too?"

"Yeah. After I ran home. I couldn't find you again, so I woke up Aunt Piper."

I nod guiltily, knowing I was out back on the lounge chair. What a failure of a mom.

"Aunt Piper dried me. She changed me."

My body is racked with guilt. Stabs of regret as I remember criticizing Piper for overreacting. I feel a deep shame that I wasn't there for my daughter.

"Lana, why didn't you tell us right away this morning?"

"I was scared. I thought you would be mad. Then we found that lady . . . Now the cops are at the house . . . So I told Daddy."

"I'm sorry I wasn't there for you. I'm so glad Aunt Piper helped you. You did the right thing to get Piper. You were brave. Now this is very important—have you told anyone else about this?" I ask Lana, trying to figure out how this all connects. Alexis was here to visit us, hoping if she said she was in town, she'd get an invite to the house—then what? And what is her deal, lying to Lana about a dog? "Just Daddy. And Aunt Piper. I said there was a lady at the lake, but that's all."

An icy fear crawls up my neck as I imagine Alexis bringing Lana to a boat in the middle of the night. She always caused trouble as a kid, and now it seems she's even more unhinged.

She told Lana she would talk to me today . . . I take out my phone, but I don't have any missed calls from Alexis. She wasn't at the hotel today, and she hasn't returned my calls.

I never should've let her back into my life. I shouldn't have taken her advice about the house, although, really, having Esme buy me out has saved my ass. But, still. It's not worth her stalking my daughter.

"And then she took the baby from the house," Bryce says. He tells me again about Lana taking baby Preston today out of his crib, the frantic search.

"Lana, sweetie," I say, but she looks like she's about to cry, and I stop myself from lecturing her. She's been through so much. I hug her. "It's okay, love. It's okay."

I think about Preston, missing from the house, how Piper would've been gutted. How she helped Lana, and what have I done? Criticize Piper and lash out at her.

* * *

Bryce paces around the room. "Should tell the cops about all this? Maybe that guy you know, Ben something? Maybe he can help. Put out an alert for this lady at the lake?"

A horrible thought occurs to me. The woman whose body was pulled from the water. What if it is indeed Alexis, not Brigit, as I'd guessed it must be based on what I found in Brigit's hotel room? Maybe my theory was wrong. If Alexis was here, is it possible that Lana fought against the woman from the lake? Struggled? Caused an accident as she was escaping? It's not possible that Lana, such a small girl, could have killed her. Is it?

She's always been a fighter, Lana. I know she's tough, and resourceful. I like to think she gets that from me. But she was afraid to talk to me. I can't believe she didn't tell me what happened that night. It makes me wonder: Would she even tell me if there were more to the story?

As I glance at her on the bed, the sense that I've let her down is overwhelming.

The worst part is all of this is my fault. If I hadn't called Alexis that night, she never would have been here. What if it's Alexis's body out there, as Piper has said all along? The thought makes me shudder.

I rack my brain, trying to understand how it all connects. None of this makes sense. The missing woman, Brigit, who was sleeping with Greg. Alexis being in town. Officer Ben, who has a chip on his shoulder and has it out for our family. Lana, being tricked by Alexis to go out in the woods and again out to the lake?

"Don't call the police, especially not Ben," I say, exasperated. "Let me think. I need to talk to Piper. See if she knows anything else about last night. But I doubt the police can help." I don't tell him that I did, in fact, invite Alexis here, and that she's been in touch with me recently.

I had planned to tell Bryce about Greg and Brigit and the check and what I saw on her phone at the hotel room, but I need more time.

I tuck Lana into bed. "I'm glad you told us, Lana. You can tell me anything. You know that?"

She nods, but I'm not so sure.

"Sweet dreams."

"I don't think I can sleep," she says, but when I look over a few moments later, she's fast asleep.

And I leave to go find Piper.

CHAPTER

50

Piper

I JUMP WHEN I hear a knock at our door. I motion for Paul to get it. He sets down his reading glasses and book on the end table. When he opens the door, Regina pops her head in.

"Can we talk?" she whispers, looking at sleeping Preston.

I don't have much choice. She pushes her way past Paul.

"Downstairs," I whisper. She follows me down the stairs. In the living room, I turn to her. "What's this about?"

Regina twists the tail of her T-shirt in her hand. "Look, I owe you a huge apology. Lana said she ran into a woman lurking at the house. That night I was out back." She looks down at her feet. "You took care of her when she couldn't find me. Thank you for keeping her safe, and not finding me like that outside." She takes a deep breath. "I am sorry I doubted your story, when you said she woke you up soaking wet. I've mistreated you, and I hope you can forgive me. I am forever grateful that you were there for Lana."

I'm surprised by her apology, but I instantly want to accept it. "I was glad to help, she's my niece." I'm ashamed at how easily I forgive everything that's happened between us. Even though I'm still mad at her, I don't like conflict. I bury my feelings, as my therapist said.

Regina's not done, though. "Did you see the woman she was talking about?"

I snap my head to look at her. "No," I answer quickly. "I still don't know what happened or why she was wet. Do you?"

Her hands fly up. "No. I'm trying make sense of it. Get a straight story. The body was found in the lake the next day. Do you think . . . it's connected?"

I swallow. "I can't imagine it was."

We look at one another. Her eyes drift down to my forearm, and I pull my sleeve down over the bandage peeking out. I feel like Regina's holding back, and she probably senses there's more I'm not saying.

She reaches out and pulls me into a hug. "You're a good mom, Piper," she says into my hair. "I'm sorry."

I let her hug me, but I know I've caught her in a lie. It's then that I'm certain Regina had something to do with the dead woman in the lake.

CHAPTER

51

Esme

I'M PULLED FROM a deep, dreamless sleep. It's my cell phone ringing and buzzing on the nightstand. I reach out and pick it up.

"Esme?" the male voice says. "It's Alan."

Our attorney. What could he possibly want at this hour? I glance at the time and see it's barely past dawn. "Hi." Greg stirs next to me.

"What's going on?" I ask.

"I wanted to give you a heads-up on what's coming. But it's important you don't tell Greg."

"Fine," I say, and I hop out of bed to move downstairs to the living room.

Alan's voice is thick as he continues, "I got word this morning. The police are going to arrest Greg for the murder of Brigit Max."

I stop. "No."

"Yes, Esme. Once they identified the victim—and in light of the photos of Greg and the victim that were sent to the station anonymously—they searched her apartment. There's a forensic match for Greg's semen in her bed. That, along with the text messages showing pings from your lake house to her at the hotel, along with plans to meet up via Messenger. It all points to Greg."

"Forensic match?" I say. "How do they have anything to test him? That can't be right."

"I'll look into it, but they could have obtained a sample any number of ways. They wouldn't put out a warrant if they didn't feel the case was strong."

My mouth is dry. "This can't be happening. They can't arrest him."

"Listen. There's hotel footage of her leaving at ten PM with another woman we're working to identify. That's our only defense, that he wasn't the last one to be seen with her alive."

My stomach drops. "Oh."

"I'm only calling you as a courtesy, since we go way back. I've known your family since you were a child. Your dad was my best friend. Trust me, there's nothing we can do to prevent the arrest from happening. All we can do is prepare. Make sure your girls aren't around for it, and then we'll get him out on bail right away."

"You can do that?"

"I'm packing my bag now. I'll be up there in three hours. I'll convince the bail magistrate to get him out of custody as soon as they bring him in."

"I thought you were already on your way and you'd be here by now," I moan. "What is he being charged with? I don't understand. This doesn't make sense. Greg didn't have anything to do with this." I feel helpless.

"He's being charged with murder."

The room seems to be spinning. I stand frozen to the spot in the living room, looking out at the lake, trying to make my brain work.

"There has to be something we can do to stop this."

"Your job is to get the girls out of the house. Greg will be fine. Whatever you do, don't tell him what's happening. I've seen better men make a run for it when facing charges." He pauses. "He can't outrun this. That would only worsen and prolong things. Do you understand, Esme?"

"I understand," I say blankly.

Hanging up the phone, a million thoughts are swirling. It doesn't make sense they'd arrest him for her murder. Greg and Brigit were having an affair, that much I'll give them. But he didn't murder her. He was at the house the whole time. That's a fact. They have the wrong man.

But they must have evidence against him. They wouldn't make an arrest without a strong case, would they?

The problem with exonerating him by the video of the woman at the hotel who was last seen with Brigit, is that the woman is me.

If I were the last person to see her alive—and I have motive to kill her because of the affair—it's starting to look like I might be the one in trouble.

I slump on the couch and cover my eyes. I think hard, connecting the pieces. And it always adds up to one person: Alexis. She's the key to all of this.

Alexis must have had Brigit followed and killed. Didn't she threaten that something bad would happen to Brigit? I just need to find some proof—hard evidence—that Alexis was behind it.

Otherwise, my husband and I are in grave danger of being prosecuted and sent to rot in jail for the rest of our lives.

I walk into the hallway and knock on my sister's door gently. "Piper." I whisper. "Piper . . . I need your help."

CHAPTER

52

Before

Alexis

I SIP AT MY sparkling water and fiddle with the cherry at the hotel lobby bar, twirling the red stem around my finger. It's ten thirty PM and since Brigit's encounter with Esme, there's no sign of her. I'd hoped she'd come to the bar for a drink to ease her troubles. But I don't think she's going to come out of her room on her own.

I will have to entice her. I get out my phone and text her: "Greg is in the lobby. I see him talking to the person at the front desk. Weren't you supposed to be with him? Maybe he's trying to get a hold of you?"

I see the bubble pop up immediately that she's read my message and typing a reply.

"On my way down."

Within five minutes, the elevator door opens, and Brigit steps out. She's still wearing her heels. She scans the lobby for Greg, and her face falls as she realizes he's not there.

I run up to her, tapping her on the arm. "He just left. I watched him talk to the front desk clerk. Then his phone rang, he said something about how he was on his way home, and left," I lie. Greg was, of course, never here. But I had to find a way to get Brigit out of her room.

She looks annoyed. "Why didn't he message me he was here?" She takes out her phone and checks it again.

"I don't know. You were supposed to meet him earlier, right?" I ask.

"Yeah, but Esme showed up."

I pretend to be shocked. "Wow."

"Yeah. She told me to stay away, but clearly she can't stop him." She gives me a smug smile.

"I bet she's monitoring his messages. That's why he came to find you. In person."

Her eyes widen. "I bet you're right."

"Let's have a drink. On me. Then we can discuss next steps."

She shrugs. She absently follows me to the bar area. I've got my seltzer water, but I order her a martini. Brigit accepts the drink from me without a thank you and puts the glass to her red lips, taking a large sip. She frowns at the taste. "This is strong," she comments, but takes another sip, nonetheless.

We sit at a high-top corner table. She keeps her eyes peeled to the door, as if he might come back in.

"You really care about him, don't you?" I comment.

Her eyes briefly pass over mine. "He's the one who's head over heels for me. Maybe I've gotten used to his attention. His money. I could get used to being with him."

I see right through her. It may have started as an easy way to make money, but he's good. Persuasive. Once you have his complete and utter attention focused on you, when you believe he really sees you for how special you are, that's when you're hooked.

"Let's have our drink, then we'll drive over there."

"What? To his summer house? Esme and the kids are there."

"Do you really care?" I ask.

"Not really." Her voice is uncertain. "I guess we could go over there. But why?"

"Confront him. Make it easy for him to leave Esme. If you're there, he'll have to choose between you. He obviously wants to leave her for you." Her lips upturn smugly in agreement at this. "But he might need to be pushed into it. It's hard for a man to commit to leaving his family. Even if he wants to."

She still doesn't look fully convinced.

"Would you rather settle for a small sum of money now, or be set up for life? Forever? Greg would provide you with that. He adores you. You already know the twins. And like you said, Esme will accept you after the dust settles." I try to keep a straight face for that load.

She takes another sip, nods.

Her eyes are starting to look glassy. She's a tiny slip of a girl, she can't weigh more than a hundred pounds.

"Let's finish our drinks and get going. It's getting late." My voice is firm and calm.

Brigit drains her glass with a final swallow. When she gets up, she's a bit unsteady on her feet. She doesn't seem fazed about going to meet Greg. In fact, she looks determined.

We walk out the front revolving door together, and I lead her by the arm, giving her a squeeze. "You're doing the right thing."

She nods.

When we get outside, she heads toward the valet stand, but I stop her.

"Brigit, I think we should take a speedboat I rented. The police presence here is insane in summer. Neither of us should be driving. Can you imagine having to spend the night in lockup?"

"Take a boat out?" She looks at me as if I'm crazy. She rips her arm away from me. "No way. It's pitch black. I'm not going on a boat. Just call a rideshare."

She gets out her phone, starts scrolling through her apps.

"There won't be rideshares or cabs around here," I lie, and I'm pretty sure I see someone getting into one behind us. "It's a resort town. They don't provide service way out here."

"I'll just drive." She throws her phone into her purse.

"No," I say. "It's an amazing boat. A speedboat. It has headlights for night driving and a warm galley where you can rest while we drive over there. We'll park at the boathouse. It's the best way to go."

She hems and haws.

"Just come see this boat. It's a beauty, actually, more than a motorboat. It's pure luxury. You'll love it. Just come look. If you don't love it, we don't have to go. You can drive."

She rolls her eyes, but I can see she's tempted. A luxury boat is where she envisions herself. Where she belongs.

"There's a bedroom down below. If you want, you and Greg could even spend the night there. My treat. For all the help you've given me. Consider it an early engagement gift."

I lead her toward the marina where the yachts and boats are moored. The evening is quiet, with just a few people milling about on the boardwalk outside the hotel.

The marina is desolate. The entrance is lit with a high light post, and we cross onto the dock. The boats sway gently in the water, the thick ropes tied to the dock holding them in place. There's hardly any breeze, so the water is calm.

We walk along, and Brigit holds onto the railing, balancing on her heels. "Which one is it? I'm cold," she says impatiently.

"Right over here," I say. I flip on my phone's flashlight. It's getting darker the farther we get out on the dock toward the water and away from the shore.

"It's that big one, at the end," I say.

I glance behind us. The marina is completely empty. No experienced fisherman or boater would go out at this time of night. There are a few people on the boardwalk, but they're far away.

When we get to the large speedboat on the left, she stops. "Wow. You rented this? You know how to drive this thing?"

"Yep," I say, and I lower my phone flashlight for a moment, sending us both into pitch darkness.

"Hey, what happened?" she says.

Without hesitating, I give her a quick, hard shove into the water.

I hear her hit the water. It's at least a three-foot climb out of it onto the dock, and in the darkness, there's no way she'll get out without my help.

I flick my phone flashlight back on and spin it around to the small dingy boat I rented and tied to the end of the dock earlier today.

"Help," she says. "Please, I can't swim!" The panic in her voice tells me she means it.

I step into the dingy and set my phone light on the middle seat. The boat is large enough for two people and has two oars in it. No motor. My hands are shaking as I work to undo the knot that ties the small boat to the dock.

The splashing continues but she's not crying for help, which makes me think she's running out of air and energy.

I push off, and row the boat to the front of the dock. I see her eyes glint against the flashlight, her frantic hands splashing, reaching.

I reach out my hand to her, steadying myself with my other hand against the boat.

Pulling her over and in, she lands in the boat, heaving and shaking.

I pull out a dry blanket and throw it on her. "Here," I say.

She wraps it around herself and manages to sit propped up against the boat. I kill the flashlight and use the glow from the shore and the stars to orient myself. I start rowing away from the shore in smooth, rhythmic strokes.

"Where—" she manages to say. "What are you doing?"

"Brigit," I say, my breath starting to come in puffs. "Sit right there. I have a knife. And you're in no condition to fight with me. It's cool enough that hypothermia could set in if you don't get dry and warm." She lets out a whimper at this, and I know my psychological warfare is working. The temperature has dropped to the fifties. She's chilled, but she won't get hypothermia. However, I want her to stay complacent and not try anything. "We're not far from Greg's. We'll be there in fifteen minutes. He'll get you warmed up and in his arms in no time."

"Please. I'm wet and cold. Please take me back."

Her whole body is shivering.

"Don't talk. Save your energy. This is the plan."

She moves toward me, making a go for the oar. I shove her back down, and she easily falls back in a pathetic heap. She gathers the blanket around her again. "Please? Let's go back."

"Shut up." Now she's starting to grate on my nerves. I need to pay attention so we're not lost out here for hours. "Do what I say, and you'll be fine. If not, I'll throw you right back in the water. Is that what you want?"

"No," she says, and I hear her start to cry.

Tuning her out, I focus on my rowing. I charted the path to Greg and Esme's boathouse several times, even coming out for a test run. But now that I'm out here in the darkness with this quivering person adding extra weight and pressure, I feel an edge of panic start to creep in.

You've got this, I remind myself. *You grew up on this lake. Swam in it every summer. Rowed in it every year.* Until my mom died, of course, and Audry and Frank cast me out. I ignore the burning in my muscles. I've never been a quitter. I remember that first summer after my mom died, when I almost didn't make it swimming across the lake. Esme would have left me to drown out here. But I'm stronger than that. I'll never give up and let the Howards win. I let my anger propel me, giving my arms the energy they need to keep rowing.

The moon is only a sliver in the night sky, but now that my eyes have adjusted, it's providing enough light. I turn off my cell phone flashlight and row by the light of the sky.

The lights on the shore of the populated side of the lake are getting smaller. I row toward the darkness. Yesterday during my trial run, I rowed west for twenty minutes to arrive at the boathouse. I stop and pull up my phone compass to make sure I'm heading west. I adjust course slightly and continue rowing. It's proving much more difficult to navigate at night.

"Why are you doing this?" Brigit asks through labored breathing. Her crying has subsided somewhat. Perhaps her energy is being drained.

I ignore her. I'm not here to chat or to entertain her juvenile dreams. The time for that is over. She's where I want her, and I no longer need to ply her with platitudes and fairy tales about her and Greg.

"Please, I need help. Please help."

"Be quiet. Save your energy. Almost there."

My arms are burning now, more so than yesterday. My muscles were tight today after a day of rowing, and her extra weight is tiring me out.

Just as I'm about to check the compass again, I see a faint light emerge on the side of the shore we're headed to, and the outline of the boathouse. We're almost there. The Howards' summer house.

I stop rowing. I take a few deep breaths and stretch my hands. I turn my phone light on to see where Brigit is and plan my next move.

I turn the light off and lunge.

I wrap my hands around her neck and squeeze with all my might. She cries out and flails her fists at me: at my arms, my face, my neck. She lands a blow to my windpipe, and I let go, gasping for breath.

She takes this opportunity to pummel me, but once I catch my breath, her swipes only serve to enrage me. I lunge at her again, this time jumping on top of her. The boat rocks furiously, and for a moment I think we'll both fall in. I hold her neck steady, willing the boat to stop moving.

She tries to punch and kick, but I whack her head against the boat. I wrap my hands around her neck again, this time using every ounce of strength I have left in my limbs, standing over her, pushing. Horrible guttural sounds emit from her as she tries frantically to breathe, fighting with every inch of her body. But I'm stronger and larger. Her energy is draining. I can feel her body giving up.

There's no going back now. I press on her neck using all my body weight. She twitches, and then is still. I don't let go for another minute, wanting to be sure I've done the job. In the darkness, I look down and see that her eyes are wide open. Still. Vacant.

The lapping of the water against the boat is the only sound I hear. I listen, making sure our commotion hasn't floated over the water and to the house and alerted its occupants.

I hold my fingers to her pulse and find there's none. I wait another twenty minutes in the boat, and then I gather all my energy. I row as close to the Howards' summer house as I dare. Then, I lift her up under her arms. The boat rocks, and I stop, holding her body still. I heave again, gathering my balance. She's positioned over the boat. I lean her down, her shoulders slumping on the edge, and I give her legs a shove.

She plunks into the water with a small splash. And then silence.

I watch their house, but there's no detectable movement that I can see. The rest of the shoreline is trees, and not a single other home on this side of the lake.

After the exertion of the rowing and strangling Brigit, and then dumping her body, my arms are starting to cramp up. I painfully row those last meters to the shoreline and hide the boat on the opposite side of the boathouse, away from the view of their house.

I sit on the shore, letting my body rest. There's no way I can row back right now. I won't make it.

I can see the house, lights glowing inside on the bottom floor. Killing Brigit has brought out a blackness in me. I no longer want to wait for revenge. Who knows how many days or weeks it may take to find her? And then to arrest Greg. Even with anonymous tips from me, the process will not be immediate.

A dark rage is burning within me. Stronger. Fierce. I want Esme to suffer. Look at what she's made me do. Look at the lengths I've had to go, while she sits in her million-dollar summer house. My whole life I've sat outside, looking in at her perfect life.

Taking down her husband isn't enough. I want more.

I sit on the shore, and in that instant, it seems clear to me what must be done.

I'll gather my strength, wait until the lights go off, and then I'll go inside.

CHAPTER

53

Piper

I SLEPT WORSE THAN usual last night. Even when Preston was sleeping, I couldn't manage to keep my eyes closed. I kept hearing noises, thinking someone was outside. I peeked out our bedroom window, sure I heard the crunching of leaves underfoot. But when I looked, the yard was empty.

Sitting up in bed, I check that Preston is sleeping soundly in his crib. I remember the talk Regina and I had last night.

It's a funny sort of satisfaction in getting an apology from her. Longing for her acceptance for so many years, but finding now that it's here, I don't care. My only objective now is to get through our time here, and then pack up and leave with my baby and my husband. That's the plan.

I hear Esme's voice at my door. "Piper." She's whispering, and thankfully Preston doesn't stir.

I open the door and slip out, the monitor grasped firmly in my hand.

"What?" I cross my arms defensively.

"I need your help. Come downstairs, I'll tell you what's happening. She looks at the door. Paul's in there. Nothing will happen to the baby."

I follow her downstairs.

"Our attorney Alan just called. He has it on good authority that Greg will be arrested today. For the murder of Brigit."

My mouth drops open. "Brigit?"

"Yes," she says. "She was our nanny. She and Greg were having an affair. So they think he killed her. He didn't—he's innocent."

"How do you know?"

"He's my husband, Piper. I know."

"So it was Brigit, the body, for sure?" I ask, considering the implications of this. "That's insane. I was so sure . . ."

"I know. But it's her. The police have identified her."

I nod.

She grabs my hand. "Piper, listen. Please. Alan says he can get Greg out on bail while we clear him, but there's no avoiding the arrest. I'm taking the girls to town so they don't have to see it. But I need your help. I know that Alexis is responsible for this. I need your help proving it."

At the mention of Alexis, I feel the color drain from my face. "What do you mean?"

"Alexis confronted me the night Brigit died, at the Bergamont. She told me Brigit was going to have hard times ahead. And that Greg and I would take the blame. I think she was setting us up."

"What? Why didn't you warn Brigit? Or go to the police?" I can't believe what I'm hearing.

"She—she threatened to expose Greg's affair." She puts her head down. "I didn't think she'd hurt her, let alone kill her. If I'd thought that, I would've told—"

Esme had a chance to potentially stop this murder, and she didn't?

"Lives have been destroyed, Esme." My voice is low and filled with disgust. My sister's always been preoccupied with presenting a flawless image. But I didn't think she was capable of such gross negligence in the name of preserving her perfect facade.

"It was a huge mistake, okay? I get that. But the father of my children is about to go to jail for a crime he didn't commit. It was Alexis. It had to be. We have to prove it."

"I think this is a job for your attorney and the police." I put my hands up. "I want no part in this. I have a baby. I have to think about my own family. You can't keep sucking me into your mess." My body is shaking with anger.

"All I need you to do is reach out to Alexis. I'm pretty sure she's staying at the Bergamont. Talk to her. Convince her to turn herself in. Convince her that it's the right thing to do." She holds my hand, squeezing it. "She owes you. And the two of you have always gotten along the best, out of us three sisters."

I pull my hand away from her. "Maybe that's because I was the only one who treated her kindly. Have you ever thought it's your fault? You drove her to hate you. You got her cast out from our family. Never invited her to family gatherings, never included her. You made her an outcast, when we're the only family she had. And it drove her to extreme lengths."

"You're taking her side? You don't understand about her . . . who she is." She shakes her finger at me. "So, what, you think Greg should go to jail?"

The thought of Alexis makes my stomach turn. "No. I'm not taking her side. I'm saying she's a broken woman. You broke her." I throw my hands up. "I'm done taking sides. All I care about is protecting my child. Keeping him safe. That is my focus. Your problems are yours alone. We are leaving when the police give us the all clear."

I spin around, determined to keep calm. The pressure building in my chest feels like it might explode. Things are starting to click into place.

My anger burns toward Esme. It's her fault. The mess we're all in is her fault. Everything that has happened here is because of her choices. Who knows . . . maybe she did kill Brigit, after all? Or maybe Greg did it together with Esme.

I push down my growing sense of guilt and responsibility. I push it down. Deep.

CHAPTER

54

Before

Alexis

I SIT ON THE shore for a few more minutes, letting the silty water lap quietly against boat. I stand up and brush the sand off me. I pull the boat a few feet onto shore to ensure I won't be left stranded here when I'm finished.

My eyes have adjusted to the darkness, and the stars overhead provide plenty of light. I leave the lakefront, moving past the boathouse on my right and following the trail that winds past it and through the woods toward the house.

The short path is crowded with huge ancient spruces, and for a moment the cover of the trees makes the darkness disorienting. But I continue on.

When the path opens, I see the house up ahead. Inside the house is dark.

I follow the side of the house around to the back. There's a raised deck. A blue pool is lit with interior lights, and I see steam coming off the hot tub. The deck is empty.

I step up to the deck carefully. Then I recognize her.

Regina is splayed out on a lounge chair. As I get closer, I hear her softly snoring. I stand over her, wondering if she'll wake on her own. She doesn't move.

Moving past her, I head toward the sliding glass door. Slowly, quietly, I slide it open. I peer back at Regina, but she hasn't moved.

I tiptoe through the kitchen to the open dining area and living room. It's different from I remember. The renovations Brigit said Esme did have transformed it.

My knife sits in its sheath on my belt. I pat it to make sure it's still there.

I hear the stairs creak and I pause. It's dark in the house; the only light is the glow from the kitchen clock.

I see a small figure walk down the stairs. She looks around but doesn't see me. When I recognize who it is, I step forward out of the shadows.

"Lana, is that you?" I say, keeping my voice low and warm.

She spins around and sees me, surprised.

"Your mommy, Regina, invited me over here," I whisper. "I ran into her the other day, and we caught up. We used to be good friends, your mom and I."

She's groggy and tired, and in the dark she must sense something is off here, but she smiles. "Okay."

"I have a really cool boat out front. By the boathouse. Want to come see it? You can tell your cousins you saw it first."

"Um. . . ."

"We'll be quick."

I guide her gently to the door and open it softly. We slip into the night air. "A little farther," I say, taking her hand in mine.

When we approach the boat, I notice her look at it and then down at my belt. The knife.

"What's that for?" she asks.

"Nothing. Just for the wild animals," I say, but I see distrust on the shadow of her face. "Your mom told me to get your help, Lana. She wants you to come with me." I remember the puppy she was so adamant about seeing. "My puppy is sick, and we need your help."

I lift her up onto the boat, and her small body is stiff. I get into the boat too and my mind is racing. I'm almost there. If I bring Lana with me, back to the hotel, the family will give me whatever I want. Money. Family dinners. An invitation to the summer house every August. I'll insist they hold family dinners in my name. When Greg is in jail for Brigit's murder, I'll help Esme raise the twins, like a second mother to them. The possibilities are endless.

I'm brought back into the moment when I hear a splash. Lana has jumped out of the boat and is wading toward the shore, waist deep in the water. I to jump out too, but the water slows me down, and she's back on land. "Lana, I will speak to your mother," I hiss, but she doesn't stop. I pull the boat back to the beach and move closer to the house, watching. Lana opens the door and closes it behind her.

I stand there, contemplating if it's safe to go back in the house and grab one of the twins. In some ways, it's now or never. Lana will tell Regina what happened, and then I'll never get a chance like this again.

I wait to see if a light comes on inside the house. Eventually, it does. I move behind a bush and wait.

When the front door opens, I don't wait to see who comes out. I start running toward the path to the woods.

A flashlight shines on me.

"Hey," a woman's voice shouts. I hear the crunch of footsteps behind me, and the light is trailing me. I move as fast as

I can, but my wet clothes and aching muscles won't allow me to move as fast as I need to go.

As I approach the boat, the light flashes again.

"Hey! Stop," I hear the voice yell. "Now."

I start pushing the boat into the water. I'm out of here. Forget Esme, forget her twins. They can wait for another day.

The boat won't budge. I push again, harder, against the mud, and feel it move slightly.

Footsteps are fast approaching. In the darkness, I hear her before I see her.

I jump into the boat. As I reach for the oar, a hand reaches out and grabs it from me. We struggle and I knock her back as she rips the oar out of my hand.

"Wait right there. I'm calling the police. You took Lana! You tried to kidnap her."

She's picked the flashlight back up and shines it in my face.

"Alexis?" Her voice is shocked.

"Yes." I hold up my hands. "It's all a misunderstanding. Who's there? Put the flashlight down. I can explain."

She continues shining the light in my eyes, blinding me. Slowly, I grab for my knife.

"Stop, please," she says. "Let's talk about this. I need to know why you took Lana. What were you doing with her? I know you've been around the house, I heard you the other day, and saw your doll. Let's talk about this, Alexis. What's going on?"

At first I'm not certain I can make out the outline of the woman before me and then I recognize her voice. It's Piper.

Thank God it's Piper. I have a chance. Piper has always been weak. Soft. She's the least awful of my three sisters. But it's too late. I have to do this. It makes sense now. Killing Piper will make room for me in the family. Four sisters are too many. With Piper gone, I'll be the third sister.

I grab for the knife and unsheathe it, rushing toward the light with the knife held overhead.

I slash at her, and feel the knife connect with flesh. She's dropped the flashlight, it's hard to see. I think it's her torso I've hit, but she pulls her away from the knife and I see it's her arm. I pull the blade up again, readying it and aiming for her chest this time. I bring my arm down with my full force. Right when I think I'll connect, I feel the wooden oar crack into the side of my skull. I drop the knife and yell in agony.

My head is thrumming, but I look on the ground and reach for my knife again. I pick it up and spin around. Piper is there, panting, a look of terror in her eyes. I pull up the knife again and rush toward her.

Another *thwack*, and then I'm on the ground, the rocky shoreline beneath my face, the gravel biting into my cheek.

I feel her body on top of me.

"Why are you trying to destroy our family? Why are you attacking me?" she yells. I manage to wrestle her and turn over, but she's still on top of me. I see blood on her arm.

"Please, you have to believe me. It's Regina!" I say, panting for breath, the pain searing in my head. There's something sticky in my eye. I need medical help, and quickly. Piper will help me. "Listen. Regina invited me here. Ask her! She wanted me to help bring down Esme. She wanted money. For her part of the house. Ask her. Look at her phone! We've been talking for weeks! Planning."

"She'd never let you take Lana," she says, panting. "You're a liar."

"Regina would hardly notice! She's not a good mother to that girl. She's never around."

"Stay here. I'm calling the police. I feel the weight of Piper lift off me. I need to overpower her and stop her. Now.

I rally a last burst of energy. I lift up my head and shoulders, hoist myself up. From behind, I give her a shove with all my might.

I pull her by the arm and drag her into the water. I push her head under. She's surprisingly strong. I feel her fight back, her hands on my hair, on my wound. The searing pain is back. She's up and pushing me under the water.

I reach around and strike out at her, flailing my arms. I flash back to earlier this evening, with Brigit. But this time I'm the one being overpowered.

I can't breathe. My lungs feel like they'll burst, screaming for air.

"Leave me alone," she yells.

She eases up enough that I come up for air and catch a breath. Panting, I tell her, "Okay, okay. I promise. Call the police. I'll turn myself in." The moment I feel her ease up and start to move away from me, I reach toward her and with all my might, I pull as hard as I can at her hair. This is it. I'm going to have to drown her. I can't go to jail. I can't let her live. I need to take her place.

I pull her down, her body splashing into the water, and hold her head under the water again. But she manages to get up. Before I know it, she's pried my hands off her head, and is now pushing me back under.

The cold water hits my face, and I struggle against it. My lungs are going to burst. I flail my arms and legs, but it's useless. I hear her saying something above the water, yelling, but I can't hear her. I can't breathe. I try to open my mouth to cry out, and water enters, causing me to flail harder.

Air. I need air. The water is everywhere, and suddenly I'm back to that summer. I'm ten and Esme is racing ahead of me. I don't know if I can keep up with her. I keep swimming, exerting myself, but I can't catch her. The water goes over my head and the blackness is everywhere.

I want to go home. Go home to my dad and my mom. I can feel the dark water creeping into my lungs, but somehowI don't care. I'm in the sun, baking on the soft sand, and my mom and dad are there. I see my mom smile, arms outstretched, and I smile up at her.

But then she's still reaching for me. I stretch my hand out to be with her, but she's slipping away. Farther away. Suddenly she's gone, and my lungs feel like they're exploding. The sun and the warmth disappear. Agony. Pain is searing through every pore of my body, every cell is on fire. I'm helpless to stop it. Helpless, rage-filled, and impotent.

Then the blackness comes.

CHAPTER

55

Esme

I'M SITTING ON the front porch, and even in the shade, the noonday sun causes beads of sweat to gather on my brow. It could also be my nerves.

In the end, Piper and Paul agreed to at least keep Brielle and Gracey out back in the pool with them while I wait out front for the officers to come to arrest Greg. I thanked Piper, telling her I owed her.

"You do. I'm happy to help with Brielle and Gracey; we'll take care of them while you deal with Greg. But promise me something?" Her voice changes.

"Yes, anything."

"When I need your help, you'll be there for me. Whatever it takes. You help me. You help Preston. Protect him as if he were your own."

"Of course," I say, putting my arms around her. "We're family."

Regina, on the other hand, was not as helpful, but then what did I expect? Earlier this morning, I took her aside and told her, quietly, what is happening with Greg's arrest. Regina's face went blank, and she nodded. "Today? They're arresting him, like, now?" she said.

"Yes, likely with a search warrant as well," I said. "So if you could keep Lana out back by the pool, or better yet take all the girls into town, that would be great."

She didn't even answer me. She ran upstairs to her room. As if it were she who had something to hide.

I shake my head. Waiting for something I don't want to happen is a cruel trick. I abandon my post out front, walk into the house and peer out back. Regina, Bryce, and Lana are in the pool, and so are Paul and Piper, the baby, and my girls. I wave at them, and return to the front porch to wait.

I see Greg on the couch, oblivious that he's spending his last moments of freedom scrolling the internet. Just then, I hear the crunch of tires.

When the first police car arrives, a gray SUV, my heart beats out of my chest with such ferocity I'm sure they can hear it.

"Greg, I need you here," I say as I open the front door and step outside.

"We're looking for Greg Wimberly, ma'am."

"Yes, he's inside." I see the gun at his hip, and raise my hands in fear. I don't want to get shot.

Another officer joins him, and they approach, their black boots clanking on the wood of my porch. "Greg Wimberly, police."

Within seconds, Greg is at the door.

"What's this about?" he asks. He catches my eye, and I shake my head no at him. I can't bear to watch. I look away, out to the water.

They pull him onto the porch. "Greg Wimberly, you're under arrest for the murder of Brigit Max. You have the right to remain silent." They turn Greg around, against the siding of the house. The officer takes his hands behind his back and secures them with handcuffs as he reads him his Miranda rights.

I move closer to him, slowly.

"What is this about?" he says, fear entrenched in his eyes.

"Greg, don't say anything. Alan is on his way; he's going to get you out right away. Do not speak to anyone. Understand? Wait for Alan. He has a plan." The last I whisper.

He struggles to understand, shaking his head. The officers move him toward the car. His face is drained of all color.

"I love you, Greg. I'll meet you at the station, with Alan. You'll be home soon. I promise."

It's a promise I plan to keep; I just don't know how. Greg has done so much to put himself in this position. He lied. He cheated. Anyone can see the evidence doesn't look good for either of us.

But I know my husband isn't a murderer. He's the father of my children, and I need to clear his name.

As the officers duck Greg's head into the back of the SUV and then climb into the front, I watch helplessly, my arms hugged to my chest.

They pull out of the driveway, and just as they are out of sight, another large vehicle appears at the edge of our drive. As it approaches, I see that it's a police SUV with a black boat hitched to the back. A second police SUV follows behind it. They pull into my driveway, and two men holding black wetsuits get out. The first man pulls out a tank from the back and begins to hook it up. The other man does the same with a second large tank.

When I spy officer Ben Sherman emerging from the second car, I rush to him.

"They arrested Greg."

"I'm aware." His expression is not unkind, but he says no more.

I motion to the men and their equipment. "What's happening here?"

His radio squawks, and he listens in before turning back to me. "We were cleared for sonar use on the lake yesterday afternoon. Yesterday morning, the helicopter's sonar detected an object that we believe to be a body. We have reason to suspect there is a second victim in the lake."

I'm so numb from Greg being arrested that I hardly register what he's saying. "So these men are . . . ?"

"These men are divers, ma'am. They're searching for human remains."

I shake my head, not registering what he means. "Please, do they know who they're looking for?"

The knuckles of my balled fists are white. I need to know what's going on.

He looks down at me, and I see a flash of genuine pity.

"You didn't hear it from me," he lowers his voice. "There's a guest at the Bergamont who never checked out of her hotel room; her belongings are still there. The boat she rented was never returned—we're checking that against the boats you have here on your property." He shifts uncomfortably, as if he knows he shouldn't be sharing this with me, but he continues. "If another woman is in that lake, as we believe her to be, well. We may be looking at a double homicide."

CHAPTER

56

Piper

WE'RE OUTSIDE IN the pool. The girls are swimming with Paul and Bryce, while I wade on the steps with Preston in his blue baby float.

Today is surreal. Everything is changed.

There's a loud banging and I hear shouts. It's happening. The police are here. I get up, lifting Preston with me, and I turn up the music on the loudspeaker. The children don't seem to notice the commotion at the front of the house.

I wrap Preston in a blanket and tuck him on my lap, sitting on a lawn chair. I can see the pool, but I can't tell what's happening in front of the house.

A cold fear settles into my chest. Will it be me they come for next?

Two nights ago, I drowned Alexis here at the lake. I didn't mean to—I was trying to stop her from attacking me. But it happened. It feels like it could have been a dream. I'm half-convinced it was just a nightmare. But now Greg is getting arrested for the murder of Brigit.

I look down at my baby, smiling up at me. His cheeks are so round and deliciously kissable. I was just trying to save myself from Alexis; if I were dead, I couldn't be his mother.

I was in a state of shock and of self-preservation. There's no doubt in my mind that if I hadn't drowned Alexis, she would have killed me. She'd already tried to kidnap Lana. The look in her eyes was unmistakable. She wasn't going to let me go alive.

When I held her down, I kept shouting, "Stop fighting me, stop fighting me!" But the more I shouted, the harder she fought. When she finally went still, I flipped her over. But she wasn't moving at all. She wasn't breathing. I tried to give her CPR, pulling her to shore and pressing her chest with my fingers laced together. But she didn't move.

I should've called for help. But then rather than call the police, I did the wrong thing.

I panicked. I was scared I'd go to prison.

I ran home, back to the house, convinced that if I just left her there, she'd disappear. It'd go away like—I couldn't bear to be hauled away from Preston. He needs me. So I left her body there, the water lapping at her lifeless body. And I ran.

I ran to the house, and I shut the front door, locking it behind me.

I peeled off my clothes and saw blood dripping from where she stabbed me. The gash in my arm was about two inches long and quite deep. I bandaged it up then gathered up my bloody shirt and wet pajamas and threw them into the washer. I changed into dry clothes, and I fell into a fitful sleep on the couch.

I shudder now at the memory.

The sliding glass door opens. Esme emerges, her face pinched with stress. "They've taken Greg to the station. Divers are at the lake. They think there's a second body."

A wave of sickness permeates through my entire body.

Paul heads over to us, wrapping a towel around his waist. "What's the news?"

"I'm heading down to the station to try to get bail. Our attorney Alan isn't answering his phone. But I can't just leave Greg there. Thank you for watching the girls. Please keep me posted on the divers."

The news about the divers sends a punch to my gut and my heart is beating wildly. Alexis's body will be found. It's simply a matter of time. I'd hoped she would stay buried in the dark water forever.

A plan starts to form in my mind. I'll go pack our bags; they're pretty much ready to go. I'll tell Regina she needs to watch Brielle and Gracey, it's urgent. Then Paul, Preston, and I will get in our car. But we won't drive home. We'll head to the bank first and get some cash; not too much, so as not to arouse suspicion. Then we'll head north. To Canada. We'll cross the border.

We can buy a house somewhere off the grid. Wire cash. Use false names. Start over.

But then I fast forward. I try to envision our future in this new life. Paul and I wanted to start trying for another child. That process may not be easy, again. We may need medical intervention. But that would be impossible if we're on the run.

And what kind of life would that be for us, for Preston, hiding away? Never being able to freely travel, or see family? Always hiding in the shadows, afraid to socialize, afraid to reveal our real names, or who we are, or why we moved there?

It's a death sentence. I can't rob Preston of his opportunity for a real life. A life he chooses. One where he can be anything he wants. Attend any college he wants; pursue any career he aspires to be in. Not a life on the run.

And Paul. What about seeing his family? His parents are getting older, and may need our help with care soon. And what about Paul's freedom, his career? I don't know what we'd do for work in Canada. Would he start another restaurant from scratch, gathering new investors, building a new name for himself in the culinary world? That could take years, and might risk us getting caught.

If not a career in the restaurant business, how would we survive financially? That's all he knows. Our savings would run out eventually.

But what's the alternative? Just stay quiet and hope they don't find out it was me? I don't know enough about forensic evidence to know if they could trace Alexis's death to me. But I know from Esme that they are planning on giving us all DNA tests, so they'll at least try.

And I'm a terrible liar. If I'm questioned with any kind of intensity or force, it will be hard for me to withstand the pressure without telling the truth.

But then I look at Preston. His sleeping face is angelic. I stand up from the pool chair and hand him to Paul, who frowns. "Everything okay?" he says.

"No," I say. "We need to talk."

He squints at me. "What's going on?"

"I'm in big trouble," I say. "Divers are scanning the lake right now out front. The police have identified a possible body on sonar. Remember how I thought the dead body in the lake was our cousin, Alexis?"

He nods.

"Well, I'm positive that the body they recover today will be Alexis."

His face looks ashen. "What are you trying to say?"

"Remember when I said Lana woke me up, and she was all wet?"

"I do."

"Well, when she woke me up that night, she said she was afraid of the lady in the lake. She said, 'She's still out there.' I wrapped her in a blanket, grabbed our flashlight, and told her to wait for me. When I went outside, I saw a woman. It was Alexis. She turned to flee, but I followed her to a boat. I asked why she took Lana. She attacked me. Forcefully. With a knife." I hold up my arm and roll up my sleeve, showing him the bandage. "Then I fought back. I overpowered her. When I agreed to let her go, to call the cops, she went for me again. She tried to drown me. She wanted to kill me. I caught her trying to take Lana, she must've been the one who took Preston and put the note, 'Watching,' on him." I swallow. "She was attacking me. Preston needs me, he needs his mommy . . . She just kept coming at me. So then I held her underwater. Not to kill her, just to make her stop. I yelled at her to please stop, but she kept fighting me. I held her until she stopped fighting. But when I turned her over, she wouldn't move. I took her to the shore, tried to do CPR. But it was too late."

I don't tell him about the burst of strength I got at the end. How she kept attacking me, and attacking me, and something within me snapped. All the years I've put up with everyone always coming at me, dismissing me, taking advantage of me, and I always let it go. I forgive, and I let people beat me down. But enough is enough. If I didn't defend myself, Alexis would have killed me. And like my therapist said I would, I let all that emotion, finally, burst forth. I stood up for myself, letting years of pent-up rage and emotion out, my body stronger than I ever knew it could be. I wasn't going to be the victim anymore. Preston needed me too much. I didn't mean to kill her, just stop her. I wasn't going to let her kill me.

"This is insane. Why didn't you tell me?"

I wring my hands. "I don't know. I should have. I was scared the police would take me away from him." I gesture to our baby.

He groans in frustration. "Piper . . ." But he doesn't finish, just shakes his head.

"And now they've arrested Greg for Brigit's murder," I say. "They're closing in. If they know Greg murdered his nanny, they must be further in the investigation that we thought. The sonar will find Alexis. I have to tell them the truth. Anyway, what's the alternative? Run? Or say nothing and live my life paranoid, worrying the other shoe will drop?"

"I don't know. I don't know! You should have told me. We could have called the police. What did you do . . . after?"

"That's the thing. I panicked. I just left her there. I ran back to the house. I bandaged my arm, put on dry clothes, and fell asleep on the couch."

"That's a crime," he says, looking at me. "Killing her may have been self-defense. But to leave a dead woman and not report it? I'm pretty sure that's not allowed, nor is withholding evidence from the police."

"I know," I say. "I see that now. But I was terrified."

For the first time since it happened, the reality of my situation sinks in. The reality of what I've done.

"I don't know what to do," I say. He wraps his arm around me, the other one holding Preston. I lay my head on his shoulder, trying to gather my courage. I'm going to need every ounce of strength for what comes next.

CHAPTER

57

Esme

THE STATION IS quaint in a way that only a vacation town police station could be. It's adorned with old-fashioned wood trim and fresh flowers hanging in baskets. The sidewalk has black streetlamps dotted against the storefronts.

Inside, the wooden floors are polished and the front desk sits in the center of a large room. The desk is encased in glass, with a metal microphone for speaking.

The man at the front desk greets me without a smile. "I'm Esme Wimberly. My husband Greg Wimberly is here . . . in custody."

He nods.

"I'd like to post bail for him."

A thinly veiled smile crosses his face. "Bail hearing will be set tomorrow," he says.

"Our attorney said he can get a bail hearing today," I say.

"Officer Ben Sherman is in charge of the hearing, and he's out for the rest of the day. You'll have to wait until he's in."

"But our attorney assured me it would be today."

"Is your attorney present?" He looks around at the empty station waiting area.

I put up my finger. "One moment."

Alan should be here by now, but I haven't been able to reach him. Grabbing my phone, I dial Alan for the third time today. Finally, he picks up.

"Where are you?" I say, clutching my phone.

"Esme, listen. My phone's been ringing off the hook. This case is already garnering national attention. A neurosurgeon accused of killing his mistress while on vacation with his family. AP, *New York Times*, all the major TV networks are calling the hospital where Greg works, and now they're calling me. They're outside my office. They'll be up there soon, I'm sure, so prepare yourself and your family."

There are about to be dozens of national news cameras in my face. I run my hand over my head to smooth my hair, noting that my makeup has all but rubbed off by now, wishing I'd thought to reapply.

"You'll be up here, soon, though, right? How far away are you? They're saying bail isn't until tomorrow. He can't sit all night in a jail cell."

There's a pause. "Esme," he says, and I don't like the tone of his voice. "You know I'd do anything for you. Your dad was my dear friend, and I've always helped your family. But this case, it's going to require more than I can provide. You need a criminal defense attorney."

"You've defended criminals."

"White collar criminals, Esme. Tax evasion. Fraud. This is murder he's being charged with."

I turn and look back at the guard, and lower my voice again. "So what am I supposed to do? When will you be here so we can discuss this in person?"

"I'm not coming."

"You're just leaving us here?"

"I can do more good from here. I've put in calls to the best law firms in the country. I'll do what I can to find you the right person for the job."

I look around helplessly. "And what do I do until then?"

"You have to wait. The bail hearing will be tomorrow. Worst case scenario, they'll assign him a public defender until he can obtain his own council. He could still make bail tomorrow." He sounds doubtful.

I want to throw the phone. *So much for loyalty, Alan.* "Thanks for your help," I say through gritted teeth, trying to hide my growing panic. "Please call me when you find a suitable defense lawyer for us."

I hang up. The room is quiet, and the officer at the front desk doesn't bother looking at me. I'm alone. My husband is in jail, my attorney isn't coming.

Times like these, I wish my mom was here. She always knew what to do in an emergency. My dad, too.

The door opens to the police station, and a nice-looking young man walks in. I half smile. Maybe he's a defense attorney, here to help already.

"Mrs. Wimberly?" he says.

"Yes?" I say expectantly.

His face lights up, and he motions with his hand to someone outside, and the door swings open. A man carrying a black camera with a light on top enters the room, the camera pointed at me.

"Mrs. Wimberly," the handsome young man says to me. "How does it feel that your husband conducted an affair with a gorgeous girl half your age? A young woman who has been found dead outside your family summer house, who he's accused of murdering?"

My mouth drops open, but no sound comes out. Why would he attack me like this? Humiliate me? For all the world to see? My cheeks flush red.

My husband is a respected neurosurgeon. People are kind to me. They respect me. They give me what I want and bend over backward when I'm displeased.

But this man. This horrid, awful man, how dare he?

He takes a step closer, a smug expression on his chiseled face. "Was it a loveless marriage? Sexless?"

The heat rises again in my face and I turn from him. I quickly approach the officer behind the glass at the front desk. I can feel the reporter close behind me, and the camera pans around to follow the entire interaction, the camera pointed so close to my face that it feels like it will hit me.

"This man is harassing me," I say.

The officer looks up blandly at the reporter. He motions to him. "Wait outside."

The reporter nods. "We'll talk more outside, Mrs. Howard," he says, as if we're good friends. The nerve.

When it becomes clear, after an hour of waiting, that no bail hearing will happen today, I take a deep breath. I go into the bathroom. I apply a bit of concealer and lipstick, digging through my purse for my blush compact. I do my best, and then I stare at my reflection in the mirror.

This time, when I push open the doors to leave the station, and the young man yells questions at me, I'm ready. "I have no comment," I say in my best, most injured voice.

I am the victim here. And the world will see me with my head held high, bearing my burden with grace and beauty.

CHAPTER

58

Regina

THE GIRLS ARE exhausted, cheeks pink from a day in the sun. Paul is grilling hot dogs and burgers outside.

"Lana," I say, flipping on the television in the living room. "Why don't you guys watch a movie? Dinner will be ready soon."

The girls climb onto the couch. With them occupied, I turn my attention to outside. The last of the diving vans is pulling away. I see Officer Ben Sherman outside, and much as I hate to do it, I know I need to talk to him.

"Ben," I call. "Er, Officer Sherman," I correct myself when I see his furrowed brow. I come down the porch steps toward where he stands by his patrol SUV.

"Regina. What do you need?" He squares his shoulders.

"Can you tell me what's going on? The divers were looking for another body?"

"The search was called off."

"Oh. Why? Did they find something?" I take a step closer.

"I'm not able to discuss that," he says shortly.

"I just thought," I look at him, trying to conjure up the friendliness we had years ago, "since I know you, you could, you know, fill me in."

His face hardens. "That would be convenient for you, now, to cash in on our relationship. Now that you need a favor." His words come out bitter.

"No, man. Hey." I take a step back. "Sorry."

He looks me up and down, as if considering something. He puffs out his chest. "Look, I have business to attend to. It's a busy time for me, obviously," he says.

"Okay. Thanks anyway," I say. As I turn to go, I catch sight of movement in his car. From my vantage point, I see the light hair of a woman in his passenger seat, but she's facing away from me.

Is that Esme? I turn again to look at Ben, the question on my lips. He looks at me triumphantly, and I don't like his expression at all. I wave and turn around quickly, making my way back to the house.

Inside, I peer out the window. I watch Ben get in his patrol car and lean in. His windows are tinted and from this distance, I can't tell what's happening or who is next to him. The car starts and he pulls around, and drives off.

"Any news?" Bryce asks, sideling up to me.

"No." I roll my eyes.

Piper comes inside. "Dinner will be ready in five," she says, and I nod.

I hear another car approach, and when I look out the window again, I expect to see Ben's police SUV returning. Instead, I see a black SUV and a gray van behind it. Behind the van is a sedan.

The cars pull to a stop, but no one gets out.

"Bryce, look at this," I say. "What's this all about?"

He shrugs. "Dunno."

"Can you go see?" I give him a little push toward the door.

I watch as he walks outside. A handsome young man gets out of the black SUV. Behind him, from the van, a man with a camera gets out. I know immediately what is happening. I have to get Bryce out of there.

"Bryce," I call, and sprint toward him from the steps. I can see him opening his mouth, talking to the man, a microphone to his lips. "Bryce, stop," I say, and I pull at his sleeve. He looks down at me like I'm a stranger assaulting him.

"What gives?" he says.

"Don't talk to them," I say, giving him a death stare. "Come on."

Reluctantly, he follows me inside the house. The man follows us, shouting questions at us, asking which sister I am and if we have anything to do with Brigit Max's murder.

Once inside, I slam the door shut in his face.

"Bryce, what was that?"

"You told me to go check it out."

"I didn't know it was reporters. Never talk to them. Anything we say can be totally bent and twisted the wrong way. Come on."

I pull the curtains shut over the two large front windows. What a pain. The other reporters have made their way out of their cars. They have coffee and to go food containers. They look like they're settling in for a long stay.

"Just what we need."

"What is?" It's Piper behind me.

I open the curtains and show her. She hugs her arms around her waist and moves away from the window.

"It's about to get ugly," she says.

CHAPTER

59

Piper

I bite into my hamburger, forcing myself to eat at least a few bites, grateful that Paul has grilled us all a nice meal despite these circumstances. We all eat our hot dogs and hamburgers in silence inside the house, the only sounds coming from Preston from his bouncer chair, getting increasingly fussy.

"I don't like hot dogs." Brielle pushes her plate away. "Where's Mom and Dad?" she says. "I want to go swim."

Ever since the reporters showed up, we've all been trapped inside. "I know you're antsy to get outside," Paul says gently, "but we need to stay in here for a while."

"I'm bored," Gracey chimes in.

Preston's fussing turns into a low cry. It's about to get louder if I don't head it off by picking him up.

"Girls, have some food, please," Regina says, and I note she's filled up on margarita mixture and poured herself another large cocktail.

My stomach churns with the lone bite of hamburger mixing with acid in my stomach. Every moment, I expect the police to come back to the door, banging it down, shouting at me to put my hands behind my back. Reading me my rights like they did to Greg. I feel so sick it's almost past the point of physical exhaustion.

I lay Preston against my chest and hold him close, inhaling the clean scent of him.

Brielle murmurs something to Lana, and she calls out to Regina, "Mom, Brielle's making fun of me," she says.

"Be nice," Regina says. Both Esme and Greg are gone, and without their parents' supervision, and being cramped inside the house, the twins' behavior is worsening.

"Maybe someone can take them into the game room?" I suggest. Paul starts collecting dinner plates, asking if the girls are finished. "I'll clean up and then take them," he offers, and I nod gratefully back.

There's a sharp rap on the door, coming from the garage, and I almost lose my grip on Preston, I jump so hard.

My eyes meet with Paul's, a deer in headlights, and he nods. He opens the door to the garage, and I see his shoulders relax.

Esme walks in, slamming the garage door behind her.

"Awful people," she says, her face slightly flushed. "Bottom feeders, is what they are. I could hardly park my car. They tried to enter the garage. That's trespassing! Is their whole life simply to sit out there and hound us?" she scoffs.

Brielle and Gracey run up to her and tug on her. "Mommy, we're bored. We want to go outside, but Uncle Paul is making us stay inside."

"Listen to your uncle," she says sternly. "You mustn't go outside. There are bad people out there."

The girls quiet down, but Brielle kicks at the couch and pouts.

Paul comes to the rescue. "Want me to show you how to play checkers?" The girls don't look very excited, but they reluctantly follow him into the game room.

"What happened with the divers?" Esme asks, looking around at us.

"Ben said they were finished," Regina says.

"Did they find anything?" she asks.

I sit on the couch and feel like I might faint. I grip onto Preston tightly.

"You got more out of him that I did. When he was wrapping up, he was very tight lipped. Acted very rude, considering our history. If they found anything, he didn't tell me."

"What history?" Bryce says.

"I told you I used to know him," Regina says, annoyed. "We went out once. A teenage fling."

Bryce puffs out his chest at that, frowning. "You didn't tell me that part."

Esme interrupts. "Whatever, the point is we need to figure out if they found a body or not. Whoever killed Brigit could be who they're looking for. We need to build a case for Greg's innocence, an alternative to him murdering her."

"What's happening with Greg?" Bryce asks.

"It's really bad," Esme says, sitting on the couch. We all move toward the sitting area and gather around her. "The bail hearing isn't until tomorrow at the earliest, they haven't even set it yet. Alan isn't coming up. He doesn't want to represent him. Says he needs a criminal defense lawyer."

"Alan is a criminal lawyer," Regina and I both say.

"But not," she says it quietly, "murder."

"Maybe Alan thinks he's guilty," Regina says, taking a sip of her drink. "Doesn't want to go down with a sinking ship."

Esme's eyes look like they might burst into flames. "What the hell is wrong with you?"

Regina holds up her hands. "He slept with her, right? You told me yourself. And she's dead, here outside our house. Looks bad."

"I've always known you were lazy, and stupid, but now I see you're also disloyal." The vein in Esme's neck is throbbing and her face is flushed. "I wish I never gave you a cent. But you'll blow through that money, and be evicted out of your home soon enough."

Bryce looks nonplussed. He catches my eye and backs out of the room without a word.

"At least my husband isn't a murderer," Regina says and turns to me. "Piper, tell her. Even you, always nice and polite, can't defend Greg."

"I have my own worries," I say. "Not that you two would ever notice anyone but yourselves."

Esme turns to me, probably mad I didn't defend her. "Like what? We know, we know, having a baby is tough." She rolls her eyes.

"How about that the body out there in the lake is Alexis. And I did it," I say quietly. It just spills out.

"What?" they both say.

It's all too much. I get up and take Preston upstairs and place him in his crib. I feel like I'm losing it. I leave him in the room, grab the monitor and close the door behind me. My throat is on fire, trying to hold back my tears.

I walk downstairs and my sisters are staring at me.

"Piper, what the hell are you talking about?" Regina says.

I tell them about Lana waking me up and what happened when I went out to confront Alexis. How it was self-defense, but I had to stop her.

"Are you sure you're not having one of your episodes?" Esme says. "Maybe the pill I gave you had an adverse effect on you?"

"I wish. I'm sure it's real."

My sisters both stare at me. "Piper, this is serious. They're searching the lake. You'll be caught."

"You think I don't know that?"

Esme looks slightly hopeful. "Did you kill Brigit that night, too?"

"As much as you'd like that, Esme, no. I am certain I didn't kill Brigit. I didn't even know her, never met her. Did you kill her?" I snap.

"Of course not," she snaps back.

"The worst part is I know why Alexis was here. After all these years. And why she would try to take Lana." I look at my sisters. "You guys are not being honest with me."

Regina stares at the floor with a guilty expression.

I say, "Regina—just spit it out. Alexis already told me."

Regina looks like a trapped animal. "Okay. Okay. I invited Alexis over. She was helping me get money from Esme, to sell my portion of the house. And I knew it would piss off Esme to have her here."

Esme explodes. "What? You've been best buddies with Alexis behind our backs? She's been poisoning you, you know. Mom always told me to watch out for her. She tried to kill Piper. She's insane! And you let her into our house?"

"Exactly!" I add. I feel my voice rising, all the anger I've held in for the past few days—years in the making—finally erupting. "If you hadn't brought her here, Regina, she wouldn't have attacked me. Now I'm going to prison, and Preston won't have a mother. I hate you," I practically spit the words. "You were always a screw up. Now you've screwed up my life, too."

Regina looks like she's been slapped. "At least you're finally being honest," she says.

I turn to Esme, and can hear the anxiety in my voice. "You said you'll take care of Preston for me, right? Like he's your own?"

"I will, don't worry," Esme says, but the way she won't meet my gaze makes me wonder. "But there's something you should know. Maybe it will help in your defense, if the police connect you to Alexis's death."

"What?" I say, afraid to get my hopes up.

"It's about Alexis. Who she was. When her mom was dying in the hospital, Mom took me aside. She said that Alexis was our half sister. Dad had a one-night thing with Mom's sister. Alexis was the product of that."

My mouth drops open. My dad, who was always a gentle, faithful man. It's hard to believe. But worse is that Alexis was our half sister. The way we treated her. I cover my mouth.

"No wonder she hated us. Esme, you should have told us. We were her only family, and look what we did to her. No wonder she followed Regina around, trying to get close to us. We ruined her life. And Regina let her destroy us."

"Hey," Regina says, offended. "More like I'm the only cool sister she could relate to. You guys are dreadful."

Esme laughs, a hollow sound. "Mom said it all along. When I was ten, she bent down and she told me the truth about Alexis. I'll never forget her words. She said, 'My sister, and that child, Alexis, are wicked. They will tear apart the love and strength and unity of our family, if we let them. I tell you this so that you may be prepared: You must keep Alexis at arm's length. Do not let her in your life, or your sisters' lives. It can only end in heartache. My sister is no longer my sister. Her betrayal severed that tie.'"

"Mom said that her sister was an addict, and that's all she cared about. Mom's one wish was that we never let Alexis come between us—and look, that's exactly what she did! All Mom wanted was for us to come every year to the summer house. Two weeks a year. Be close sisters. Have a strong bond. But because of Alexis, that's a far cry from reality."

Esme continues, and I sit listening with my mouth open trying to process what she's saying. "And Alexis, just like Mom said, has been trying to destroy my family. She was here—she threatened Greg and I about Brigit. She's the reason he's in jail."

"I wouldn't go that far," Regina retorts.

"Just wait, Regina, listen. She's ruined my life. She's ruined Piper's. She tried to take Lana from you. She wanted to destroy us. We should be thankful Piper took care of her."

"I can't believe Mom didn't take Alexis in," I say, narrowing my eyes. "I can't imagine. It's like our situation. Will you keep your word, and care for Preston, Esme? If I go to prison?" I glance over at Regina, knowing she'll be worthless.

Esme's silence speaks volumes.

I throw my hands in the air. "Thank goodness Preston has Paul," I say. "You two won't be bothered with him." I sit down and cover my ears, feeling like my head is about to explode.

Everything is a mess. If I'd had any idea this trip would turn out the way it has, I would never have come. Stipulation or not. Was it only a week ago that everything was fine? My biggest worry was if Preston would sleep an extra hour or not.

A sharp knock rings out at the front door.

"Paparazzi again," Esme says, cursing.

The knock sounds again, more insistent this time. It must be the police coming for me. I feel like I might actually faint.

A voice calls out. A woman's voice. "You're going to want to open the door," she calls from outside the house. I recognize her voice instantly.

And that's when everything changes.

CHAPTER

60

Esme

My eyes shoot to the door, then back to my sisters. They heard her, too. I walk to the door. I open it half an inch. I inhale sharply when I see her.

"Hurry up, before I start talking to the media," she says. I feel my nostrils flare as I open the door.

Alexis saunters in the house. Her hair is much lighter, like she's copying me, and she's dressed very expensively. Her perfume wafts over me as she walks into the house and makes herself at home on the sectional sofa.

"Not a very warm reception from my sisters," she says. "Those paps out there would love to interview me. But that just wouldn't be right, to hang my family out to dry."

"Alexis." Piper's face is white. She looks afraid, but there is relief there, too. "Esme, I—I think we need to call the police," she says, taking a step back. "She's dangerous." Her hands are shaking, and she reaches for her phone.

"Piper, there's no need for that. The police are right outside, with me," Alexis says.

"What?" Piper says. I open the curtain and outside, sure enough, is a gray police SUV. I see an officer leaning against it, staring up at the house.

"Is that Officer Sherman?" I ask.

"I call him Ben," she says with a wink. "He's very protective of me. You're welcome to talk with him, but I think he'd be more likely to arrest you than me."

Piper scoots around the edge of the living room to look out the window herself, and Regina joins her.

"Why is he here? What's going on? I thought you were dead, Alexis," Piper says.

"Yes, you tried to kill me. Really nasty. But don't worry, I didn't tell Ben the extent of your vicious attack on me."

"Did you tell him how you attacked me first?" Piper says, and when Alexis ignores her, she continues. "What about the sonar, the body in the lake? What was that all about?"

"I don't know," Alexis says, glancing at each of us. "Did you guys kill someone else?"

"Of course not," I say, and immediately regret sinking to her level to even answer her.

"Well, when I heard from the hotel that Sergeant Ben was looking for me, I came to him here. I explained that I've been staying out of the way of my sisters because I'm fearful of you guys. But that I'd never want money wasted on divers searching the lake. He really appreciated my bravery for coming to him. It was an instant connection with us."

Alexis stretches her pouty lips into a sly smile and continues. "He understands strained family relations can quickly turn messy, especially, he said, with you three who think you're so high and mighty. He even shared with me how his ex-wife—soon to be ex—was making his life difficult. I offered to pay her a visit. And guess what? I bet it'll work out, and she'll agree to settle with no alimony."

Piper's voice raises an octave. "Guys, we need help from the police. Someone who's not Ben. She's dangerous. She tried to take Lana in the middle of the night. Tell them, Regina. She attacked me, over and over again." She holds up her arm. "She cut me with a knife."

Regina seems to have lost her voice. "Yeah, it's, uh—"

Alexis cuts her off. "Not true. Regina invited me over. I have the phone records to prove it. When I arrived, she was asleep drooling on herself by the pool. Lana woke up and was trying to wake her poor mom up. Lana fell in the pool, and I jumped in to save her. Who would believe you over me, Piper? You have a history of mental illness, and didn't you see things that weren't real? I tried to tell you I was helping Lana, but you were out of it." She shrugs. "It's a good thing I'm forgiving. I forgive you. And I have no idea how you cut yourself, but it wasn't me."

"Enough," I say. "Alexis, I will call the police myself. You have a lot of explaining to do. You followed me, and at the hotel you told me something would happen to Brigit! And that blame would be placed on Greg and me. You're behind all of this somehow."

Alexis smiles calmly and shakes her head. "I have no idea what you're talking about. I never said any such thing. I've never met her. Brigit, did you say her name was? Is that the one Ben was telling me about? Your nanny who Greg slept with and killed?" She blinks at me and I want to smash her face in.

She leans in toward me. "Though I will admit," she says and raises her hands up, "I'm not surprised to find that Greg moved on after our affair. You know we had a thing, right? For about seven months, right after Audry's funeral. He couldn't keep his hands off me. I broke it off. I'm glad he found someone else to fulfill him, since you couldn't. Shame he killed her. Seems I dodged a real bullet."

I see red. My body lunges toward Alexis, and my hands are on her. I feel her small, delicate neck and I wrap my fingers as tightly as I can, squeezing. I smell her perfume and I see her eyes bulging and I've never hated a human so much in my life. I hold onto her neck and everything goes black.

* * *

When I come to, Alexis is on the couch with a cold compress on her neck. Piper is sitting in the corner of the opposite couch, and Regina is next to Alexis saying something.

"What happened?" I ask.

"You tried to kill me, you fool," Alexis says indignantly. "Our sisters had to pry you off me like a wild animal."

"Stop saying that. You're not one of us," I hiss.

"But I am. We share blood. We've even shared your husband."

I clasp my hands together, willing myself to stay calm. I can't go to prison, as well as my husband. *My husband.* I cannot believe he slept with Alexis. And yet, part of me knew. When he said he paid her off, and his eye twitched, I knew he was lying . . .

"You need to leave," I say to Alexis. "Haven't you done enough?"

She sets down the ice pack and smooths her hair. "I do have a date with Ben, he's waiting, so I have to be going. But I wanted you all to know that I don't hold any hard feelings. We're sisters. We need to stick together."

Piper and I exchange looks, and Regina doesn't bat an eye.

"I'll see if I can get any helpful information from Ben." She stands up. "He said it's pretty conclusive that it's Greg." She pauses. "It's always the lover . . . a cliché, but so true."

One year later

Piper

PRESTON WADDLES OUT of the car and I follow close behind him. "Not so fast, mister," I say, scooping him in my arms. Paul carries our bags to the door.

We're at the summer house. After everything that happened last summer, Esme has had contractors out here and is talking about redoing the entire thing again, new paint, new kitchen concept, reconfiguring the upstairs, the works.

It's August now, almost a year since that chapter in our lives. I knock on the oak door, the memories flooding back. Esme is inside, greets me at the door. Preston runs in, and Paul follows after him.

Esme joins me on the porch. She embraces me in a quick hug. "Sit," she says, motioning to the deck chair. She looks different, more serious. The past year has taken a toll on her. Greg, the trial, the constant media scrutiny.

Greg's new attorney was a top dog, a shark known to defend—and win—all his high-profile criminal cases. When the jury came back hung, Esme called me with the news. Paul and I drove up for the judge's final comments to close the trial and rule on whether there would be a new one. The judge said that the prosecutors were declining to retry the case; Greg was free to go. After almost a year in jail, his skin sallow and his hair completely gray, he looked like a changed man.

The money for the trial, and, some have speculated, to pay a lone juror to refuse to convict him, set them back. Esme had a nest egg, and Greg's family had some dwindling family fortune left, but I know they're hurting financially. Greg lost his job at the hospital, and they just moved here, to our summer house, to live full time. I don't think they can afford anyplace else. Certainly not the lifestyle Esme was accustomed to before. She already bought out Regina last year, and Paul and I don't mind if they stay here full time. I'm not totally sure how they'll afford a second remodel, or if it's just talk from Esme, the reality of her situation not fully fitting in with the lifestyle she's accustomed to.

"How are you guys doing?" I say. I can't even imagine the stress she must've gone through this year. Especially Esme, whose image and social standing mean so much to her. It must have been hard when all her so-called friends turned their backs on her, sources close to her sold stories to the press, and the invites to social events dried up.

She sits very still. Her hair is still shiny and coiffed, and she's wearing a nice dress and makeup. "We're doing well. Being at the summer house is a nice change for our family. The girls will go to the local school. Greg is at an interview right now at the urgent care center. The media attention has died down, on to the next big story. Our lives will resume. Normalcy. Peace and quiet."

She stiffens as her eyes pan over to the left, at the end of the lake, where there are several cars. There's a slab of cement framed in the ground, and several workers with hard hats are hoisting up lumber and nailing the frame up around it. It looks to be a large structure.

"That," she says, her voice steely, "however, is unacceptable."

"What is it?" I ask her.

"It's zoned as a residential structure," she says.

"It's so large."

"It's a monstrosity, and ruins our pristine view, and is totally illegitimate. I'm having Alan pull the papers as we speak. Apparently, someone in local government pulled strings to get it approved. We'll have to contest it. I can't wait to have them tear it down and replant the vegetation, at their expense. This won't do at all." She shakes her head.

"What about you?" she says, glancing at me for the first time. "You and Paul, Preston? All is well? I haven't seen you since the hearing." She reaches out a hand. "Thank you for being there for us, by the way."

"Of course. We're good. Paul is actually thinking of opening up another restaurant."

"Is that right?" She raises her eyebrows. "Where?"

"Right here," I say. "In town. We were thinking maybe it would be nice to move out here, too. To our own place," I'm quick to add. I can see the panic in her face ease that we won't be moving in with her family to the summer house. "We'd live in town. The food scene is really exploding here, and Paul has a new vision he wants to execute. He has the investors lined up and everything. And he's been offered a recurring guest spot as a judge on a cooking show. I can stay here while he films that six weeks of the year. They even talked about filming the show at the opening of his restaurant."

"Wow," she says. There's a shadow of something—is it jealousy?—but then her expression returns to a smile. "That's great."

"Have you heard from Regina?" I ask.

Her expression doesn't change. "No, I haven't. You?"

"About six months ago. They're still at the house, they were able to keep it. Lana is doing well. She didn't say much else. Do you think she'll come?"

Esme shrugs. "I guess we'll see. I doubt it."

Both our heads turn when we hear the tires of a car coming up the road. The large black SUV pulls to a stop at the edge of the construction of the new house. A thin woman gets out of the car in a flowy dress and flats. A man comes up to greet her from the house, maybe a contractor, and he points and shows her plans. She nods. Then, suddenly, she turns toward us. She smiles widely and waves her arms toward us.

Esme's face is frozen. "No," she says. "No."

The woman below us says something to the contractor and he nods, shakes her hand, and returns to the house. I watch as she goes to the car and pulls something out, holding it between her hands. Then she starts walking toward us.

The woman approaches with a bright smile plastered on her face, and as she gets closer up the road, both Esme and I are glued to our seats as if some force is holding us there, forcing us in place, unable to escape.

"Hello, neighbor," she calls to us.

Esme grips the seat of the deck chair. She swallows, but doesn't move.

"I brought you a pie!" she says. "Though, aren't you supposed to bring me the pie as a welcome gift?" She winks. "No matter. Plenty of time for that."

She sets the pie down on the step. Esme regards it as if it's a dead mouse dropped by a cat.

"What. Are. You. Doing. Here." Her voice is flat and cold.

"What. Do. You. Think?" The woman laughs. "I'm your new neighbor. Well, Ben and I are."

Alexis turns her eyes to me. "Hello, Piper. Nice to see you. How's the arm?"

I reflexively touch the small scar on my forearm. "I'm going inside to get Paul," I say to Esme, ignoring Alexis, and standing up.

"I'll come, too," Esme says and also stands. "I should get a restraining order against you," she says to Alexis.

"Ben did suggest we might not want to move near you. With Greg's criminal history and all." At that Esme flinches. "But I told him, in a court of law, Greg has been acquitted and that's enough for me. After all, you are family. I don't need a restraining order against you guys."

I shake my head at the gall of this woman. Brazenly attacking me and never being held accountable. I know our family treated her poorly, but it doesn't excuse attempted murder.

Esme was right about one thing: Alexis had it out for our family. Alexis was in our house that night with Lana, and even if Regina did invite her, I don't think it's a coincidence she was there the night Brigit was murdered. But when I mentioned it to Esme to take to the lawyers, that and Alexis's threat to blame Greg, Esme said they tried, but failed, to find evidence. The attorneys did an extensive forensic search; there was no connection between Alexis and Brigit Max. No phone records, no friendship or connection existed. They never knew one another, and Alexis would have no motive to murder her, even with the short-lived affair between her and Greg, which was over before Greg started up with Brigit. Alexis wouldn't have even known about Brigit and Greg. Furthermore, Alexis had an airtight alibi that night; the local police sergeant named Ben Sherman had vouched that they'd been together the entire night after she left here. In fact, he said that he drove her here, waited outside while she checked on her inebriated sister, and left together.

So the defense had declined to call Alexis as a witness or use her as a potential alternative suspect at all, believing that a second affair would paint Greg's character as even worse. No evidence suggested she was anything other than an invited guest to our home that night, my word against hers. The prosecution didn't introduce her as a witness against Greg, either, so she slithered out of any involvement in the whole trial.

The hair on my neck stands up being this close her. I know what she's capable of. I look at her now, smiling and chatting like nothing's happened.

Alexis knows very well that we don't want to talk to her. She just doesn't care. She continues, "I'm opening an art gallery in town to feature my paintings. I've got some pieces that would be perfect for your house, Esme. Add some color. I'll bring them by."

"I'm not doing this with you," Esme says, shaking her head.

Alexis winces. "I think you are. You don't have much choice. Oh, and before you go," she says and holds a large, thick cardstock envelope out to us. "I wanted to give you this."

She shakes it at Esme, indicating she should take it, but Esme regards it without touching it.

"Now that Ben's divorce is settled and his pesky ex-wife moved out of town, thanks to me," Alexis says and does a little bow. She climbs the porch steps then takes Esme's hand and forces the envelope into her palm. "An invitation to our wedding. We'll have it here, next August, at our new house. It will be a new tradition. Every year we'll host an anniversary party here. To commemorate and celebrate our love. It's what this place is all about, isn't it?" She smiles triumphantly. "I told Ben the other day, when it comes to life, I feel like I've won." She takes a step closer and leans in toward Esme's face. "It does feel good to say it—I win."

ACKNOWLEDGMENTS

I WANT TO THANK those who I owe this book to because without your help, I wouldn't have been able to write, edit, or publish this novel.

Thank you to my awesome husband and beautiful children. I love you so much. My husband is the reason I'm an author. Years ago, he encouraged me to take a writing course and keep going. And as I wrote this book, he continued to be supportive as ever. Also, I'm thankful to my kids, everything I do is for you two. I feel very blessed to have such amazing kids.

Huge thanks to a kind friend and terrific writer, Carol Willis, for being an early reader of the first several chapters of this manuscript. Your thoughtful suggestions and encouragement were exactly what I needed.

Thank you to the book's editor Denise Zaza whose insightful feedback and keen eye helped to revise, polish, and deepen this manuscript. I've learned a great deal from working with you and it was a wonderful experience.

As always, I'm very thankful to my literary agent Jill Marsal for your buoying support and expertise. I am lucky to have my dream agent as my agent.

And a special thank you to Minka Kent, my writing sprinting partner, valued mentor and amazing friend. You're one of those beautiful people, inside and out, who uplifts others even when you're insanely busy.

Thank you so much to the outstanding team at Crooked Lane Books who worked on this novel, including Dulce Botello, Julia Abbott, Thaisheemarie Fantauzzi Perez, and Mikaela Bender. And thank you to Lauren Harms for designing a perfect book cover for The Summer House Murder.

Thank you, readers, for picking up this book. I appreciate you spending your time with my characters.